"Our new interim director is a stickler for rules..." Daisy winked.

"Thanks for the cookies," he added from the doorway.

Daisy turned around and grinned. "Thank the kids. They insisted."

Ben watched them all leave and then reached for the tin of cookies to sample one of the golden stars. The cookie melted in his mouth.

Cavernous silence engulfed the house that was noisy and full of laughter just minutes ago. It was as if Daisy and the triplets took the light and warmth with them.

The Stanley family seemed to turn this house into a home, with Daisy as its heart and soul.

It would be easy to ask her out, except he was reading too much into her being nice.

And he didn't want to do anything to ruin the atmosphere at the playhouse. They'd been thrown together because of Lily, Aspen and Rosie.

Any attraction to the pretty brunette was simply wishful thinking on his part...

T0284487

Dear Reader,

Welcome to a Violet Ridge Christmas!

I love the hustle and bustle of the holidays. When possible, I attend community events, especially concerts and plays, as music and stories capture the spirit of the season for me.

Military veteran Ben Irwin finds himself at a crossroads while celebrating his first Christmas back in his hometown. He volunteers to help with the set design for the annual play and gets more than he bargained for with the Stanley triplets and their mother. Daisy is determined to make this the best Christmas ever for her triplets following her husband's death two years earlier. Both Ben and Daisy have to confront their pasts to find love in their future.

This is the first book in my new series about the Virtue siblings and the Lazy River Dude Ranch, with three more books to follow.

I love connecting with readers. Please follow me on Facebook (Tanya Agler Author) or email me at tanya.agler@tanyaagler.com.

Happy holidays!

Tanya

THE TRIPLETS' HOLIDAY MIRACLE

TANYA AGLER

HEARTWARMING

If you purchased this book without a cover you should be aware that this book is stolen property. It was reported as "unsold and destroyed" to the publisher, and neither the author nor the publisher has received any payment for this "stripped book."

Harlequin®
HEARTWARMING™

ISBN-13: 978-1-335-05136-3

The Triplets' Holiday Miracle

Copyright © 2024 by Tanya Agler

All rights reserved. No part of this book may be used or reproduced in any manner whatsoever without written permission.

Without limiting the author's and publisher's exclusive rights, any unauthorized use of this publication to train generative artificial intelligence (AI) technologies is expressly prohibited.

This is a work of fiction. Names, characters, places and incidents are either the product of the author's imagination or are used fictitiously. Any resemblance to actual persons, living or dead, businesses, companies, events or locales is entirely coincidental.

For questions and comments about the quality of this book, please contact us at CustomerService@Harlequin.com.

TM and ® are trademarks of Harlequin Enterprises ULC.

Harlequin Enterprises ULC
22 Adelaide St. West, 41st Floor
Toronto, Ontario M5H 4E3, Canada
www.Harlequin.com

Printed in Lithuania

Recycling programs for this product may not exist in your area.

MIX
Paper | Supporting responsible forestry
FSC® C021394

Tanya Agler remembers the first set of Harlequin books her grandmother gifted her, and she's been in love with romance novels ever since. An award-winning author, Tanya makes her home in Georgia with her wonderful husband, their four children and a lovable basset, who really rules the roost. When she's not writing, Tanya loves classic movies and a good cup of tea. Visit her at tanyaagler.com or email her at tanyaagler@gmail.com.

Books by Tanya Agler

Harlequin Heartwarming

The Single Dad's Holiday Match
The Soldier's Unexpected Family
The Sheriff's Second Chance
A Ranger for the Twins

Smoky Mountain First Responders

The Firefighter's Christmas Promise
The Paramedic's Forever Family

Rodeo Stars of Violet Ridge

Caught by the Cowgirl
Snowbound with the Rodeo Star
Her Temporary Cowboy

Visit the Author Profile page
at Harlequin.com for more titles.

During the writing of this book, two important women in my life passed away. To my mother-in-law, Meredith Agler, your love of Christmas was as much a part of you as your love of family. Thank you for welcoming me to my first family Cookie Day and then inviting me back for many more. And to my agent, Dawn Dowdle. Thank you for all your advice and patience. I can still hear your gentle admonition that a smile is always found on the face and you can only shrug your shoulders. This book is dedicated to both of you.

I also want to thank the kindness of jewelry designer Ilene Kay. When my family was vacationing in North Carolina as I began plotting this book, we stumbled upon her giving a demonstration of how she designed and created her artistic earrings. After showing me her tools, she took the time to answer my multitude of questions. Thank you so much, Ilene. All the mistakes in the book about jewelry making are mine.

CHAPTER ONE

IT WASN'T AS if Ben Irwin's life depended on this meeting with Zelda Baker at the Smokehouse. The days of his air force military career when he had undertaken flying missions that put him at actual risk of injury or death were permanently over as of two months ago. Through the wool of his heavy navy peacoat, Ben rubbed his hip. That last crash had forced his honorable discharge. No longer was he Colonel Irwin with the respect of his fellow service members bolstering him. Now, he was just plain Ben, living in his hometown of Violet Ridge again.

A mere six weeks ago, he'd purchased a historic house two blocks from downtown, and not just any house either. He had loved the stately Victorian manor from the first time he'd seen it while walking to Gregson Hill after sharing roasted chestnuts with his mother, who'd since passed. At closing, Ben had been convinced he'd gotten a bargain when he paid for the house in full. With large airy rooms and lots of light, the building had more than enough room for him with its six bedrooms and five baths, almost too much for one person. But after living next door to the curmudgeonly, seventy-something-year-old Constance Mulligan for a little over a month, he understood why the former owners had given each other a high five once he signed the contract. They'd received a pittance of what the home was worth, but they no longer had to deal with Mrs. Mulligan.

Living next door to Constance might not be so bad if he had somewhere to go during the day, but his employment prospects had fizzled out.

Until now. The current mayor had just announced he was retiring next year. Becoming the next mayor would be the perfect fit for Ben and his skill set. This morning he'd arranged to have lunch with his former boss and mentor, Zelda, who had served as mayor two administrations ago. Without a doubt, she'd help him launch his campaign. With Ben's military background as a negotiator and his family's ties to the region, he'd finally found his best chance to give something back to the area that had provided so many opportunities for the Irwin family.

Shaking a few snowflakes off his coat sleeves, Ben approached the Smokehouse, his favorite burger place in town. It had been four years since he'd paid this restaurant a visit. That was way too long for one of their legendary meals. The austere interior had always been no-nonsense, a little like him. Instead of frou-frou frills, the owners concentrated on what they did well: burgers and French fries. He could always count on a good meal with no fanfare.

He entered the restaurant and blinked. Was he in the wrong place on this Friday afternoon? Nope. The smell of grilled meat and grease was exactly as he remembered. Everything else was different.

For one thing, a row of wire reindeer with clear twinkling lights occupied the back wall. Overhead, giant green balls, red bells and humongous cardboard-cutout peppermints swayed over each table, along with crimson lanterns glowing bright. Every booth and table was occupied, and laughter carried over Christmas music playing in the background. This was a far cry from the uncluttered white walls of the past.

Ben approached the attendant's stand, covered with strands of brightly colored holiday lights. The attendant, wearing a Santa hat and holding a pen, greeted him.

"I'm meeting Zelda Baker," he said.

The woman's smile broadened. "You must be Ben. Right this way." She grabbed a menu and a set of silverware wrapped with a red paper napkin covered with candy canes and led him to a booth with a window view.

Ben would have known his former boss anywhere. Two years after his mother had died, Ben
had searched for a job away from the ranch, preferring to make his name on his own merits. He
found one downtown as an intern to Mayor Baker,
a position that had lasted until he entered the Air
Force Academy. Many a summer morning, he
headed into town before daybreak and arrived
at City Hall as Zelda was unlocking the building. Every night, he stayed until she wrapped up
for the day.

At least she hadn't changed. Her kelly green
hair was styled in a pixie cut and framed an elfin
face that never seemed to age. Her hair matched
her bright green velour sweat suit. She scooted
out of the booth and gave him a warm hug, her
head coming up to his chest since she was a foot
shorter than his tall, rangy frame.

"Merry Christmas, Ben. Welcome home."

He hung his coat on the post hook across from
the one holding Zelda's bright patchwork coat of
every color imaginable. "Thank you."

She slid back into the booth. "If I remember
correctly, you ate here at least twice a week under
its previous ownership. I take it you haven't been
here since you've come home? You look flabbergasted at the changes to the place."

He unwrapped the utensils. "I've been busy."

"Thank you for your service for our country."

Zelda patted his hand, her age spots more prominent now than when he'd worked with her. "It's good to have you back. How's life on the ranch? Are you and Lizzie getting along?"

"We agreed five weeks ago that my hip injury wasn't conducive to long rides in the saddle. I saw Lizzie yesterday when she and Lucky hosted Thanksgiving."

He was still reeling from how his family had grown over the past year. His younger sister, Lizzie, was expecting a baby with her husband, Lucky, a part-time instructor at Ben's stepsister's rodeo academy. His older brother was settled in Boston with his wife and two energetic children. His father had married a famous singer, whose daughter lived nearby with her husband and toddler. Everyone had gathered at the ranch for a joyful holiday.

For the most part, he had enjoyed himself. When he wasn't staggering from the extensive changes to the ranch, that was. Somehow, after consuming all that delicious food prepared by the ranch's cook yesterday, he was hungry again.

Ben picked up the three-page menu and studied the new offerings. Barbecue brisket sandwiches. Reubens. Chicken salad on a flaky croissant? What happened to sticking to what you did best? He placed the menu on the plastic tablecloth decorated with bright red poinsettias. Everything had changed while he was away serving his country. Why couldn't things just stay the same?

At least the Smokehouse still served hamburgers. There was nothing like them anywhere else in the world, and he should know, having been stationed in over fourteen countries and sent on missions to a number of others. Nothing was as good as the first bite of a Smokehouse hamburger. He could almost taste the crinkle-cut French fries drizzled with ketchup.

Zelda set aside her menu and studied Ben. "The Double I is in good hands. Lizzie's attracted new employees with the addition of the guesthouses. Keeping up with the times. She's done well with introducing the Simmental cattle to the ranch, too." Zelda had always known the details of every ranch and family in the surrounding township. "What's next on the horizon for you?"

That was a good question.

After working for a week at the Double I Ranch, where he'd grown up, it became obvious his sister, Lizzie, ran an efficient enterprise. He'd quit the ranch, and then headed to the Irwin Arena, another of his father's business ventures, only to find his father's staff was a close-knit group who ran the operation smoothly. He cleared out his office in less than a week.

Before he had a chance to answer, the server

came over, pencil and pad in hand. "Zelda! What a wonderful surprise! I didn't notice you here."

"I'm glad to see you back at work." Zelda scooted out of the bench and embraced the server before settling back into the booth. "How's your dad doing?"

The server grinned. "Much better. Your chicken noodle soup helped. So did the news that my sister is expecting a baby."

"How wonderful." Zelda clapped her hands. "I'll start knitting baby booties this afternoon."

The server wrote down their drink orders, but before Ben could get in another word, an older couple came over to talk to Zelda, followed by more patrons stopping by while he sat on his side of the booth, feeling left out. It seemed like everyone in the restaurant knew Zelda and/or her identical twin, Nelda, and either had a question for her or simply wanted to wish her a happy holiday. Somehow, in the midst of it all, they ordered their meals, but those were the only words he'd uttered since they arrived. Zelda was more popular than ever, and she listened to each resident about every little thing. Neighbor disputes. The recent senior center community bus breakdown. Advice about a Christmas present. To each, Zelda doled out sage words of wisdom.

Their meals came, and Ben stared at his plate, the standard white dishes swapped out with holiday ones. The hamburger was there, along with a fruit cup and homemade potato chips.

"This isn't what I ordered." Ben pushed his plate to the edge and motioned for the server. "I ordered fries."

"They started serving homemade potato crisps. They're delicious." Zelda reached over and popped one in her mouth. "Try one."

The server returned with a smile and asked if everything was okay.

Ben pointed to his plate. "I received someone's fruit cup by mistake."

The server laughed. "You must be new around here. That's standard with every lunch order."

"It's been a while since Ben's been home." Zelda interjected and waved her hand. "He has to get back into the Violet Ridge groove."

The server scurried away, and Ben turned his attention to his meal. He pushed the fruit cup aside and turned to Zelda. "Finally. People are leaving us alone, and we can talk."

"This is a mighty fine meal. Eat up before it gets cold." Zelda took a bite of her turkey and cranberry sandwich and smacked her lips. "For the record, I've been watching you this whole time. Tell me what's bothering you."

That was Zelda. She cared about everyone who set foot in Violet Ridge, taking each resident under her wing. Ben picked up his hamburger. "Lizzie's efficient and running the ranch like a five-star general. Dad's staff at the arena is a well-oiled machine. There's no place for me at the ranch or at the arena, but I have another job in mind."

"Let me guess." Zelda chewed another bite of her sandwich and squinted. He didn't squirm or flinch. Instead, he waited patiently during her assessment. She could read people and a room as well as any lieutenant general. "Stellar military career. Family connections out the wazoo. The ability to organize like no other. You want to run for mayor."

"I've worked at City Hall before, and I can bring something to the position."

"You should know right off I never endorse candidates. Still, even without my endorsement, you have a good chance to win with your military experience." Zelda placed her sandwich on her plate and settled her elbows on the table, leaning forward. "I've been watching you as long-time residents came over. You didn't introduce yourself, and you didn't insert yourself into the conversations."

Ben chewed on his hamburger, the long-anticipated treat suddenly feeling like cardboard in his mouth. "I didn't want to interrupt."

"People change. Towns change. You have to get to know us all over again." Zelda's eyes were kind even if her tone was brusque.

"Any suggestions?" Becoming mayor was more than just about winning an election; it was about giving back to the community that had been there for him when his civic-minded mother died. Cards. Meals. Pats on the back. That had meant so much to a gangly teenager who was closer to his mom than his workaholic father.

Zelda plucked out a plump raspberry from her fruit cup and popped it into her mouth. "Volunteering would be a way to give back to the community."

She then outlined other ways for him to get back into the thick of the town's activities. Once she started advising him, his hamburger regained its flavor. The quality of the meal hadn't changed. It was just as good as he remembered.

"You sold me. So where am I needed the most?" Fortunately, he had time and money to commit to whatever volunteer position she recommended. Finding his purpose in Violet Ridge meant everything to him.

Zelda finished her lunch and pushed away her plate. "You going to eat those crisps?"

He piled half on her dish. They smelled good, but he liked the old fries. "Consider that payment for your assistance."

They both chuckled. Zelda munched on a crisp, her face blissful. "These are my granddaughter Sofia's favorite. She just turned seven." She showed him pictures of Sofia on her cell phone. "There are days she's going on seventeen. They grow up so fast."

He wouldn't know about children, having never been married. He'd come close a couple of times to asking a woman to marry him, but his career had kept him busy.

"She has your facial expressions," he said, handing the phone back to her. "So, do you have any recommendations as far as volunteer positions?"

Zelda tapped her last crisp against her plate before popping it in her mouth. The crunch filled the air, and Ben couldn't help it. He tried one. It was surprisingly good.

"The Snow Much Fun festival will be taking place soon." She leaned back against the red pleather of the booth and winced. "Then again Monica and Kim are organizing that. They're both go-getters who like being in charge. You don't want to get in the middle of one of their heated discussions and ruin your chances of becoming mayor before you even run."

"Then that's out." Ben finished the fruit cup and moved on to the crisps. To his surprise, he found himself wanting more. "Anyone else looking for someone like me?"

She snapped her fingers. "Frank Craddock

called me yesterday. He's in need of extra volunteers at the Holly Theater."

Ben instantly recognized the name of the local community playhouse where the annual production of *The Santa Who Forgot Christmas* was the must-see event of the season. "Volunteers who don't have to act, right?"

He still shuddered at the memory of his short time on the Holly Playhouse Theater stage. He'd been cast as Nicky, one of the two lead child roles. Stage fright didn't even begin to describe the intense knot in his stomach and the sweat that dripped down his brow. His legs had been like lead weights as he stood there, silent and shaking. Nothing in his twenty years of serving in the military had matched that moment when every audience member stared at him, waiting for him to deliver his lines. The curtain had gone down, and his understudy filled in for him.

"They need crew members, too. You'd be busy from now until Christmas Eve when the play is performed," Zelda said.

The server brought the bill, and Ben reached for it before Zelda could. He presented his credit card, and the server accepted it. Ben dismissed Zelda's objection. "It's my way of thanking you for your time."

"How was the meal?" His mentor raised her

eyebrow almost as if the question had a deeper meaning.

He looked down, every crumb and food speck gone. "It was delicious."

"Change isn't as bad as you think." Zelda winked at him, then scooted out of the booth and donned her coat. "Even for someone who likes everything to stay the same. Good to have you back in town, Ben. Merry Christmas."

Ben signed the bill and then walked the two blocks to the Holly Theater. Zelda's advice had never steered him wrong. He nodded at a street vendor selling hot chocolate and peppermint mochas. Still full, he didn't stop, but it might be nice to purchase something on his way home. Maybe he'd surprise Mrs. Mulligan and buy her a cup of hot cocoa. He had offered to install lights on her house as she was the only one who didn't have any decorations, but she had glared at him and turned away, pivoting those boots on the snow and ice. Who knew why she was like that? Some around here speculated she was tight with her purse strings. Others said she was just getting by. Perhaps a gift would break the ice between them.

He resolved to remember to buy her something before stopping in front of a two-story whitewashed brick building. The marquee, announcing that *The Santa Who Forgot Christmas* was coming soon, jutted out over the entry doors and box office windows. His hip ached with an intensity not experienced since he finished his physical therapy. Perhaps that was a sign he should just return to the vendor and buy two hot cocoas. He'd leave one on Mrs. Mulligan's front doorstep, ring the doorbell and run.

But Ben wasn't seven anymore. If he wanted to be mayor, he couldn't let the fear from that isolated incident of stage fright hold him back. Twenty years in the military had changed him. It instilled a sense of pride and confidence he hadn't had when he was a kid. Any challenge inside the playhouse would be conquered with the stiff spine he'd perfected over the years. He looked down at his plain navy wool coat and jeans. He'd have felt a sight more confident in his dress blues, but those were now hanging in a closet, retired on a permanent basis, same as him.

No one told him how hard the first Christmas was away from the military. He missed the soldiers who served with him, and their families. Okay, he needed a position as a volunteer here more than he acknowledged to Zelda.

Corralling his nerves, he opened the door and found an empty lobby. He followed voices and entered the auditorium that could accommodate two hundred patrons. Plush red curtains surrounded the stage that was much smaller than he remembered.

The owner of the playhouse, Frank Craddock, approached him. In his fifties with a receding hairline and hair that was more silver than brown, Frank had changed over the years. "Ben Irwin! Merry Christmas!" He patted Ben on the back before clutching his clipboard to his chest. "Good to see you again, but the auditions were yesterday."

He then met Ben's gaze and they laughed, as it would be a good long time—preferably never—before Ben acted in another play. "I'm here to volunteer for a crew position. Zelda Baker suggested it."

"I never turn down a pair of able hands." Frank let out another boomer of a laugh. "Are you good with a paintbrush?"

Considering Ben repainted every room in his house, getting rid of the dark gray walls with a soothing creamy white, he nodded. "I'm pretty good with a blowtorch and miter saw, too."

"Can't pay you." Frank raised his eyebrow.

"Wasn't expecting anything." Except to get to know the residents of Violet Ridge better.

"You're hired. Why don't you have a seat in the auditorium." Frank gestured to the rows of empty seats. "I have one matter to handle and then I'll get you some waiver forms to sign."

Frank hustled away, and Ben looked around. This theater wasn't the bustling hive of activity he anticipated. That didn't matter. He'd made himself available, and so volunteering here was now a part of his holiday season.

Ben approached a row and went to lower himself into one of the cushioned seats when a young boy, most likely six or seven, jumped out at him.

"Boo!"

Ben almost stumbled before righting himself. "Wrong season, don't you think?"

"You're funny." The boy laughed and hunkered back down. "Shh. Don't tell anyone where I am. I'm trying to frighten my sisters."

"No deal." A boy this age shouldn't be left unsupervised in a theater. "I'll take you back where you belong."

The boy remained crouched on the floor. "I want to stay here. We can hide together." The boy gave one more half-hearted protest before taking in Ben's resolute expression. He sighed with acceptance and rose off the floor. "I wouldn't have told anyone."

Ben gave the boy credit despite his flawed logic. After all, if you were hiding, you weren't talking. He smiled and reached out his hand. "Come along. Someone's probably worried about you."

The boy's shoulders slumped, but Ben was determined to find the lad's caregiver. A quick glance at the lobby proved fruitless. Then Ben headed backstage while the boy trudged alongside him. He heard voices from behind the door where Frank had disappeared earlier.

Barging in, Ben found himself at the back of a crowd. Frank was congratulating everyone on being cast in this year's production of *The Santa Who Forgot Christmas* before launching into the rehearsal schedule.

Ben sought out anyone who seemed to be missing something valuable in terms of one little boy. His gaze settled on a woman with curly, light brown hair that fell past her shoulders. Long swirly silver earrings dangled on either side of her swanlike neck. He admired her pretty yellow sweater paired with a swirly skirt that extended to her ankles. Slim and of average height, she held on to the hands of two little girls who appeared to be about the same age as the boy beside him.

Applause pulled his attention away from the woman. Cast members milled about the room, trading phone numbers and asking about yesterday's Thanksgiving. No one came forth to claim the boy, and Ben started to worry until the woman released the hands of the two girls and rushed over to them.

"Aspen! I thought you were behind me." The woman placed her hand over her heart. "Don't run off like that."

That was her entire lecture? No admonishment for escaping her notice. What if he'd left the theater? Without a coat? And with residents distracted during the rush of the holiday season? Aspen could have been hurt. Or lost. Or freezing. Or worse. Any of those alternatives were painful, as Ben could attest to, having experienced all those things and more during his time in the military. He cleared his throat. "I found him in the auditorium, playing hide-and-seek."

"All's well that ends well." She smiled and reached for Aspen's hand.

"Something bad could have happened," Ben warned with a voice that usually sent fear through anyone in his midst.

"Nothing did, though. Good is all around, if you look for it." Those brown eyes almost seemed to twinkle. "Thank you."

She moved past him. Her dismissal of him rankled, but there wasn't much he could do about it. With his lips pursed in a straight line, he simply nodded and walked to the other side of the room to await further instructions from Frank.

If she was part of this production, he was wrong about one thing. There was something in this theater that could cause his stomach to twist into a knot even tighter than when he experienced stage fright. Actually, it was a someone.

And he didn't even know her name.

DAISY STANLEY WAITED for Frank Craddock to finish talking to the actor who was set to play Santa in this year's production of *The Santa Who Forgot Christmas*. She had to admit Teddy Krengle was perfect for the role with his rosy red cheeks and rounded white beard. Even his name sounded similar to Kris Kringle.

In the meantime, she scanned the room until she set her gaze on the man who'd returned Aspen to her a few minutes earlier. Tall with a commanding air, he glared at her as if she was a menace on the same level as the Bumble from *Rudolph the Red-Nosed Reindeer*.

What had he expected her to do? Scold her seven-year-old son in front of his sisters and everyone else? That wasn't her style. And by the time they arrived home later, Aspen would have forgotten about this infraction and probably would have done something else worthy of a scolding, anyway.

As a single mom of triplets, she waged her battles carefully. One victory a day was all she expected and wanted.

Daisy kept an eye on her children while clutching the waiver and schedule Frank had handed out at the start of the meeting. There was some mistake. She intended to rectify the issue before the first rehearsal started.

However, Teddy and Frank were chatting up

a storm. Beside her, Rosie and Lily started bickering over Lily's doll, Winter, a cowgirl wearing blue jeans and two long yellow braids. If Daisy didn't do something, their behavior would get them kicked out of the production before it even started.

While that sounded like it might be for the best, considering they'd be giving up most of their holiday season for rehearsals, Rosie had set her heart on auditioning and was ecstatic over being cast as Noelle. As the natural leader of the triplets, whenever Rosie wanted something that badly, the other two went along with her.

Still, she had to straighten out this misunderstanding with Frank Craddock. It would be a sight easier to do if someone else was watching the triplets. Since the newcomer was the only other person not speaking to someone else, that narrowed her options to him. He'd have to do. She was sure that if he ever smiled, he would be quite handsome with that head of dark brown hair and those piercing green eyes.

Daisy gripped her daughters' hands and motioned at Aspen to come with her. Then she forced her brightest smile on her face and approached the man with determination. "Excuse me. We haven't been formally introduced, but you and Aspen are already fast friends. Would you watch my triplets for a minute while I get everything straightened out with Mr. Craddock?"

The man seemed ready to say no when she spotted the other two gentlemen going their separate ways. Frank was heading toward the auditorium, but she couldn't let him leave yet. Daisy sent a quick thanks the man's way and rushed toward the theater owner.

"Mr. Craddock. Frank! There's been a mistake." Daisy thrust the papers at him. "The volunteer at the audition said there'd be no outside people present at the rehearsals."

"That's correct." Frank glanced toward the man who was being roped into a round of "Ring around the Rosie" with the triplets. "If you're talking about Ben, he's a new volunteer."

Good. He could take her spot, then. The owner started walking again, and Daisy followed. "I was talking about me. I'd be an outside person."

"No, you're not. Your children are acting in the play. Every parent of a minor actor has to volunteer." Mr. Craddock gave a curt nod.

Was it really volunteering if it was mandatory? Daisy wasn't quite sure about that, and she needed the time from the rehearsals to get back to silversmithing. More than just her creative outlet, her jewelry business would supplement her income from her job at her family's dude ranch. With her babysitter heading to college next fall after a gap year so she could earn money for tuition, the extra income was essential to pay for childcare and necessities for three growing children.

"How often do I have to be here?" she asked.

"Whenever one of your children is rehearsing. You'll love it." Mr. Craddock opened the door and sailed into the auditorium.

She glanced at the rehearsal schedule, and her eyes almost popped out. With Rosie and Aspen having the two lead juvenile roles, she should just set up a tent in the lobby. Their presence was required almost every evening and Saturdays. They'd spend more time here than they would at home until Christmas Eve.

Exhaling, she faced the man keeping watch over the triplets. "We all fall down!" Rosie announced with glee.

Rosie, Lily and Aspen tumbled to the floor, laughing, while the man rolled his eyes and then joined them. At least she left them in the hands of a good sport.

Daisy hurried over and thanked him. "You're a lifesaver. I'm Daisy Stanley."

"Are all of these yours?" he asked.

She was taken aback at his abrasive tone. "I don't rent them, if that's what you're asking."

The trio giggled and popped up off the floor, surrounding her with hugs from every side. Looking disheveled and out of sorts, the man remained on the ground, rubbing his hip. Just because she was used to the triplets' antics didn't mean he was. She reached out her arm. "Need some help?"

"I'm more than capable of rising on my own merits," he said.

He was prickly to say the least. Too bad. That dark hair had a slight wave to it, and his face held a touch of earnestness. Those good looks could use a dose of manners, though.

"Everyone can use a hand sometimes. Life's the sweeter for it." She kept her hand outstretched, used to being met with attitude by her three older brothers.

Her youngest, Lily, tugged the bottom of her yellow cardigan. "Mommy, I thought only cookies and desserts are sweet. How can life be sweet?"

"It's an expression, like that Christmas song you like. The world isn't made of marshmallows, but it's sweet and gooey. Like you, Lilypad." Daisy tweaked Lily's nose. "A marshmallow world means we can look forward to Christmas the whole year round."

"Okay." Lily smiled at her, looking so much like her late father with those big hazel eyes and curly blond hair. She and Rosie were technically identical, although Lily's eyes were slightly closer together, making it easy to tell them apart.

Their brother resembled her side of the family with brown hair and dark eyes.

Daisy returned her attention to the man on the floor. He was still rubbing his hip. "Are you hurt? Do you need me to get someone?"

He clenched his jaw and finally accepted her hand. On his feet again, he released her and wiped off his jeans. "Are they always this rambunctious?"

She laughed that away with a shrug. "If you're asking whether they're creative and energetic and happy, the answer is yes. If you'll excuse us…"

The man stared at her as if she was an elf, newly arrived from the North Pole. Thankfully, she'd only have to endure him until the play was over and they went their separate ways.

Until then, she wouldn't let this person ruin her holiday spirit, although the prospect of having to volunteer here every night and weekend was putting a small dent in her resolve. With a month until Christmas, she was trying her hardest to make this the best one yet for the triplets. They'd changed so much this year, and this was the first holiday without the spirit of grief hanging over them as it had for the past twenty-four months. Aspen was finally acting like his former self, and Lily's speech was coming along. She wouldn't allow anything to set them back.

They'd come so far, changing for the better. Change was a necessary part of life.

Holding her head high, she grasped Aspen's hand while the papers fell onto the floor. Daisy retrieved them, her exit with her daughters trailing behind her less than graceful. But her dignity was intact, and she'd take that as her victory of the day.

CHAPTER TWO

WITH NO SNOW clouds in sight, rather unusual for the last day of November in this part of Colorado, the weather was cooperating with Ben's plan to add more lights to his exterior display. Whistling "It's Beginning to Look a Lot Like Christmas" and holding a box of supplies, he headed toward the side of his Victorian house that faced the dormant garden.

This morning he used his blower on the driveway and sidewalk to clear away yesterday's snowfall accumulation. Then a trip to Lafayette's Hardware in town provided him with extra strands of lights so he could make his holiday spirits—and his house—as bright as possible.

Going big for the holidays was his new mission. Come January, he'd devote the same kind of energy to the mayoral race.

As for today? The next phase of his life was here. For the past twenty years, the air force had been his life, and every ounce of his energy had been devoted to his service. Somehow, though, every holiday season, he was either assigned to a mission that lasted until the new year or he'd rented a house with vinyl siding where he couldn't hang anything on the eaves. The moment he set eyes on the for-sale sign in front of this house, he knew he'd found his permanent home. He'd always admired the exterior gables and gingerbread wainscoting, but the interior crown molding and original cherry woodwork sold the house. When he toured it with his real estate agent, he envisioned happy evenings and family gatherings. The sprawling Victorian was a welcoming house, the white siding offsetting the black shutters with lattice work at the cornices. Come spring, the garden would be bright with columbine and violets, but for now, a thin blanket of ice and snow covered the front lawn.

What he hadn't counted on was how empty the house was. It was as if it called out for more people, and here he was, the only occupant.

With six bedrooms, if he counted the attic alcove, this was just the type of house suitable for a large family. The triplets popped into his mind, followed by a fleeting image of their mother. Over the past few rehearsals, he'd already discovered that Daisy had a way of turning a person inside out. He hadn't met anyone who ruffled his feathers like her and then smoothed the situation over with a smile and an expectation that everything would work out for the best. It was as if she was able to corral chaos with grace and a grin. Ben couldn't decide if her husband was the most fortunate man alive, or something else.

He blinked and found the pile of lights ready to be hung. He had just enough time to tackle this side of his house before the evening's rehearsal. Now all that was left was anchoring the ladder in place.

Returning from his garage, he hefted the ladder to the side of the house. His hip ached, the full brunt of his injury reminding him of why his military retirement was a necessity. After tonight's rehearsal, he'd take a long soak in his whirlpool tub to ease the deep ache. With that in mind, he extricated a bag of gutter clips and started up the ladder.

"Mr. Irwin. May I have a word?" The strong voice of his next-door neighbor carried across the yard.

He sighed and climbed off the ladder, taking care to step on the pine straw, which was free of ice. "Constance, how many times do I have to insist? Please call me Ben."

He turned to find her standing there, hands on hips, not a silver strand of her short hair out of place. Her cream-colored puffer coat with huge green buttons and blue, yellow and orange stripes near the top made her look as though she stepped out of a 1980s magazine ad.

Ben smiled in an effort to break the ice. If he could win her over, everyone else in Violet Ridge would be a breeze.

The wrinkles in her forehead deepened in an obvious dismissal of his efforts to befriend her. "We have to talk about your light display, Mr. Irwin."

His grin widened, and he tapped the box of lights next to the ladder. "It's great, isn't it? I'm making up for the displays I missed while I served in the air force."

"I, for one, have only gratitude for your years in the military, but that doesn't excuse the fact that I could see your lights through my window all night long." Her piercing gaze deflated his spirit. "I didn't sleep a wink."

He hadn't considered that his display might keep anyone awake. What he believed to be luminous and cheery was hardly that in Constance's eyes. Compromise, though, was his middle name, a skill he'd learned and perfected throughout his military tenure.

"This is my first display at my new house. You'll have to forgive me if I went a little overboard." Which he hadn't. Not yet. The last six hundred LED lights would help him achieve something impressive.

She tapped her foot and he relented, as he wanted to be a conscientious neighbor. "I'll purchase a timer so the lights will automatically turn off at eleven. How's that?"

"Nine would be better." Her brown eyes narrowed. "It would save on electricity costs, and you wouldn't overload the circuits. Last thing we need is a citywide blackout."

Looked like the wrong person possessed the name Ebenezer. If he ever had children, the family tradition of naming the second son Ebenezer—Ben for short—ended with him. He took a deep calming breath, the cold mountain air exactly what he needed for peace and patience to return.

"These are the best LED lights Lafayette's Hardware carries. They're energy-efficient and carry the UL seal." He tried to sweeten his tone with a smile. "How about ten thirty?"

She held her chin in the air, and her lips twitched. "Ten fifteen."

In his opinion, he received the better end of the bargain, and he stuck out his hand to shake on their agreement. She ignored him and started for her house, muttering under her breath every step of the way. Maybe she needed a hobby or some activity to get into the holiday spirit.

He threw out another olive branch. "Constance." She paused and swiveled back, one lone eyebrow raised in a look of dismay. "As you know, the Holly Theater is hosting its yearly production of *The Santa Who Forgot Christmas* on Christmas Eve. I'm working with props and set design. Frank Craddock said he and Rhonda could use some help with costumes and makeup. Would you be interested?"

She huffed. "Who wants to spend money on a play on Christmas Eve when you could be at home? I expect you to keep your word about those lights. Good day."

She stomped away before he could respond. While he'd always prided himself on his diplomatic nature, probably as a result of mediating discussions between his older brother, Jeff, and his younger sister, Lizzie, Constance would try the patience of most anyone.

Except maybe Daisy. She'd laugh it off and then probably get the older woman to do her bidding. Once again, he couldn't stop thinking about the mother of two of the lead actors. As Ben attached the gutter clips near the roofline, he shook his head. He wasn't thinking about Daisy because of any glimmer of attraction for the woman with lustrous hair and wide eyes. For all he knew, she was married, and that meant she was off-limits. Instead, she represented what he longed to have: a loving family. More than ever, he was glad he realized this and focused again on the lights.

Families came with strings attached. The best relationships involved love and trust, neither of which were part of his childhood. No matter how much he wanted to fill this house with laughter and booming voices, he wouldn't rush into anything, let alone into a relationship without love simply to have children underfoot. He remembered too well the rocky relationship his parents had before his mother succumbed to cancer too young when he was twelve and Lizzie was only six. Toward the end of his mother's life, only cold-stone silence dominated the breakfast table. He never wanted to live that way again.

He finished his task and stepped off the ladder. He couldn't wait for dusk to see the latest strands all aglow although he'd have to wait until after the rehearsal. Speaking of which, he'd best hurry as he was due at the theater in an hour. He stowed his ladder in its usual spot and then drove to Lafayette's Hardware. There he purchased a timer for the lights. A promise was a promise.

From there, Ben walked to the Holly Theater, ready for a productive Saturday afternoon. If he did say so himself, he was rather handy with a hammer and a paintbrush.

At the intersection of Main Street and Maple Valley Drive where the theater was located, the smell of roasted chestnuts permeated the air. He inhaled a shaky breath as he remembered how much his mother loved the simple holiday treat. Whenever they headed into town for last-minute shopping, she always stopped and purchased two servings. He'd share his final one with her, and she'd smile, claiming that was the best of the lot.

When was the last time he'd eaten roasted chestnuts? He stood there, deliberating whether to buy some when the vendor called out to him. "Ben, Ben Irwin! Long time no see."

That was Ben's cue to approach the small cart that was positioned near the corner.

"Hello." Ben read the menu written in long-hand on a slate, then pulled out his wallet. "One small serving."

"Good to see you. Hunter asks about you all the time." The vendor extracted his scoop. "What's your choice? Spice-buttered? Cinnamon sugar? Plain?"

His mother always ordered cinnamon sugar, so Ben followed the tradition. He offered a bill to the vendor, finally recognizing him as the father of one of his former classmates. "How is Hunter, Mr. Hoffman?"

"Call me Oren. Hunter lives in Denver with his wife and their three kids. My oldest grand-child just started high school, and the other two aren't far behind." The vendor kept chatting while scooping out the chestnuts.

Ben stuffed the change in the tip jar and walked away with a small basket of chestnuts along with a promise the man would pass on Ben's well-wishes. Finding a bench, he ate the first one, the flavor sweet and satisfying, and continued to work his way through the whole basket. With the theater in sight, he peeled the last chestnut out of its shell and rolled it around the cinnamon sugar lining the paper bottom. Then he popped it in his mouth. *Delicious.* The only thing that would have made the snack better was sharing it with someone. Yet he was in no hurry to rush into a relationship just to share his chestnuts with somebody.

Last week at Thanksgiving dinner, he'd seen the spark between his sister and her husband, Lucky. Even when they were pretending to be engaged, he knew he was witnessing the beginning of something rare and wonderful. He was happy for his sister, who'd found a love that would grow deeper with each passing day. Ben was sure Lizzie and Lucky would laugh every morning at the breakfast table, no stony silence between them. Likewise, he was determined not to settle for anything less than true love, and he simply didn't have time to go looking for that kind of bond.

Not with his sister's baby due in the next few weeks, a house to decorate and a mayoral campaign to plan. He folded up the cardboard basket and threw it in the trash.

Ben entered the auditorium and heard a hushed voice near the back. A glance around showed no one in sight.

Following the sound of the shushed murmurs, he found a little girl sitting in the middle of the next-to-last row, an open book in her hands and a doll in the folded burgundy theater seat beside her. Was this one Rosie or Lily?

The girl raised her head and smiled. "Can you read to me? I like reading more than games. I play Ring around the Rosie 'cause that's my sister's favorite, seeing as how it's her name and all."

Thank you, Lily.

She kept him from having to admit he didn't know which sister she was. "Not right now. Maybe later." Who was watching her? He surveyed the auditorium and didn't see anyone else. "Shouldn't you be with your mom and siblings?"

"Mommy's helping Aspen and Rosie. She told me to stay here with Tatum. She's going to help me write my Christmas letter to Santa tomorrow. Tatum's the best." Lily picked up the doll with long yellow braids hidden under a red cowgirl hat and hugged it. "I love her."

Ben kept from clenching his jaw. It was bad enough that he'd been contemplating Daisy this morning, but why had he been thinking about a woman who trusted a doll as a babysitter?

"Let's find your mom." Ben resigned himself to another encounter with Daisy. "Bring Tatum with you."

"I don't see Tatum. I guess she had to leave." Daisy's lilting voice came from behind him. He turned and found her standing there, dangly silver earrings showcasing her long neck. Her teal sweater had a Christmas tree with lights in pink and purple with a large gold star on top. Almost as if it was guiding everyone toward her. "Hi, Lily. Did you have a good session at speech therapy today?"

For some reason, however, that same bubbly tension as the other day brewed in his stomach. He blew out a breath until he felt settled, then positioned himself between Lily and Daisy. "Lily was reading to Tatum when I arrived. She shouldn't be left alone with a doll."

Daisy tilted to the left, and Lily brushed by him. The little girl ran over to her mother, hugging her with an intensity Ben envied. Military life hadn't provided him with many opportunities to cultivate that type of connection.

Or was it his personality that was off-putting?

After all, he knew other officers who were married with families.

Lily stopped hugging her mother and started bouncing on her heels. "Mommy, guess what? Miss Annabelle says I'm graduating at Christmas."

Daisy clapped her hands together. "How wonderful. All that reading to Winter paid off. I'm so proud of you, Lilypad." She turned toward Ben, a questioning look on her pretty face. "What are you talking about? Lily's not alone. She has Tatum."

Frustration laced through Ben at Daisy's casual dismissal of his concern. "She obviously needs more attention than what *Tatum* can provide." He whipped off his gloves and stuck them in his pocket as a young woman, most likely still in high school, her ebony hair styled in a ponytail, rushed over toward them. Lily hugged the newcomer, who returned the embrace.

"I told you I'd be right back," the teenager said. She met Daisy's gaze, and a huge grin showed off her braces. "Annabelle said to tell you Lily is making great progress with her speech therapy. She'll call you tomorrow about an end date, maybe as soon as next week."

"What a wonderful early Christmas present! Thank you so much, Tatum. I'll see you tomorrow, then?" Daisy asked, placing her hands on Lily's shoulders.

Tatum nodded. "And next week. I'll drive them here for rehearsal."

"Perfect! I'll come straight here after work since Seth agreed I can leave earlier than usual." Daisy watched until Tatum left the auditorium but not before the teen waved one last time at Lily. Then Daisy switched her gaze back to Ben. "You were saying something?"

He shuffled his feet, feeling rather foolish. "Tatum's a person."

"She's more than that. The triplets simply adore her, and the Delgado family is the best. They're my next-door neighbors. After Dylan—" her gaze lowered to the top of Lily's head, and Daisy's fingers tightened ever so slightly around her daughter's thin shoulders "—my husband and their father, passed away, the Delgados practically adopted us."

It was only then he noticed her left ring finger was bare. She was a widow.

He sought some way to leave with at least a modicum of grace.

"Glad to hear you have neighbors who help you." He'd never take that for granted, especially after living next door to Constance, who criticized Ben's every decision about his house. She still reminded him on a weekly basis that she disagreed with his landscaping company's decision to plant flax and take out the chokeberry plants, calling that an absolute shame.

Ben exited the aisle, bumping his leg on the end seat. Wincing in pain, he rubbed the spot and gave up trying to leave on a graceful note. He nodded before making his way to the set design area. Greeting his fellow volunteer, Ben donned the safety apron and goggles, relieved to be around the familiar scent of wood shavings and the buzz of the table saw.

He'd take his chances with the tools and woodworking equipment. They seemed far less dangerous to him than the chaotic calm of Daisy Stanley.

PLAY REHEARSAL WAS done for the evening. Good thing, too, as the triplets were hungry and starting to fidget.

"Mommy, this is Aspen's coat."

Rosie's voice registered, and Daisy blinked. She'd been so engrossed in reliving her last encounter with the intriguing Ben Irwin that she had, in fact, put Rosie in her brother's massive neon orange coat rather than her smaller fuchsia one. "You were paying attention. Good job, Rosie."

Daisy gave her daughter a high five before extricating her arms.

Rosie's giggles counted as her victory for the day. That, along with the good news that Lily was graduating from speech therapy.

Frank clapped from the doorway, bringing the roomful of volunteers to a standstill. Even the triplets stopped fidgeting.

"May I have everyone's attention?" Frank called the group to order.

Daisy shepherded her crew together while Frank's wife joined him. The only available spot was next to Ben, and Daisy brushed against him. For some reason, she seemed to have gotten on his bad side. This was a new experience for her. She prided herself on getting along with nearly everyone, even Constance Mulligan, Violet Ridge's version of Scrooge and Mr. Potter rolled into one.

And yet Ben was an enigma. Nothing seemed to faze him. He wore the same stony expression each time they encountered one another. She made it her personal mission to make him smile before the play was over.

There was no time like the present. She sidled up to him. "Whatever happened, the triplets didn't do it."

She kept her voice low, so that only Ben could hear her, and she thought she glimpsed a glimmer of a smile. Perhaps he did have a sense of humor under that stern exterior.

Frank began talking again, and Daisy paid attention. "Rhonda and I want to thank everyone for their voluntary participation in this year's production." He stopped when his gaze fell on the triplets.

He murmured something in his wife's ear, and she nodded.

"Lily? Aspen? Rosie? How about we take a trip to the concession stand? If I'm not mistaken, there are some animal crackers there." The triplets looked up at Daisy.

"One pack of animal crackers each won't ruin your dinner." Daisy winked at them as they skipped off with Rhonda. That left her next to Ben.

Something troubled her about their earlier exchange. Her blood froze. He didn't really think she'd leave Lily alone and unsupervised for hours with only a doll, did he? "Ben, did you think…"

Before she could finish her question, Frank called the group back to order. She was still close enough to Ben to smell wood shavings with a hint of spicy lime, no doubt his preferred aftershave. In spite of her consternation with the troubling man, she found the combination was rather pleasant.

"As many of you know, our daughter, Cheyenne, moved to Kansas earlier this year when her husband accepted a position in Topeka. Rhonda and I found out our first grandbaby arrived two and a half months ahead of schedule." Frank stopped and wiped a tear from the corner of his eye. "Noah Francis Johnson is currently in the NICU and weighs three pounds, four ounces. The soonest we can fly out is Friday night. Rhonda's already counting down the hours until we leave."

Daisy remembered the kindness of the nurses in the NICU after the triplets were born. Little Noah was in good hands.

The actor who played Santa, Teddy Krengle, forged forward and embraced Frank in a massive bear hug, and the others came and patted Frank on the back. Everyone offered their best wishes and congratulations.

After that continued for a few minutes, Frank motioned with his hands until the room fell silent once more. "Thank you, but there are issues concerning the play I need to address."

The actress who played Rosie and Aspen's mom stepped forward, a concerned look on her face. "Will this impact our production schedule? My boss is already letting me take off from work an hour early. Will the interim director keep the same schedule?"

Frank cleared his throat. "That's the problem. Rhonda is my backup and the assistant director. In a normal situation, she'd step in for me."

Murmurs rippled through the air, and Daisy

couldn't help but glance at Ben. Why she expected someone who'd just returned to Violet Ridge to ask the next question, she wasn't really sure. Maybe it was because he was imposing with his wavy black hair and piercing eyes that seemed to observe everything. Maybe it was because he wore an air of authority with an underlying strength that could seemingly handle anything, even the three lovable imps who were the cornerstone of her heart.

Maybe it was because he was the first man she'd noticed since Dylan died.

"Who's Rhonda's backup?" Teddy Krengle asked the obvious.

Frank scrubbed his face with his right hand. "Cheyenne was our backup until she moved. We're very proud of keeping the Holly management in the family. The Holly has belonged to the Craddocks since we bought it from the Sims family in 1973."

Once again, noise dominated the space with people talking over each other, drowning out whatever Frank was trying to say. Beside her, Ben stood still and observed the melee breaking out around them.

"What's going to happen to the play?" someone called out.

Frank exhaled and shook his head. "We're concerned about our grandson and Cheyenne."

People interrupted him, chiming in their agreement family came first. He motioned for silence and continued, "As of now, tomorrow evening's rehearsal is on as scheduled, but if I can't find an interim director, I'll cancel rehearsal until I can fly back to Violet Ridge."

"What happens if you need to stay in Kansas? You need to be with your family." Teddy frowned, a jarring sight as if Santa himself were frowning.

"If that happens, I don't know if the show will go on."

A chilling silence broke out. No one could fault Frank and Rhonda for their concern over their family. Still, this production meant so much to the community. Truth be told, it meant so much to Daisy and her children. This play had given them a lifeline in the month after Dylan's death, a way to cope during the worst of circumstances. Who knew if it would help someone else in the same manner this year?

"The show will go on. It always does," Teddy reassured Frank. "We just need to find a director."

Everyone looked at each other. Some shrugged while others focused their gaze at the ground, obviously unwilling to take the reins. Daisy couldn't blame them. A play of this magnitude would require a full-time effort. She'd love to step up, but her job at the dude ranch and the care of her three children precluded any more obligations. As it was, she struggled to find time for her silversmithing.

Rhonda returned with Rosie, Lily and Aspen, each of whom carried a bag of animal crackers. Rosie ran to Daisy and reached out her bag. "Hi, Mommy. These are so good. Want to share with me?"

"I'd love one." How would she break the news to them this year's production might not happen as planned? Just the thought of their disappointment sent her reeling. This could ruin Christmas for them.

Aspen headed over to Ben. "Want a cookie? I'll share."

She brightened at the connection Aspen was already forming with someone new. Normally he held back until he trusted the person would stay in his life for longer than a few days. He'd been like that ever since Dylan died.

Ben shook his head. "Thank you, but I had some roasted chestnuts before I came here."

Daisy's lips thinned into a straight line. Couldn't he see Aspen was trying to connect with him?

Then again, Aspen was persistent, and he didn't prove her wrong. "Come on, Mr. Irwin. You've never had one of Miss Rhonda's special cookies. They're really good. They have frosting and everything. You gotta try the tigers. They're my favorite."

Ben met Daisy's gaze, and she arched her eyebrow. Sure Ben was handsome on the outside, but how a person responded to a child's offer of animal crackers was often a good arbiter of what was on the inside.

"One frosted animal cracker shouldn't ruin my dinner." Ben's deadpan voice lifted Daisy's spirits. He reached inside and pulled out a cookie. Sampling it, he crunched with extra effect. "I've always been partial to camels. Thank you, Aspen."

Her son's grin stretched from ear to ear, and Lily and Rosie then insisted on sharing theirs with Ben as well. If he won over the triplets this easily—a tough audience if there ever was one—he could do anything. She had it! Ben should serve as the interim director. If so, he'd knock this production out of the park. And the Irwin family's word counted for so much around here, so he'd have the community's support, too.

If this was only about what was best for her, she wouldn't ask Ben to take over as interim director. After all, canceled rehearsals would have given her extra time in December to jump-start her jewelry business. Crafting her signature dangly earrings and fashioning those one-of-a-kind necklaces filled her creative well and provided an income boost, one she'd need for more expensive childcare once Tatum departed for college. One look at the radiant faces of her children, though, and she knew. This play wasn't only about her. It was about the happiness this play was bringing the trio, along with the joy it would provide to Violet Ridge residents on Christmas Eve.

With her resolve intact, Daisy looked up at Ben, and he stiffened. "What are you going to ask of me? Charades? Relay races? The Hokey Pokey?"

"That's what it's all about, isn't it?" Daisy smiled at her own joke and then considered the man before her. Authoritative, in control, personable. Weren't those directorial traits? "And helping people. That's definitely what life's about."

Ben reached for another cookie. "That's my plan."

She gasped at the idea that the two of them were already on the same wavelength. This was working even better than planned. After all, he was the ideal solution. Frank could go to Topeka without any worries, and the triplets wouldn't be disappointed. "Are you about to throw your hat in the race?"

He munched the head of a tiger. "I prefer to keep it private until I'm committed. There's a lot riding on my decision, and people might not warm up to me. While I was serving in the military for twenty years, Violet Ridge moved on. It's almost unrecognizable."

"I think you're perfect for the position."

Ben pulled out another cookie and studied it and then glanced at her, the fine wrinkles on his forehead forming frown lines.

"It's a hippo," Daisy said.

"I know." He bit off the head and chewed. "I've only told a few people about this. Then again, nothing stays a secret around here for long. I suppose I shouldn't be surprised my intention to run for mayor is out there."

"Mayor? I thought you were volunteering to take over as interim director." So much for being on the same wavelength. They weren't even in the same building!

He broke off eye contact with her. "Oh, no… no. I don't know anything about directing a play." A hush fell over the room, so much so that everyone must have heard what he said. Ben forced a laugh and pantomimed dipping an imaginary brush in a bucket of paint. "I get stage fright so I'm about the last person you'd want for this job. I'm just the paint guy, the muscle you need to lift the sets into place. Elf at work."

Lily tapped Daisy's arm. "Mommy, I'm hungry. Is it dinnertime?"

Rosie nodded while Aspen rubbed his stomach over his coat.

Daisy gathered them together, moving them past Frank. "Congratulations on your grandson. I hope you find an interim director before you leave."

Too bad it wouldn't be Ben. He seemed to bond with almost everyone in the building, but he obviously didn't want the position. On the plus side, if the past week was any indication of his ability to get along with a varied group of performers and crew members alike, he'd serve the town well if elected mayor.

Why he couldn't step into Frank's shoes and direct the play, especially since there were only twenty-four days left leading up to Christmas Eve, was beyond Daisy's comprehension. He'd be a natural, but that wasn't her decision to make. This week she'd find some way to keep the triplets' minds off the canceled rehearsals and hope Frank found someone so he could visit Topeka with a clear mind. She'd leave it at that. Somehow, the play would go on.

With or without Ben, as far as she was concerned.

CHAPTER THREE

"NO WORRIES, BEN. I intend to call the high school drama director tonight and ask her to take over as interim director." Frank tapped an ancient Rolodex on the corner of his office desk. "I also have some other contacts to try. Past cast and crew members. People who know their way around here."

Frank looked too relieved at not having to take Ben up on his offer to direct. He rose and shook the older gentleman's hand. "Good to know."

Reassured there were other options on the table, Ben took his leave, the roasted chestnuts and animal crackers no substitute for a filling dinner.

He patted his coat pocket, the timer still secure in its place. After he ate, he'd install it and keep his promise to his neighbor. He was almost out of the auditorium when something caught his eye. There, on the ground, was Lily's doll. The one not named Tatum.

He sighed. Earlier he'd seen the love in Lily's eyes for her doll, Winter. The thought of her being disappointed when she couldn't find Winter didn't sit well with him. Neither was it sitting well how Daisy had been disappointed in his response to her asking him to take over as the interim director. Delivering Winter to Lily and updating Daisy about his conversation with Frank might return him to Daisy's good graces.

He picked up the doll and found a tag on the back of Winter's shirt. "If found, please return to Daisy Stanley." Her phone number and address were listed there.

Dinner could wait until he made a little girl happy, and maybe her mother as well. Not that there was anything between him and the lovely Daisy. He wanted a family someday, but not this soon and not with Daisy. For one thing, he'd be getting an instant family without any time for him and Daisy to get to know each other better. *If* he were to start dating someone, he would want to take it slow, make sure their personalities meshed before getting in too deep. He thought about his dad and his new stepmother, Evie. She brought out a mellow side of his father Ben never knew existed. While Ben hadn't been able to return to Violet Ridge for their wedding last year, he'd spent time with them since then. They balanced each other, with Evie reminding Ben's father to relax and enjoy life while Dad adored Evie, sharing early-morning horse rides with her on the open range.

The two were so much alike Ben could see why they fell in love. They suited each other far more than his father and his mother, who were opposites. His mother was a night owl who preferred spending time in Violet Ridge, seeking out civic causes. She'd even been allergic to horses. His parents had been total opposites, and he'd always vowed never to fall for someone so different from him.

When he settled down, he wanted someone like him. Relationships were hard enough without overcoming personality differences. Daisy was appealing with her dimples and wavy light brown hair, but mellow didn't begin to describe her. Life happened around her, and Ben wanted someone relaxed. Not the tumultuous maelstrom that swirled around whatever room she occupied.

For now, though, he'd get another taste of Daisy's bright personality before settling in for the evening at his house. The empty one with lots of rooms, waiting for occupants to grace its presence with love and laughter.

Somehow, he'd have to start making that happen. *Hmm.* His spring garden would be the ideal backdrop for kicking off his mayoral campaign. His family was well-known in these parts, and people would come to support his father and end up liking what he could bring to the table.

On that note, he tucked the doll under his coat

and headed outside. During rehearsal, a light snow had begun falling. The upper part of the theater marquee had a fine sheen of ice. Downtown, the black lampposts glowed in the early-evening gloaming with strands of twinkling lights attached in a diagonal pattern over the streets. With Winter safe and sound, he started for his SUV but stopped when his father's accountant welcomed him back to Violet Ridge. After a few minutes, he resumed his journey and was almost at his car when a high school classmate approached him to ask if he would consider joining the reunion committee. After getting roped into helping with refreshments for the next event, Ben kept his head low and arrived at his car.

He was deicing his windshield when someone else approached. Ben tensed until the older man explained his compact wouldn't start. He pulled out his jumper cables and recharged the compact's battery. As much as Ben wanted to concentrate on the task at hand, the older man chattered away about his wife's pot roast and a warm fire. Before the elderly gentleman went on his way, he thanked Ben and wrote down his address, insisting Ben drop by soon for a slice of his wife's gingerbread cake.

Ben just smiled and placed the cables in the trunk, knowing he'd do no such thing.

Before he knew it, he pulled into a driveway on Canyon Outlook Avenue, the address on the doll's shirt. The snow had ceased with only a light dusting dotting the bushes. There wasn't enough to build a snowman or impact transportation. His attention was drawn to the cozy home covered in a bright display of colorful lights. Even the window boxes, filled with daisies rather than poinsettias, were outlined with twinkling lights. In fact the whole yard was a testament to the holiday. In the middle of her front yard were eight wire reindeer and Santa in his sleigh, the frames covered with white LED lights.

Apparently they both loved Christmas decorations.

He retrieved Lily's doll and headed for the front porch, taking care on the slippery front steps. At the door, he searched for the doorbell, which was somewhat difficult to locate due to a huge pine wreath with holly berries and a big plaid bow taking up half the door. Finally, he found and pressed the doorbell, and a lone howl reverberated through the house. Ben kept from rushing inside to make sure nothing was wrong. After a minute elapsed, he paced the length of the front porch, taking note of the three-foot snowman standing between a pair of rocking chairs, its black scarf illuminated with small white lights.

Another minute went by, and no answer. Nobody was home. Lily might have convinced Daisy to return to the theater to look for Winter. He fingered the doll, wondering what to do next. When his sister, Lizzie, was young, she couldn't sleep without her cherished teddy bear. There was that one time he and his brother retraced every step of her day until they found the beloved bear in the chicken coop with an egg resting on the stuffed animal's bright red bow.

Lizzie had hugged Jeff and then Ben with an intensity she still possessed today. He couldn't wait to meet her baby in a few weeks.

Tomorrow he'd stop in at Reichert Supply Company and pick out the largest, softest teddy bear for his impending niece or nephew, but that didn't solve his new dilemma. Would Lily be able to sleep without Winter?

He checked the back of the doll again and found a phone number. He texted a message that he had located Winter. Why he didn't start with that, he wasn't quite sure. If he was honest, maybe he'd just wanted to see Daisy again.

Grasping Winter in hand, he was more than satisfied he'd done all he could do tonight. Besides, he still needed to install the holiday display timer. He headed to his car when he heard the door open behind him. A long brown blur of a dog ran past him before coming to a halt in front of him. Then a line of drool passed from the hound's mouth into the snow before the dog, most likely a bloodhound mix, sniffed him as if expecting him to bear treats instead of a doll.

"Pearl! Come back here." Daisy's soft voice was soothing yet insistent.

The dog let out a bawling howl and then jumped onto Ben's jeans, more drool dripping from her mouth onto the dark denim. Ben turned and found Daisy at the doorway.

"What are you doing here?" She clapped her hands. Pearl reluctantly left his side and joined Daisy, a look of disapproval on her pretty features.

"I found Lily's doll." He held up Winter, and Daisy's face softened.

"Thank you for bringing Winter home." Daisy stood at the threshold and reached for the doll.

During the exchange, his hand brushed against hers. The warmth of her skin seeped into him, sending a shock through his body. He checked the soles of his shoes. Static electricity, pure and simple.

Aspen appeared in the foyer and reached for Pearl's collar. A grin spread across his face. "Hey, it's Mr. Ben." He turned toward the staircase. "Rosie! Lily! Mr. Ben's here."

A door slammed, and Rosie and Lily stormed down the stairs, throwing themselves at his side.

Daisy handed Lily her doll. "He found Winter and brought her home."

Lily squeezed his side especially hard. "Thank you." She let go and embraced Winter. Then she glanced up at him, her big hazel eyes large and luminous. "Do you like tomato soup? Mommy's making that and grilled cheese."

Aspen started nodding his head up and down so hard Ben feared whiplash might set in. "It's gooey and melts in your mouth."

An acrid odor filled the air, and Pearl let out a low, long howl.

"The sandwiches." Daisy said, raising her hand to her mouth.

Daisy rushed into the kitchen with everyone, including Ben, on her heels. She grabbed an oven mitt and removed the pan from the burner. Wisps of smoke wafted off the sandwiches. Without a word, she stepped on the lever of the trash can and disposed of the problem.

Pearl rushed forward, obviously hoping some food dropped on the floor, but Rosie waggled her finger. "No, Pearl. That's not for you."

The dog slunk away as if she understood. Then she perked up at seeing Ben again. The hound sat in front of him, her dark brown eyes soulful and pleading, as if expecting him to produce food out of thin air. He held up his hands. "I only brought Lily's doll. Nothing else."

He watched as Daisy doled out tasks to her three children. In turn, Rosie retrieved cheese from the refrigerator while Aspen found a stool and lowered a loaf of bread from the cabinet. Lily plucked a tomato from a bowl of fruit and handed it to her mom. Ben found himself drawn to the family moment. He'd never taken part in anything like this at the ranch where the long-time cook reigned supreme in the kitchen.

Daisy raised her eyebrow while slicing thick slices of tomato. "Is there something wrong?"

He didn't want to burden her with his child-hood and focused on something happier: her family. "I was just thinking that your children are all so different. Rosie's obviously a natural leader." Something he could appreciate well after serving under some of the best officers. "Aspen's a go-getter, and Lily loves hugs. I'm guessing she's quieter, more of an introvert?"

Daisy nodded and walked over to the stove. She stirred the soup and then switched off the burner, turning back toward Ben. "Rosie and Aspen are more outgoing while it takes Lily time to form bonds. At least those are their natural tendencies. Aspen has only recently come out of the shell he built around himself two years ago. It's taken them time to find themselves again after Dylan's death."

Lily sent him a shy smile while giving Winter another hug. "Thank you for finding her. I wouldn't have been able to sleep without her."

That smile twisted his insides into a pile of goo. Thank goodness no one from his unit could see him now.

Rosie came over and tapped his side. "Are you staying for dinner?"

Aspen rushed over and echoed Rosie's invitation. "We're going sledding after dinner. You can come with us."

"I'm sure Ben has something else to do." Daisy wiped her hands on a dish towel. "Right, Ben?"

Her tone made it clear she was dismissing him, yet he didn't want to leave this homey kitchen just yet. He liked the Stanley household. "Actually, I'd like my next mission to be devouring a grilled cheese and tomato sandwich. Then I can tell you about my conversation with Frank."

Daisy cleared her throat and sent him a furtive look of warning. Even though they hadn't known each other long, he received the message to maintain silence about that subject around the triplets.

"Everyone wash up with actual soap and water, especially Aspen," Daisy said.

The trio filed out of the room with Aspen muttering something about his hands already being clean. Pearl followed behind, her claws clattering on the hardwood floor.

Ben held out his hands. "How can I help?"

"You have a good six inches on me. Reach up and grab that bag of croutons, please." She pointed to the top shelf, and he handed them to her with ease. "Thanks. We like them on our tomato soup." She emptied the bag into the bowl. "What happened with Frank?"

Ben filled her in on their conversation, starting with how they'd bonded over talk about babies, namely Lizzie's impending arrival and little Noah in the NICU, and finishing with Frank's list of contacts for an interim director. "He's positive the drama teacher will take over the play."

"I know her. She was in the same graduating class as Lizzie and me." Daisy spread butter on the bread and placed the sandwiches in a pan on the stovetop. "Please tell Lizzie I said hello. It seems like yesterday I sat behind her in biology class. Back then, she was Lizzie Irwin and I was Daisy Virtue. You had already joined the air force."

If the constant motion that hovered around Daisy wasn't enough of a reason to fight this rising attraction, the reminder of their age difference was. He was six and a half years older than his sister. If Daisy and Lizzie were classmates, Daisy was also that much younger.

"Yeah. I went straight from high school to the Air Force Academy. I loved serving my country." Even now, he missed the discipline and purpose. He'd heard from some of his fellow officers and wished he could have left on his own terms. "I'm settling here for good. It will be nice to be around family, even more so now that I'll have a new niece or nephew."

Thanksgiving had provided some much-needed time in reestablishing his relationship with his sister. Better still, he'd be around from the beginning for his baby niece or nephew.

"Family is important. I hope my brother Jase moves back someday, but at least my other two brothers are here." She flipped the sandwiches and then ladled soup into bowls, garnishing each with croutons and a pinch of shredded cheese. "Sorry if I became emotional this afternoon. For some reason, I latched onto the idea that you'd be the right choice for the interim director, but I should have talked to you about it in private first. Glad to hear that Frank has it under control. This production means so much to me. To the whole town, really."

Hearing her say that, it took all of Ben's willpower not to call Frank and offer his services on the spot, but the Holly Theater stage was a place he'd prefer to avoid. One bout of stage fright per lifetime was enough.

Limiting his involvement with the Stanley family was also becoming something he'd be wise to do—he was already starting to get attached. It was just that the surroundings were so inviting. A dog in the kitchen, a crackling fire in the adjoining living room and triplets making noise up and down the staircase. Daisy's sunny personality countered his gruffer side. And yet there were too many reasons he should cut his losses and leave now. Their age difference. The children. His promise to Constance Mulligan to install the timer. With his hip, he should have installed it in the daylight.

"Thanks for the invite." Ben backed away until his leg came in contact with something. Pearl yelped, and he realized he'd stumbled across Daisy's dog. He rubbed the spot where Pearl collided into him, and then petted the hound. "But I'll be on my way before I cause any more accidents."

"Nonsense. The triplets invited you, and you accepted." She reached up and brought down another bowl. "There's plenty of soup."

Her stress on the word *triplets* gave him pause. He liked Daisy's children, but it was their mother he wanted to get to know better. "Tomato soup is my favorite, but…"

Lily came into the kitchen and hugged him. "Thanks for bringing Winter home." She dug into her pocket and shoved something at him. "I want you to have the candy cane I got at school today for helping the teacher. Can you sit next to me?"

"No, sit next to me!" Aspen emerged next and yanked on Ben's arm. "I saw you first."

Rosie entered and stomped her foot. "He hasn't spent time with me yet so he should sit next to me." She smiled at Ben, her bottom adult tooth already emerging, another way to tell her apart from her sister, along with the eyes.

"I can't sit next to each of you, but I can tell Lily and Rosie apart now. It's the eyes. Lily's are closer together."

"You're perceptive." Daisy handed him a bowl of soup and tilted her head toward the dining room. "Triplet, Mr. Ben, triplet, Mommy, triplet. We'll invite him another time so everyone can have a turn next to him."

How could he tell her this was a one-time occasion? From now on, he'd steer a wide berth from this house with Daisy's soft edges on full display. Twenty years in the military, something he'd never regret, some of the best years of his life, had hardened him. He'd seen things that still haunted his dreams, waking him up in cold night terror, drenched in sweat. He wouldn't expose anyone to that.

He stuck the candy cane in his coat pocket while the triplets bickered about which two would be the fortunate ones.

"Whoa!" Ben brought his index finger and thumb to his mouth for a loud whistle. The triplets and Pearl fell into attention. *Good.* "You're forgetting that someone needs to sit next to your mom, especially since she made this meal for us."

Lily went over and hugged her mom's side. "I don't want you to feel bad, Mommy. Aspen and Rosie can be near Mr. Ben."

Daisy returned the embrace, and Ben already felt the love in this close-knit family, a taste of what he wanted someday in the far, but not too far, future. After he met his new niece or nephew. After he figured out how to serve Violet Ridge.

After he got his life in order.

DAISY GAUGED THE scant amount of snow accumulated on the steep slope of Gregson Park. The exterior floodlights on tall wooden poles provided plenty of illumination on the outdoor hill, a town favorite that was within walking distance of her home as well as equidistant to downtown. Generations of Violet Ridge residents had partaken of winter fun by sledding and building snow forts here. With temperatures never rising past the freezing mark since the last snowfall, she assumed there'd be enough powder for sledding. The lack of residents in the vicinity should have been an instant clue she was wrong. Three disappointed faces stared back at her. Four if you counted Pearl.

Five, if you counted Ben.

Not that his disappointed face was different from his troubled expression or his happy countenance. Come to think of it, he was hard to read, not like Dylan at all. Her stomach wrenched at the comparison. It wasn't fair to compare gruff, military Ben to her lighthearted, easygoing late husband.

The past two years had been the hardest of her life, even harder than losing her parents in a car crash when she was eight. But this year marked a turning point. Dylan would have wanted her to find happiness again. She'd have wanted the same if the tables had been turned, and he was raising the triplets alone.

Yet she'd been the one to receive the knock at the door from the police officer informing her of Dylan's death the weekend after Thanksgiving. With Rosie sniffling and Lily running a fever, she insisted Dylan go by himself on the skiing trip with their mutual best friends. He had wanted to stay home and help take care of the triplets, but their friends had been visiting from London, and she wanted one of them to have fun. That last day, though, he was caught in an avalanche, never to return.

Accepting happiness without strings or comparisons was easier said than done. No one told her at Dylan's funeral that the goodbye she said to him then wasn't the last goodbye she'd ever say in her mind. There were lots of little good-byes. After two years, she was beginning to live again.

And that first holiday without Dylan? Her empty shell had come face-to-face with three preschoolers who needed to latch onto some semblance of happiness, especially when their friends were beaming with hopes of sugarplums and Santa. A huge chunk of her heart may have been buried with Dylan, but three pieces of her heart stared back at her every morning at the breakfast table, each looking to her for stability and comfort. Needing a distraction from the numbing pain, she purchased tickets to that year's production of *The Santa Who Forgot Christmas*, and they all laughed for the first time since Dylan's death.

That lighthearted moment was the lifeline that helped her through that first Christmas. This year, though, the holiday seemed different. Rosie, Aspen and Lily were finally old enough to have permanent memories. Rosie insisted on audition-ing for the play, hoping for a role in the annual production. Whatever Rosie did, Aspen and Lily were sure to follow. That type of enthusiasm had paid off with all three being cast, with Rosie and

Aspen getting the plum roles of the brother and sister who guided Santa through a comedy of errors until Santa finally remembered Christmas. Just as a cloud of gloom hung over Santa for most of the play, so too did that same cloud hover over their group at that moment.

"Sledding may be a no-go because it's too wet," she said, gathering the triplets close, "but that doesn't mean we can't have fun."

Raising morale was her role, first with her brothers after their parents died and then with the triplets after Dylan. She didn't mind, except sometimes she yearned for someone to do likewise for her.

Rosie trilled her lips together and then plopped into the snow. "I want to go home."

Her siblings followed her lead and rested in the snow, their ski pants keeping them from being soaked to the skin. Daisy wrinkled her nose until it came in contact with the soft knit yarn of her candy cane scarf. "We just arrived."

Even Pearl, hopefully warm in her doggie coat and booties, seemed to throw in the towel, settling on her haunches near Rosie, who petted the hound's bristly fur and scoffed. "There's nothing to do. We can't go sledding," Rosie said.

"Not with that attitude." Daisy tapped the bright fuchsia cap hiding Rosie's curly blond hair. "We can still make a snowman. Who's with me?"

Careful as dusk was claiming the area, she climbed down the steep slope until she found her footing in a flat area. Her coat reflected the dim light in the soft shadows. Pearl followed, the retractable leash giving her plenty of room to go at her own pace. Daisy twisted her body and found the quartet still waiting at the top.

"Come on! There's more snow in the shade." She'd discovered the best way for the triplets to fall and stay asleep was plenty of vigorous evening activity that expended the remainder of their vast energy reserve. The problem was, it wore down her supply as well, preventing her from pulling out her silversmith tools and returning to her favorite pastime. Soon, though, that would have to change, as she'd need the income for childcare once Tatum departed for college.

But this visit to Gregson Park was about so much more. Daisy would do her best to make sure this was the best and most memorable Christmas ever for the triplets.

After some grumbles, the foursome proceeded down the hill and congregated around her. She scooped up snow and packed it into a ball before placing it on the ground and rolling it around to add heft. "This here is snow-dog snow."

"Huh?" Ben grimaced. "I've never heard of a snow dog."

Daisy stopped what she was doing and pretended to act shocked. Then she placed her gloved hands over Pearl's ears. "Don't let Pearl hear you say that. She knows what I'm talking about, don't you, girl?"

Pearl thumped her tail and ran around Daisy.

"I love snow dogs." Lily imitated her mom's actions and glanced at Ben. "Can you help me make a snow kitty cat?"

"What about a snow T. rex?" Aspen got into the fun and started packing snow into a ball.

Ben did the same. "We'll come back to do that another time. Let's build a giant snow dog together. Pearl would like that, wouldn't you, Pearl?"

The dog howled her approval as the cold air invaded Daisy's lungs and froze her insides. Another time? Was that promise for the triplets? Or did he want to spend time with her?

She looked at him. Tall and rather imposing, Ben wasn't bad to look at; he was actually quite handsome. That scar on his chin added more character. A quiver that had nothing to do with the cold shot through her system. Someone like Ben might be perfect for her, though. Strong and solid, he radiated security. If they ever dated and agreed to a relationship, she could keep her heart intact with him.

It had been over ten years since she'd been out on a first date with anyone. A few men had invited her out this year, but she'd always used the excuse she'd need to find a babysitter for her triplets. No one had asked twice. Really, she hadn't found any of the offers appealing, let alone the men behind the request. Until now. Not that Ben had asked her out. It was quite obvious he was bonding with her children, but there was no sign he found her attractive.

Aspen yanked her coat, bringing her out of her thoughts. Everyone seemed to be waiting for her to accept Ben's offer. She laughed away the tension and packed enough snow to create one of her dog's long ears. "That's one thing you can always count on. Snow and Colorado go hand in hand like Santa and cookies. Hey, Pearl, you'll be famous."

Her dog howled and then plopped in the snow. Together they created a snow mound that slightly resembled Pearl, enough so that a few passersby complimented their snow dog. Enthusiasm spread through the crowd with another family creating four snow puppies that trailed behind their original. Daisy might be biased, but she liked their rendition of Pearl the best, not that it compared with the actual canine, who was far superior.

Ben took out his phone and snapped a picture of the snow dog. The triplets clamored to be in the next one. "And Pearl." The three of them clapped and beckoned the hound, who bounded over to them, her tail thumping on the snow, sending ice chunks in the air.

Daisy rushed to get her phone and snapped many pictures so she could figure out which was one didn't have Aspen in motion later. "I hope it's okay we waylaid your evening like we did."

"I enjoyed getting to know the triplets better." Ben pocketed his phone and smiled. "Besides, I only had one thing to do tonight, and it won't take long to install a timer on my holiday display."

"Good. Then you have time for one more activity."

Without another word, Daisy fell backward onto the snow and moved her arms up and down.

"Snow angels!" Rosie came over and did the same.

The four of them stood and oohed over their creations. Daisy sidled over to Ben and nudged him. "What are you waiting for?"

"I'll get wet." Ben stared at her as if stating the obvious.

"It's fun." She narrowed her gaze. "Haven't you ever made a snow angel before?"

"It's late. Don't the triplets have school tomorrow?" Ben looked at his watch with a stern look. "A regimented schedule is a good indicator of future success."

While Ben's argument was compelling, she stood there, tapping her winter boot. "You didn't answer my question."

"I gravitated toward snow forts and snowball fights with my older brother." Ben looked wistfully at the four imprints on the ground. "But I did make snow angels a long time ago."

"It sounds like you made them with someone you cared about," Daisy prodded, seeking out something personal even though they'd only known each other a short time.

"My mother. She died when I was twelve. Winter was her favorite season." Ben sighed and fell backward in the snow.

Having Ben reconnect with his childhood definitely counted as her victory for today.

The triplets cheered and encouraged him to move his arms up and down. Their energy and enthusiasm were Daisy's constants in a world where everything else changed from day to day. She wouldn't have it any other way. Life without finding joy in the little things was rather dull, and not for her.

Ben rose and looked down at his snow angel. She saw his jaw click, and she sidled next to him. "Your mother would love it."

"She would." He smiled and then looked out at the group. "Do you always keep them out this late on school nights?"

"They're only little once." Now it was her turn to be on the defensive.

Daisy called the triplets together, and they

started heading home. "This school week is filled with holiday parties, and I just attended their first-grade teacher conferences. They're on track for second grade, and they would have been out this late if Frank hadn't canceled tonight's rehearsal."

Her skin prickled as she rushed to her own defense. Why she did that, she wasn't quite sure. He didn't know anything about their bedtime rituals or holiday traditions or anything personal. And yet there was something about him that made her want to become acquainted with him, find out more about personal details like the one he just shared with her about snow angels.

That simple act sparked the attraction inside her, the flame growing stronger by the minute.

They turned onto her street, and Ben held up his hands. "You can tell me to back off."

It was Daisy's turn to reevaluate her rush to a hasty conclusion. He must have attached himself to the triplets if he was already concerned about their bedtime.

"You haven't said anything I haven't heard before." They were now halfway to her house, and she could already see her decorations, a sight that inevitably lifted her spirits. "I'm used to listening while people express their opinions about my children."

Because no matter where she went in Violet

Ridge, there were residents who felt compelled to advise her about what she could do differently in terms of the triplets' upbringing.

"I'm still adjusting to civilian life and becoming more diplomatic." Ben strolled along, keeping pace with Pearl although the triplets were a few paces ahead of them. "The air force is prolific in terms of schedules and discipline."

"There's a place for that, but childhood only comes along once. There's something special about the first trip of the year to Gregson Park. When there's more snow, it'll be packed with people. I'm glad we went tonight before everyone in Violet Ridge descends on the best sledding hill around." They reached her front door, and she unlocked it. The triplets and Pearl ran inside, but Daisy lingered on the porch with Ben.

"There can be something special about a schedule and a set routine," Ben countered, concern written on his face, expressive for the first time since she'd met him. "Good night, Daisy."

He started down the steps, and she called out, "Make a snow angel in your front yard tonight. Incorporate it into your nightly routine until Christmas." He turned around and stepped up the stairs leading to her front door.

Chills that had nothing to do with the weather raised goose bumps under her coat. Was he going to ask something personal? Ask her out on a date? Maybe if he could kiss her?

The answer to each would be a resounding yes. Then a crash came from inside her house. Alarm skittered through her, and she yelled out, "Good night, Ben."

She slammed the door in his face and ran to the source of the noise. There was Pearl, munching happily on her kibble that had fallen to the kitchen floor, the storage bin open and empty beside her. A good distance from the mess, the triplets pointed their fingers at each other, claiming the other was responsible. Relief no one was hurt registered, as did Pearl's crunching happily away without a care in the world.

Daisy reached for the broom and started cleaning. Even if Ben had been interested, she was sure this antic would run him off. Her chaotic life had no room for anyone else. Making this holiday perfect for her kids came first, and that kept her plenty busy.

CHAPTER FOUR

BEN DUSTED THE snow off his navy wool peacoat and entered Mi Casa Mexican Restaurant. There wasn't anyone at the attendant area, but it wasn't hard to find his sister among the crowded tables. Lizzie was so intent on studying the menu that her hands flew to her chest when he sat across from her. She exhaled a surprised breath. "I wasn't expecting you for another five minutes."

"If you're not early, you're late." This military expectation had always served him well. She started to rise, but he shook his head. "Don't get up on my account."

"Thank you for agreeing to eat here instead of the Smokehouse. The baby wanted guacamole, and I didn't wait for you to order some."

As if on cue, the server brought a basket of chips, a bowl of guacamole and two glasses of water.

Lizzie thanked her with a smile as she reached for a tortilla chip. "This is perfect for now."

"Where's Lucky?" Ben looked around for

Lizzie's husband, who was supposed to join them for lunch.

"He and Sabrina are busy at the rodeo academy. Sabrina and her husband purchased a mare for training the clowns a few months ago, and she and Lucky are teaching Miss Lightning new tricks over the holidays. This week they're teaching her how to give kisses." Lizzie flipped over the menu and tapped the laminated plastic with her thumbnail. "I can't decide between the chile rellenos and the tamales."

"Have both. What you can't finish, take home to Lucky." Then Ben's curiosity got the better of him. "How can a mare give kisses?"

"By bussing the clown on her cheek. As part of the entertainment, the rodeo clown performs between events. Sabrina rode around in a clown car as part of her routine, but she and Ty want to incorporate horses into their training. When the classes aren't in session, they teach their horses new tricks, like bowing, giving the clown a kiss and so on." Lizzie placed the menu on the table and dipped another chip into the guacamole. "Mmm, this is delicious. Have some."

She pushed the bowl toward him, and Ben obliged. "You're right."

"Of course I am." Lizzie smiled and reached for his hand, giving it a squeeze. "You'd make a great addition to the ranch. I can find a place for you."

Ben froze with his second chip already immersed in the guacamole. This was what he was afraid of. That she'd pressure him back to the ranch, and they'd end up fighting since they were both stubborn. He knew too well his hip precluded any hard physical labor, and everyone on the ranch earned their keep. As much as he loved his sister, he didn't belong at the Double I. "Thanks, but I like being a guest rather than an employee."

"You're not a guest. You're family." She directed a look of frustration in his direction. "Same with Sabrina. You're her stepbrother, but she considers me her sister and you her brother. If you want a job at the rodeo academy, we can go straight there after lunch."

Lizzie's persistence made her an efficient yet conscientious manager of one of the largest ranches in Colorado, but now was the time to confide in her about his future plans. "Thank you for your concern." Eating lunch with her and seeing her glowing eyes made him feel wanted. He appreciated that, as well as her loyalty to Sabrina. "But I've decided how I want to give back to Violet Ridge."

After delivering their orders to the server, he launched into his intention to run for mayor. The

Irwin family had formed a good bond with the residents of Violet Ridge, and he wanted to keep that going. Lizzie sat back, tears in her eyes. "Mom would be so proud."

"I'm not officially in the running for mayor yet." And he wasn't sure the play was the best way to help his campaign.

Gaining community support, though important, was no longer the reason he was committed to the play. He liked being part of something bigger than himself again. Cutting wood, pounding nails and creating Santa's North Pole Workshop weren't the daily activities he envisioned for himself earlier this year when he was deployed to a support base in Afghanistan. But in a little over a week, he'd established a routine around the theater. There was just enough variety to keep things interesting.

"Let me know what you need me to do for your campaign, and I'll get it done." Lizzie licked her lips as the server brought their food.

Ben thanked her and inhaled the cilantro and spices of his loaded burrito. He pointed his fork in the direction of Lizzie's baby bump. "You do know you'll be otherwise occupied."

Lizzie waved away his objection. "You're important to me. I make time for people I love. You're my brother, and you're home. I'm so happy." She wiped away a tear at the corner of her eye and reached for her fork. "I hope you don't want a bite of my tamale. I'm eating every bite on this plate by myself."

He laughed and dug into his meal. In no time, he passed an empty plate to the server while they waited for the bill. He caught sight of Frank and Rhonda entering the restaurant. Frank whispered something in Rhonda's ear before Rhonda kept walking behind the attendant to their table.

"Ben." Frank looked troubled, dark circles lining his eyes.

Oh, no. Had something happened to his grandson? To his surprise, he was hanging on Frank's response, caring more than he would have a few weeks ago. "How are Cheyenne and Noah?"

Ben set his cloth napkin next to his plate while Lizzie echoed her concern over Frank's family.

"They're improving. Cheyenne is being released from the hospital tomorrow morning, and Noah's doing well." A glimmer of light shone in Frank's eyes. He pulled out his phone to show off pictures of his grandchild. "Rhonda's been worried, so I thought a meal at her favorite restaurant would do her good before we leave tomorrow."

"I'm looking forward to meeting the interim director tonight," Ben said.

"About that." Frank unbuttoned his coat and sank into one of the empty seats.

Ben pushed the remainder of the chips in Frank's direction. "You sound serious."

Lizzie excused herself to talk to a friend at a nearby table.

"No one can take over as interim director." Frank dipped a chip in the guacamole and ate it, followed by a second, then a third. "I've called the high school drama teacher, band director and principal. I've talked to every theater owner in a hundred-mile radius, and they have their own holiday productions. I even called Zelda Baker to see if she or Nelda could direct, but they're busy with the Snow Much Fun festival."

"What are you going to do?" Ben asked.

Frank shrugged and finished off the last of the guacamole. "If no one steps up, I'll have to cancel this year's production." He wiped the crumbs off his shirt. "This is our biggest moneymaker of the year, too."

Stunned, Ben sat back and stuck his hand into his coat pocket, coming in contact with something hard. What was it? Oh, yes. It was the candy cane Lily had given him last night. She, Rosie and Aspen had gone out of their way to make him feel included at dinner. They regaled him with stories about how they were now legends in the first grade with their classmates asking for their autographs. Almost everyone in their class had promised to attend the play on Christmas Eve. The triplets would be devastated if the show didn't go on.

Before Ben could offer to step up as the interim director, Lizzie returned, her hand cradling her back. "I think I ate too many tamales. Will you drive me home, Ben?"

Concern for Lizzie overtook anything else. He promised himself when he returned home that he'd do everything he could to be there for his family. So far, Thanksgiving and this lunch were signs he was succeeding. Ben grabbed his keys and said a hasty goodbye to Frank.

IN THE WARDROBE room at the Holly Theater, Daisy measured Aspen's neck and then his arms for his costume fitting. Next up would be Rosie. Normally backstage was a bustling area where Frank conducted his nightly production meeting. So far, though, there'd been no sign of Frank or Rhonda.

Worse yet, she hadn't spotted Ben either. Not that she was looking for him. Last night he'd come to her home to return Lily's doll and stayed at the behest of the triplets. He hadn't shown anything beyond a friendly interest in her. He was going to run for mayor, and she was a resident in a town where everyone looked out for each other. That was all.

"Ouch." Aspen wriggled and squirmed. "That's too tight."

"Sorry." Daisy loosened the cloth measuring tape from around Aspen's waist. "My mind was in the clouds."

That brought giggles from Rosie and Lily, and Daisy pushed away any thoughts about a handsome veteran. Instead, she focused on recording Aspen's measurements on the chart.

Rhonda entered the room without her usual smile. "Meeting in five. Frank wants everyone there."

Rhonda didn't sound like her usual self either. "Is everything okay with Noah?" Daisy asked.

The older woman's face lit up. "He and Cheyenne are doing well. I can't wait to fly to Topeka tomorrow."

The triplets crowded around her, asking questions about Kansas, but Rhonda put them off so she could tell the rest of the crew. Daisy worried about the announcement, but Ben had assured her Frank had leads on an interim director.

She already had faith in Ben, and that scared her.

After the measurements were done, she led the triplets to the paneled room set aside for cast read-throughs. Daisy found herself on the edge of the crowd, the triplets craning to see. Aspen jumped high for a better view. She placed her hand on Aspen's shoulder. His body tensed but he stayed still.

Frank stepped onto a raised dais and clapped four times until everyone's gaze rested on him. Rhonda joined him and placed her arm around his waist. He smiled at her, their love obvious. Then he faced the cast and crew, a long sigh tying Daisy's stomach in knots. This wasn't going to be good. "Rhonda and I want to thank each of you for your willingness to devote your holiday season to *The Santa Who Forgot Christmas*. Unfortunately, this will be the first time in forty years it won't be produced in Violet Ridge."

Gasps and murmurs rocketed through the crowd. Rosie burst into tears and dug her head into Daisy's side, her shudders sending a shot of pain through Daisy. She placed her arms around Rosie's small frame, hoping to provide some comfort as Frank continued, "I've reached out to at least twenty people, but no one can take over as interim director."

His voice faded. He stepped back, obviously needing a moment to compose himself. Rhonda continued for her husband, "And that's on top of what I do with the concession stand, operating the lighting board and more. We can't be worrying about the theater in Topeka." Her jaw clenched, and Frank wound his arm around her frame. "Not when Cheyenne and Noah need us."

Daisy remembered the time when the triplets were in the NICU. Daisy's blood pressure had soared, and her doctor induced labor at thirty-two weeks. As soon as she was well enough, she and Dylan, their hands joined, had stood in front of the incubators, willing each baby to grow and thrive. Since then, she'd had challenging days, unique moments and jaw-dropping split seconds of panic, but never did she feel anything less than thankful for the three graduating from the NICU with only minor issues.

Aspen tugged at her other side, alarm in those big brown eyes. "Why's Rosie upset?"

Rosie pulled away from Daisy's side, only to give her brother a piercing stare. "There's not gonna be a play. We're not Nicky and Noelle no more."

She burst into a new set of tears. Aspen finally comprehended the situation. Then he quivered and tried to keep a stiff upper lip. As if Lily knew she needed to comfort her siblings, she held out her arms, and the three joined together in a big circle.

"I'll take over as director," a man's voice heralded from the rear.

Everyone seemed to turn in the same direction at once. Ben stood there, his navy peacoat accenting his dark hair, slightly mussed from the knit hat he was fingering. "I was going to speak to you earlier, but Lizzie had a touch of indigestion that turned out to be, well, indigestion."

Rosie, Aspen and Lily released one another and rushed over to Ben, enveloping him in a big hug.

Frank must have had some qualms as he shook his head. "That's a nice gesture, Ben, but you've been gone from Violet Ridge for quite a while, and you don't have any experience at the playhouse."

"Actually I do," Ben said, irony in his voice. "This time, though, I'll be directing instead of acting."

Ben stood straight, firm in his decision. The frisson of attraction that pulsed through Daisy scared her more than she wanted to admit. It was one thing to take off her beloved wedding ring in the sanctity of her bedroom; it was another thing to feel something for another man. Ben might radiate security, but what she was starting to feel for him was anything but safe. When Dylan died, her heart had shattered into a billion pieces. She never wanted that level of pain over losing someone she loved again. Only by guarding her feelings would she keep herself from experiencing heartbreak.

No wonder she was attracted to aloof Ben. Who was safer than this veteran who revolved around schedules and discipline?

She looked away and turned her attention back to Rhonda and Frank.

Rhonda whispered something in Frank's ear, and he nodded. "Looks like the show will go on."

The room erupted in a loud cheer. Daisy focused her gaze on Ben as the cast and crew offered their help. He looked most uncomfortable at being the center of attention, another indication he might flounder as the interim director.

But he was stepping into the role. She gave him credit for that.

Frank reminded the cast and crew there were only three weeks of rehearsals remaining. Crew members scattered away to build the sets and sew costumes and follow through with the other activities Daisy was learning about, all instrumental in coordinated synchronization toward a successful production.

Rhonda huddled with Frank while Ben remained with Rosie, Aspen and Lily glued to his side. Little did he know he now had three people who would follow him to the ends of the earth for taking over as director. Four, if you counted her. Ben's offer did more than salvage the triplets' holiday season. This play was a testament to how lighthearted fun could change a season of grief to a season of hope.

Daisy reached the trio at the same time as Rhonda.

"We shouldn't keep Teddy Krengle waiting." Daisy held out her hand.

Rhonda tapped Daisy's shoulder. "After you get them settled, can you come back for a minute?"

That tone gave Daisy pause, but she nodded. She led the triplets to the stage and explained Rhonda's request to Teddy and his wife, Jessica, the actress who was playing Mrs. Claus. They agreed to include Lily in the acting warm-ups.

Procrastinating since she didn't particularly want to hear what Rhonda was going to say, Daisy watched the group begin their stretching exercises. Teddy showed the triplets how to expand their facial muscles, and they went through a series of face elongations that made Daisy rumble with laughter. Next they roared like lions. While they pretended to taste sour lemons, Daisy could no longer put off the inevitable.

With reluctance, she left her vantage point and went back to the read-through room. There she found Ben sitting at the side table, examining a script with a pair of glasses ensconced firmly on the bridge of his nose. Like Clark Kent, the glasses added to his appeal, making his face more angular and bringing out his quiet intelligence.

He glanced in her direction and stood. "A shipment arrived, and Frank had to sign for it. They'll be right back."

"I'm surprised you didn't go with them, considering you're filling Frank's shoes," Daisy said.

"Frank is irreplaceable. I'm just keeping the seat warm." Ben removed his glasses, and she tamped the urge to place them back on his face.

This was the first time they'd ever been alone, and she quelled the reindeer prancing in her stomach. He'd taken off his peacoat, and his navy sweater emphasized his broad shoulders. She tore away her gaze and walked over to the row of cast pictures from previous productions of *The Santa Who Forgot Christmas*. The hairstyles and costumes may have changed, but the heart of the production was always the same. Each photo showcased the actors playing Santa and Mrs. Claus at the center flanked by the actors playing Nicky and Noelle and the rest of the cast.

She felt Ben's presence behind her, and those reindeer hooves danced once more as if they were about to take off pulling Santa's sleigh. But why? All she wanted was to make this the happiest Christmas ever for Rosie, Aspen and Lily. She barely knew Ben. Her strong reaction to him was merely manifested nervous tension about the rehearsal meeting. After all, Ben had saved the day. Who wouldn't respond to such a selfless act?

Welcoming any distraction while she composed herself, she concentrated on the pictures.

Something in one of the older photos caught her eye. The little boy who played Nicky looked a lot like Ben, but that couldn't be. He'd grown up on the Double I. Ranch chores must have occupied most of the day. Surely, he hadn't acted in the play. She turned around and bumped into the solidness of his chest. That was not the type of solidity she craved. When she found someone to spend time with, she wanted someone boring, someone who wouldn't break her heart.

He steadied her and then stepped backward.

"Thank you." She smoothed her red-and-green-plaid skirt, her favorite this time of year. She took another look at the cast photo and then at Ben once more. "Is that you?"

He blushed a deep red, rather endearing of the stiff former air force colonel. "I'm surprised that picture is there."

So he did have a history with the theater. "You were Nicky?"

"Yes and no. My mother drove me to the rehearsals with my baby sister in tow." He stared at the picture. "But my understudy performed as Nicky."

"What happened? Were you sick? Were you snowed in at the ranch?" Ben didn't seem like the type of person who shirked his commitments.

He shook his head and squirmed. "Stay fry." He mumbled the words and avoided her gaze.

"What's a 'stay fry'?" Then the truth hit her with the force of Santa's sleigh. "Oh. Stage fright."

"My father was rather upset that an Irwin let down the community. My classmates teased me about it for quite some time."

It made so much more sense now why he hadn't stepped forward when Frank put out his call for an interim director. And yet he'd come through for the cast and crew.

It took courage to return to the site of a childhood disappointment. Without giving it a moment's thought, she stepped toward him and pulled him into an embrace, the piney scent of his aftershave mixing with the fresh smell of his shampoo. This was the first time since Dylan died that she'd initiated close contact with a man who wasn't related to her. Her head felt as though she was cheating on Dylan while her heart reminded her Dylan would have wanted her to keep living. No one said it would be this hard to go on with the rest of her life.

She broke the contact as Frank and Rhonda walked into the room, both carrying boxes.

"Good. You're both here." Frank laid his box on the table and reached for Rhonda's load, setting it next to his. "Ben, thank you for agreeing to fill in for me."

Rhonda brushed her hands and sat in the closest chair, fanning her face, red from exertion.

"Whew. Glad to be sitting down, although I'll be sitting long enough on the plane tomorrow. I can't wait to meet little Noah and see Cheyenne for myself." Daisy would have loved for her mother to have been there with her in the NICU. As it was, her brothers had surrounded her with love, even though Jase had returned at the earliest opportunity to his job as a detective in Denver.

"It's scary when you see the baby in the incubator, but he's in good hands. Hopefully, he'll be released in time to spend his first Christmas at home." Daisy sent reassurance to the older woman along with some wisdom she wished someone had shared with her all those years ago.

"Thanks, Daisy," Rhonda said.

Daisy pointed toward the door. "I'd best get back to the triplets."

"I have a special request of you." Frank rifled through the box until he pulled out a binder. "The triplets will be fine during the rehearsal. Teddy and his wife have been acting as Santa and Mrs. Claus for the past ten years, and they're professionals with the child actors."

Then why was she needed as a volunteer? Frustration swept through her once more at how productive she could be in even one hour. Last night, Daisy had examined the flyers for January's after-school programs. She added up how much she'd need for art lessons for Lily, karate for Aspen and drama for Rosie. In three weeks' time, she could finish several pairs of top-quality earrings, enough to supplement next year's increased childcare costs once Tatum started college.

Silence filled the air, and Daisy realized she'd been lost in her thoughts. Everyone looked at her, and she winced. "I'm sorry. Can you repeat that last part?"

"I told you that you needed more finesse." Rhonda tsked at Frank before coming over and patting Daisy's hand. "It sounds like more of a job than it is. With your experience managing the dude ranch gift shop, you'll knock out the assistant director duties with no trouble."

"I don't need an assistant," Ben interrupted, reaching for his glasses on the table and placing them in his pocket.

Frank laughed away Ben's protest. "Trust me, you do. Rhonda's my lifeline. You can't be everywhere at once."

Ben opened his mouth, but Daisy was faster. She couldn't risk Frank and Rhonda canceling the play if she refused. "I'll do it."

She wanted to take back the words as soon as they left her mouth, but Frank and Rhonda seemed pleased with her decision. They launched into Daisy's new duties and tasks.

One look at Ben, and Daisy worried about

what she'd agreed to do since it sounded like she'd be working by his side quite often. She'd do the same all over again, though, if it helped the show go on. This meant too much to the triplets and to the Craddocks, not to mention the residents of Violet Ridge who made this play a part of their Christmas Eve tradition.

Somehow, she'd have to find as many excuses as possible to distance herself from the man who unsettled her heart.

CHAPTER FIVE

SATISFIED WITH HIS exterior illumination display on this crisp December morning, Ben turned his attention to sprucing up his interior decor. At Thanksgiving, Ben had carted away totes of ornaments and decorations that had belonged to his mother with his father's blessing.

Over the past few mornings before rehearsals, Ben had strolled down memory lane. His mother kept his preschool ornament, the one with his gawky picture set among a hundred puzzle pieces glued together. She also saved his toilet paper angel and the dough fingerprint plates. However, there were also unexpected treasures, including her Santa collection and her special ornaments. Every year, she'd added one unique glass ball, each painted by a local artist, some with violets, some with columbine, others with horses or buffalo. Next week, he'd purchase a second live Christmas tree from a local lot and showcase them.

This morning, Ben hung strands of garland intertwined with fairy lights along the top of his windowsill. From his vantage point, he saw four people walking on the sidewalk and carting something on a sled. Behind them, a familiar bloodhound stopped and sniffed a snow-covered bush. Even from here, he could tell Daisy was laughing, a happy expression on her pretty face. Her curly, honey brown hair was loose today and flowing over her shoulders. Watching her brought a lightness over him, one he hadn't felt since he was a teenager.

The Stanley family must be attempting another trip to Gregson Park. It was a perfect day for it since the snow had tapered off before dawn, leaving a cold winter day ideal for sledding. He could stay inside and finish decorating or catch the quartet and ask to join them. It was a no-brainer.

Ben rushed upstairs and threw on a sweater, snow pants and boots. By the time he donned his coat and reached the sidewalk, they were already gone, but no matter. They'd be easy to spot. If nothing else, he'd listen for Daisy's distinctive laugh and Pearl's bark.

Arriving at the hill covered in white from last night's snowfall, he looked around for Daisy or Pearl but couldn't find them. He clomped to the top of the hill. Still no dog or triplets or Daisy. His search yielded no trace of them.

Dejected, Ben returned home and caught something out of the corner of his eye. He stomped on the pristine snow until he reached Mrs. Mulligan's backyard. There was his elderly neighbor pinning fitted flannel cream bedsheets to the clothesline.

Worry clouded Ben's mind over his eccentric neighbor. Was she trying to conserve money or electricity by hanging her laundry out to dry? Or was her dryer broken?

"Good morning, Mrs. Mulligan," Ben called out, considering the nicest way to offer her his washer and dryer.

She glanced at her watch and frowned. "Afternoon, Mr. Irwin. Time's a-wasting standing around chitchatting."

She reached for another clothespin and remained on task. Ben's concern took flight. He stepped forward and pointed toward his house. "If you need to borrow my dryer, I'm not using it."

Her frown grew deeper, the wrinkles on her forehead forming deep creases. "Why would I need to do that?" She finished hanging the last sheet and picked up the laundry basket. "It's not snowing."

She turned and began walking to her back door. Being around people had done him a world of good over the past two weeks. Although whether it was people in general or one person in particular, namely Daisy Stanley, he wasn't quite sure. Still, that connection urged him to reach out to Constance one more time.

With Frank and Rhonda leaving for Kansas, there were open volunteer positions for the production. As the interim director, he wanted to make sure the cast and crew weren't spread out too thin.

"Wait." He headed toward her before he could talk himself out of his request.

She huffed out a breath that looked like a wispy puff.

"I'm about to take my nap, Mr. Irwin. I usually go to bed a little after nine at night, but your lights are keeping me awake." Her pointed tone was intended to stall further discussion, but he wasn't deterred. Not after twenty years in the military.

"I'll switch the timer to turn them off a half hour earlier." If he budged any more than that, though, he wouldn't even be turning them on period. "I'm filling in for Frank and Rhonda Craddock at the Holly Theater, and we need extra volunteers for the concession area and wardrobe department."

She transferred the basket from one arm to the other, her lips thin in disapproval. "I said no the first time, Mr. Irwin, and I meant no. Good day."

Since he returned to Violet Ridge, many residents had gone out of their way to welcome him with open arms. Some updated him on what he'd missed while he was overseas; others thanked him for his military service. He would have to live next to the one exception.

Ben glanced at the sheets hanging on the clothesline and bit his lip. Did she have any family to contact about whether this was her usual behavior? Or to make sure she had enough money to cover her electric bill? He scratched his head for a solution when he heard a commotion on his front porch.

Heading back, he discovered the Stanley family waiting for him. Pearl made her presence known with one lone bark, a line of slobber reaching from her mouth to the snow covering the grass. Then she trotted toward him, and he petted Pearl until she seemed satisfied and returned to Daisy's side.

A goofy grin spread over his face at the sight of her in colorful ski pants and a beanie with a pom-pom on top. "Hello."

Daisy's cheeks were pink from exertion, and Lily gave him a big hug. "Mr. Ben, we're delivering cookies."

Aspen reached him next and tugged at his hand, pulling him toward the sled parked in Ben's driveway. "We made them this morning. They're so good."

Rosie stood guard over the sled, her hands on her hips as if exasperated that her role as leader had been usurped, but she wedged her way to him, her grin as big as her personality. "They're sugar cookies with frosting on them."

He smiled at the triplets, wishing he could have delivered cookies with them. "I'll have to get on the nice list so you bring me some next year."

"You're always on my nice list, Mr. Ben." Lily approached him, Winter by her side. She then wrapped her doll's arms around his waist.

Ben was taken aback at how a doll's hug was something novel to him. It was sweet, and the whole scene was a picture of domesticity he wouldn't have appreciated a few months ago while reviewing security images and flight patterns. Then the accident changed everything, including his sleep habits. His permanent hip injury sometimes woke him up, and other times he found himself bolting awake covered in sweat from a nightmare.

He pushed that away, concentrating instead on the Stanley family's optimism and kindness. Something he could get used to in a hurry, if he let himself.

"And you're good at games." Rosie gave an emphatic nod as her stamp of approval.

"Unh. You're okay at hide-and-seek." Aspen stared at him, his nose wrinkled. "But you gotta work on letting us hide more."

Daisy reached into a bag and pulled out a red decorative tin with a snowflake design. "No one should have to wait a year for them. Here you go."

They brought him homemade cookies? He couldn't remember the last time someone gifted him such a treat. Removing the lid, he found a dozen cookies in the shape of stars with yellow frosting and dusted with golden sugar. His throat was tight, but he squeezed out his murmur of appreciation. "Thank you."

The smell of sugar was almost impossible to resist, but he found his manners before he ate the whole tin. "You must be freezing." Even Pearl looked as though she was cold. "If you have a minute, come in and warm up."

"You were our final stop." Daisy picked up the rope attached to the sled. "But we should really..."

The triplets crowded around her and clamored to see his house. "Please, Mommy! Let's go inside!"

He didn't know which warmed him more: the cookies or his popularity with the triplets. Ben pushed past everyone and opened his front door, clutching his tin like a commendation from a general. "If it's okay with you, I'll rummage up some hot chocolate."

Daisy's pink blush deepened to a rosy glow. "A present is just that, a freely given gift. We didn't expect anything in return."

"I'm not asking you to come inside because you gave me cookies. We're friends, right?" He held his breath.

For the past twenty years, he'd maintained a professional distance from his colleagues, his work becoming as much a part of him as the air he breathed and the food he consumed.

He'd almost forgotten what it meant to be a friend or how to make new ones.

Her smile washed away his misgivings. "Be careful of that label. I've been known to call on my friends to help me with the triplets. Many of them have babysat them a time or two."

"I need practice since my sister, Lizzie, will have her baby soon." He ushered everyone into his house.

The sound of Pearl barking and the triplets talking over each other filled the house with something other than silence. He clutched the tin tight to his chest thinking about how quiet his home had been. The noise was perfect.

Daisy bit her lip. "They're always this noisy." Her explanation came out as an apology of sorts, and he waved away her concern.

"I like it. Welcome to my house."

The foursome and Pearl didn't need a second invitation to come inside. He set the tin on the top shelf of his built-in bookshelves. Daisy gasped and examined his mother's collection of Santa Clauses on the mantel. "These are gorgeous. I adore Christmas! I just love the hope and antic- ipation of something better around the corner."

There were six of them resting on the cherry-wood. He picked up a figurine of Father Christmas in a muted brown robe holding a small pine tree. "This one is my favorite. I like the natural aspect."

Daisy pointed to a jolly Santa with a thick white beard and a full sack behind him. "If I had to choose a favorite, I think it would be that one."

Rosie tapped Ben's waist. "Can we touch them?"

Ben shook his head and placed Father Christmas on the mantel. "I have something better. I'll be right back."

When he sorted his mother's boxes of holiday decorations, he found a toy that had kept him and his brother, Jeff, occupied for hours.

Within minutes, he returned with a long wooden toy that resembled a house chimney with pegs on the side along with a small Santa. He set it on the fireplace hearth, and the triplets huddled around him. He let each of them touch the small carved wooden Santa before he settled it at the top of the pegs. Then the toy clicked and clacked down the alternating pegs and landed in the opening of the chimney. Laughter rang out as Rosie, Aspen and Lily reached for Santa at the same time, each wanting a turn to send Santa into the chimney.

Ben found a notepad and jotted down numbers on three slips of paper, distributing them to each child to determine who would go first. While they were occupied with the toy, Ben asked whether everyone wanted hot cocoa.

"Can we bring this into the kitchen?" Aspen lifted the base.

"As long as you're careful, yes." Ben ushered them into his kitchen and gathered everything he needed.

In no time, he distributed cups of hot cocoa, saving the two largest mugs for him and Daisy. Ben opened the tin of cookies and savored the sweet smell while listening to the triplets' glee over the toy. Santa missed a peg and clattered to the floor, causing an especially large burst of laughter out of Aspen.

He guided them into his dining room, the table long and imposing. Daisy admired the heaping helping of whipped cream, garnished with chocolate shavings. "This is impressive. Thank you."

"Tammy, our cook, was one of the best parts of growing up at the Double I." He handed napkins from the holder to Rosie, Aspen and Lily. "She made sure I knew how to cook before I entered the military. Her husband, JR, is the foreman, and they're like family."

"I've only met Tammy. Seth has tried to lure them to the Lazy River, but they're loyal to your father." She smiled a knowing smile as she licked a glob of whipped cream. "It's as good as it looks, too."

Before he knew it, time had passed too quickly. Daisy thanked him and ushered Aspen, Rosie and Lily out the door so they'd make it to play practice on schedule.

"Our new interim director is a stickler for rules." She winked as she picked up the rope to the sled.

"Thanks for the cookies," he added from the doorway.

Daisy turned around and grinned. "Thank the kids. They insisted."

Ben watched them leave and then reached for the tin of cookies, sampling one of the golden stars. The cookie melted in his mouth, rivaling the cookies Tammy always baked.

Cavernous silence engulfed the house that was noisy and full of laughter just minutes ago. It was as if Daisy and the triplets took the light and warmth with them.

The Stanley family seemed to turn this house into a home with Daisy as its heart and soul.

It would be easy to ask her out, except he was reading too much into a nice act. For one thing, she'd proclaimed him her friend, a far cry from anything romantic. Daisy herself had pointed out she wasn't the one who placed him on the Stanleys' cookie list; the triplets insisted on his being a recipient of the goodies. For another, he didn't want to do anything to ruin the atmosphere at the playhouse. They'd been thrown together because of Lily, Aspen and Rosie. Any attraction to the pretty and younger brunette was simply wishful thinking on his part.

He placed the cookie tin in the back of a kitchen cabinet, out of sight, out of mind.

AFTER RECEIVING BEN'S text to meet her onstage, Daisy paused in the lobby of the Holly Theater. Her stomach was most unsettled on this late Saturday afternoon, but it had little to do with how close it was to dinnertime and absolutely nothing to do with the excellent hot cocoa she enjoyed at Ben's home earlier. Rather, it was Ben who was disrupting her normal and busy existence. At one point earlier today, she'd thought he was on the verge of asking her out when he'd stared at her as though he had something important to say.

That crucial comment turned out to be that she had whipped cream on her nose. Then Pearl did the honors of licking it off, causing the triplets to erupt into gales of laughter. Just like that, any holiday hint of romance disappeared faster than a plateful of sugar cookies.

With her hand on the massive door leading from the lobby into the auditorium, Daisy hesitated. She reached into her core, her peaceful place, and pulled herself together before entering the auditorium. There he was, measuring tape in one hand, script in the other. Those black-rimmed glasses added to his air of distinction and disrupted that peace she thought had returned after two years of adjusting to Dylan's death.

She tried concentrating on the red carpet with sprigs of holly embroidered on the sides, but her gaze was drawn back to the imposing veteran. As much as she tried not to notice little details about Ben, she couldn't help herself. Navy must be his favorite color as he once again was wearing a sweater of that hue, this time matched with dark gray pants. His shoulders were stiff with tension.

Did the man ever relax?

She cherished her hobby of making jewelry; it was a relaxing pastime for her. And believe it or not, it was quite relaxing to read to and tuck in the triplets at bedtime. After everything she'd been through, she was content with her life. Well, except for this unexpected promotion of sorts to assistant director and the lack of time to return to her silversmithing.

With each step, it became clear it was time to end any reluctance to be behind the scenes of this production. Along with every other audience member on Christmas Eve, her holiday spirit would rise to its crescendo at the pinnacle of the play when Santa recovered his memory and regained his hearty ho-ho-ho.

She filed past the rows of seats and marched up the stairs to join Ben. She ignored that growing twinge that anticipated seeing him every day. Once the play ended, they'd go their separate ways once more.

"Here I am, reporting for duty."

Daisy waited while Ben removed the pencil from behind his ear and jotted notes on the script. Then he dipped his head in acknowledgment, handed her the metal tip attached to the measuring tape and walked across the stage, the long yellow tape extending to its fullest length.

"You can let go," Ben said.

The tape retracted back into the container with a loud snap.

"What are you doing?" she asked.

"I'm reviewing Frank's notes and blocking the play in my mind." Ben placed the tape measure on the edge of the stage and then flipped the page, looking out at the audience. "Something's missing, but I can't put my finger on it."

She joined him and stared at the empty auditorium. "People."

Facing him, she watched as he suddenly went pale, his breath coming in short spurts. Concerned for him, she placed her hand in his. Finally, he blinked. "Wow. I haven't had that type of emotional reaction in years." His tone was almost sheepish, and he looked closely at her. "What is it about you that makes me confront my past?"

What was it about him that made her confront her future?

"It's the holidays. They represent hope." She moved her hand, and his larger palm rubbed against hers, raising a jolt of awareness. She flicked that away and concentrated on him, depositing his script next to the tape measure and leading him off the stage to the first row of seats. Then, she dropped his hand like a hot roasted chestnut. "The most likely explanation, though, is that you're confronting those feelings from all those years ago, the ones that caused your stage fright."

Ben started to rise. "I don't have time for that type of reflection. Frank left a mountain of work that's piled up since he found out about Noah."

"Whoa there! You're dismissing me faster than when Aspen discovers I've made stuffed zucchini for dinner." She reached for him and pulled him back to his seat. "There's too much at stake for you to proceed as if this is nothing more than putting a bicycle together at the last minute on Christmas Eve."

The vein in Ben's neck almost popped out, only affirming her theory he didn't relax enough. "Procrastinating like that only courts disaster."

"Sometimes life leaves you no choice but to put together three bikes the night before Christmas." Like last year when she stayed up assembling them into the wee hours of the morning, a red one for Aspen, teal for Rosie and pink for Lily. The training wheels had been the hardest. "You need to take a minute to let your body mold to the chair frame and envision the best possible outcome on Christmas Eve."

His body seemed like it was ready to spring into action, and Daisy tapped his shoulder with her index finger, his coiled energy rising to the surface.

"Outcomes are dependent on human variables," he said. "There should be contingency plans in place. Look what happened when Frank didn't have one."

"Yes, I know what happened. You stepped forward." She tried to make sure her smile was evident in her voice. "And now you need to think about why this play is important to the audience."

Ben huffed out a breath. "I should finish the measurements. If someone came in here, they'd think I was slacking off."

"Figuring out why you're doing this in the first place is as important as the physical labor." She wasn't going to bend on this. "If the only reason you're doing this is to advance your mayoral campaign, you should check with your stepsister or her husband or the ranch employees to see if someone can take over for you as director. People are the heart of this play and this town."

Ben arched his eyebrow and tapped the arm-rest between them. "You'd have made first lieu-tenant in no time in the air force. You don't hold back punches, do you?"

"I'm the mother of triplets. What do you think?" She broke the eye contact between them on purpose, too afraid he might see that she wanted him to stay on as interim director. And beyond that as a fixture in her life. Instead, she waved her hand around her. "What do you see when you look at the stage? At the whole theater? Take a minute and really study what's around you."

Seconds ticked by into minutes as she conducted the experiment for herself. Long heavy scarlet curtains hung on either side of the stage, offsetting the large gold-and-scarlet rectangular art deco carving above the proscenium. On both sides, a gold shelf jutted out of the woodwork, each holding an ornamental pot with poinsettias. Behind that were screens with green-and-gold latticework with a holly-and-ivy design. The same artistic motif carried throughout the theater with long scrolls of holly and ivy at every third row of seats. Her gaze went to the ceiling and the raised dome featuring fine wood carvings of intricate holly leaves. How many people had been entertained here over the years? The stories these walls could tell, both in terms of the fictional productions and the people who'd sat in these very seats, was the essence of what her youngest brother, Crosby, studied in his role as the town historian.

The silence extended until Daisy turned to Ben, eager to find out if he saw the same wonders she had. "So what did you see?"

"Four egresses with signage that needs updating. The recessed lighting in the floor also needs work so people can see when they file in prior to the show. Speaking of which, there's a slight bump in the carpet on one side. I definitely need to fix that before anyone trips." His jaw clenched as he made a note on his phone.

When he finished, she tapped his arm. "While I see the importance in that, what about the grandeur of this theater? All the stories represented here? Did you see the initials carved into the holly over there?" She popped to her feet beside him. "It's important to consider why you're here. What's duty without consideration to the people who want to capture the essence of Christmas and hold it dear? I think you need to reconsider your priorities. On Christmas Eve, this play is the heart of Violet Ridge."

CHAPTER SIX

ON THIS EARLY Monday morning, Ben adjusted his polarized sunglasses and stretched his leg muscles on his front porch. Thankfully, he could still walk and run without much trouble. It was only sitting for extended periods of time that caused his hip to ache. Last night, he tossed and turned, sleep elusive. A good long run was the solution for what ailed him, namely one determined Daisy Stanley.

Why her? His opposite in almost every way, she challenged him so much that his skin prickled. Just when he figured out the trajectory of his future, she came along. More than any four-star general, she scrambled his brain. He was starting to feel too happy, almost giddy, when she was near. He found himself thinking the same thing twice or three times, something that had never happened before. In the two days since Saturday's rehearsal, he felt discombobulated. She turned his world on end, asking him to think about people and examining the fine details of what was beneath the surface.

By any measure, he should be looking forward to Christmas Day when the play would be behind him. Instead, he realized he'd be spending Christmas morning in a too-silent house with no reason to contact Daisy.

Snapping out of it, he checked the traction device on the bottom of his running sneakers. Then he set off on the ice-covered sidewalks, the hints of a glorious Colorado sunrise peeking through the craggy mountains. Orange streaks blazed across the sky covering the white mountain caps with a soft glow that reminded him of Daisy.

Argh. He started running faster, willing her away from his mind.

Running always provided a good distraction, and this morning was no different. Perhaps he should make physical fitness a cornerstone of his campaign. To his knowledge, the local government of Violet Ridge didn't offer any 5K runs or marathons. Getting the town up and active could be one of his priorities.

In the back of his mind, he could already hear Daisy asking a litany of questions. Was he serving everyone in the community? How could he use those races as fundraisers for charitable causes that would benefit people or animals in need?

Once again, he sent Daisy out of his mind.

He headed downtown where he enjoyed seeing the soft pastel facades of the stores. Always aware of his surroundings, he knew the alleyways and sidewalks like the back of his hand. He nodded at the other early bird runners on his route, some with dogs by their side, others alone.

The quiet stillness of downtown appealed to him. There was something innocent and refreshing about the pristine snow, the holiday window displays and the red bows on the antique lampposts. When he retired from the military, he worried about whether he'd be able to see the good in the world again. Sometimes in the middle of the night, when he woke up drenched in sweat from a nightmare, that concern magnified. Yet when he viewed downtown Violet Ridge, those fears dissipated like the morning fog that hovered over the winter fields of the Double I. Just as sunlight spread over the town, so too did the feelings of goodness and serenity blossom and expand inside him.

Catching his breath, he stopped in front of Rocky Mountain Chocolatiers and examined the eye-catching train in the display window. Each boxcar held a different holiday treat, and he considered the triplets. Would they like those giant multicolored swirl lollipops...or something so sour their lips puckered? Or would they prefer something sweet like the candied apples, some with nuts, others with chocolate chips? No doubt Aspen would go for the sour, Lily the sweet and Rosie the biggest apple in the store. As for their mother?

Maybe she'd appreciate a tin of fudge or a container of hot cocoa mix. Whatever gift she received, he had a feeling she'd bestow a huge smile of gratitude to the point where the giver would be the one receiving the superior gift.

"Ben!" He was so intent on thoughts of Daisy's smile, he missed Zelda's approach.

How he'd done so when she wore a bright lime green vest over layers of protective clothing paired with running pants with streaks of fluorescent green and yellow was something the former colonel in him chose to ignore. "Zelda! I'm surprised to see you this early. I thought you didn't like exercise."

She jogged in place, little puffs of air misting around her, her bright green pixie cut not moving at all. "That was before my granddaughter was born. Now, I'm all about fitness. The change has done me a world of good. I've lowered my cholesterol, and my doctor told me I've added five potential years to my life span. In the winter, I make sure I keep Sofia's picture as the screensaver when my alarm goes off. I also set my watch to vibrate. You can never have too many backups."

That was exactly his point on Saturday when he and Daisy sparred in the auditorium. "I agree."

Zelda stopped and sized him up. "I heard you're filling in for Frank while he's in Topeka, and that Daisy is your assistant."

Ben gave a wry laugh at Zelda's intense network of Violet Ridge informants.

How had he forgotten the intricacies of small-town living? Life on a military base wasn't much different given the close quarters and the way everyone knew everyone else's business.

"Have you also heard whether the play is going to go off without a hitch?" He kept his tone light, eager to steer the conversation away from Daisy.

His former boss was too perceptive, and that look in her eye? He couldn't tell whether she was dubious he and Daisy could work together or if she was playing matchmaker. If it was the latter, it wasn't going to work. Daisy's sweetness and light were on full display on Saturday; he would only crush her spirit. He had seen far too much, experienced too much darkness, while serving in the military. Maybe he should just accept that he was a lifelong bachelor and focus on becoming the best uncle he could be to his new niece or nephew.

"I'm more interested in how it's working out with Daisy, but I'll give you a pass this time. Holiday spirit and all." Zelda scrutinized the chocolate shop's window while jogging in place. "It looks like Emma has Sofia's favorite kettle corn back in stock. I'll have to buy some this morning before she sells out of it."

"Who's Emma?" Ben was having trouble keeping track of everyone.

"She bought the Rocky Mountain Chocolatiers a few years ago. A good mayor knows every business owner. If you're serious about running for mayor, you should stop by the Rotary Club meeting in January." Zelda pulled out her phone and touched the screen. In seconds, his phone buzzed, and he scanned the text with the details. "FYI, Daisy Stanley knows everyone in this town. You should get on her good side and ask her to introduce you to her friends. What's more, she's kept her positive nature in spite of everything that's happened to her. See you around."

Zelda plugged in her earbuds once more and jogged away, but she piqued Ben's curiosity. He caught up with his mentor. "What do you mean?"

She halted her progress in front of Reichert's Supply Company. "I have a big day ahead, Irwin."

"What happened to Daisy?" He supposed he could have asked Daisy herself, but sometimes it was better to ask an old friend.

Was Zelda a friend or only his former boss? All of a sudden, he found labels weren't as clear anymore. Although everything in the military served a purpose with missions possessing well-defined parameters, he was now a veteran adjusting to life in Violet Ridge. Things were different here, after all.

"Didn't Lizzie tell you about it when it happened?" Zelda eyed him with some scrutiny as she pulled out her earbuds and placed them back in their case.

"You've met my sister. She loves talking about the horses and she always filled me in on the cattle drives." His sister loved the ranch, and he was glad that represented her future. Now if his would only fall into place.

"Lizzie can get quite excited about the Double I. Just last week I asked her about the baby, and she went on and on about the new Simmental baby calf. Apparently, the introduction of the Simmentals to the western pasture is going great. Then she finally answered my question about the baby." Zelda laughed and shook her head. "Lizzie's much more amenable to change than you. It seems like yesterday Lizzie and Daisy were knocking on my door when they were seniors in high school, interviewing me for the yearbook. Daisy's quite remarkable. She's had to adapt to major change her entire life and just goes with the flow."

"What type of changes?" As sunlight flooded

the town in a soft glow, he found himself waiting for Zelda's response.

Zelda narrowed her eyes and studied him. Then she reached for her earbuds and inserted them into place once more. "That's not my story to tell. Daisy will confide in you if you ask. She's worth the effort, Ben."

The challenge in her voice was as clear as her dismissal. He watched as she jogged away, waving at the other runners who made their way to the downtown main thoroughfare.

If Ben waited until tonight to ask, the logistics of the play would take center stage. He needed an excuse to visit her. Jogging back to the candy store wasn't much help as it was closed on Sundays and Mondays, even this close to the holidays. Then again, he did have one of Daisy's tins.

That gave him an idea. With one in mind, he resumed his morning run.

EARLY IN THE afternoon during her lunch break, Daisy exited the small wooden coal miner's building where her younger brother Crosby worked as the town historian. Constructed in the 1880s, it was the oldest surviving structure in Violet Ridge. With her older brother Seth busy checking in the newest group of guests at the Lazy River, she had volunteered to visit Crosby, who hadn't responded to their texts about whether he'd prefer roast beef or turkey for Christmas dinner. Sure enough, Crosby had turned off his phone before falling asleep in the back room the night before. Daisy had found him with his head resting on a rickety table covered with diaries and old ranch ledgers.

With Crosby's vote for turkey in hand, she donned her gloves. Should she head to Reichert's for some holiday shopping or her favorite sandwich and salad restaurant, Harvest Thyme, for a take-out lunch that she could eat next to the ice-skating rink? Her stomach growled, making the decision simple. Harvest Thyme won by a mile.

She headed toward Main Street when she saw Ben coming her way, a fierce look of determination on his face. He made a beeline for her, similar to Santa's sleigh traveling to the next rooftop.

"Tatum said I'd find you at the Miner's Cottage. Looks like I arrived just in time." His terse tone gave her pause. Was he going to replace her as assistant director? After the other day, she wasn't sure that was for the best. He needed her as much as he needed to get it through his thick skull how crucial this play was for the town, a springboard from time with the community on Christmas Eve to precious time with family on Christmas Day.

Her hands shook, and she was glad she'd already donned her gloves so he couldn't see her reaction. She wasn't sure if that was in response to him seeking her out or to the man himself. Of all the men in Violet Ridge, why was this moody air force vet the first man she'd noticed in the past two years? He might look safe, but he was proving dangerous to her heart, the treacherous organ that was beating too fast.

She pasted on a wide smile, quelling her inner turmoil at his close presence. "I only have a small window before I have to return to the dude ranch gift shop, and I haven't grabbed lunch yet."

"Can I join you? I've made notes about the play, and I can run them by you before tonight's rehearsal."

She noticed he mentioned the play, the triplets, anything but the feelings that were bubbling near the surface. For the first time in a long time, she was feeling alive again. It would be her luck that it was one-sided. She exhaled a puff of air, the cold nip biting into her cheeks. It would be easy to tell him she was in a hurry, but his look of expectation changed her mind. Instead, she filled him in on her lunch plans.

"I'm heading to Harvest Thyme and grabbing a sandwich to go." She glanced at her phone, the trip to town taking longer than expected since she and Crosby had fun discussing the merits of cranberry sauce versus green bean casserole.

"Is that a new restaurant?" Ben waited until she nodded. "I'll go with you. I ran into Zelda during my morning jog, and she told me I need to get to know the town's business owners."

Daisy sighed and set out for Harvest Thyme, located a short distance from the Miner's Cottage. In no time, they entered the establishment, the sound of the cowbell distinct and rather unusual even for these parts. The restaurant's heater delivered delicious warmth to her cheeks. She shrugged out of her coat, and they joined the line.

He gazed around the cozy space, smaller than other restaurants in Violet Ridge because it was designed mainly for take-out and delivery orders. The owners, Vaughn and Sue McKinnon, had poured their time and energy into this place, decorating the space with generations of farm implements from Sue's family farm. Rusted antique sickles rested next to pruning shears and old pitchforks. In keeping with the rustic theme, the few customer tables were covered in rustic tablecloths, even this close to Christmas.

Ben seemed to approve of the decor. "What's good to eat here?"

Daisy handed him a menu from the box on the wall. "Everything. Vaughn and Sue opened it when they retired and their son took over the family farm. They also have freezer meals, and I often pick up the vegetable lasagna. It thaws at work and then I bake it when I get home. It's Rosie's favorite, with zucchini, carrots and squash. Red pepper gives it a kick that Aspen likes."

Ben scanned the offerings. "I don't see that on here."

"It's special order only. You order it ahead of time to go. Some of their offerings need a day in advance, like their bison pasta bake or their Colorado cowboy casserole. These are their breakfast choices." She flipped over the menu. "And this is what they serve for lunch. I recommend the open-faced roast beef sandwich or the portabella mushroom wrap. All the herbs and vegetables are grown on their farm."

Someone tapped her shoulder, and Daisy recognized her as a mother of a student in Aspen's first-grade class. Daisy introduced Ben as the new interim director of the play, and Allison shook his hand.

"We already have our tickets." She leaned into Daisy with a smile. "Don't tell Aspen, but I think CeCe has a crush on him."

Daisy laughed and put her index finger over her mouth, indicating that she would keep the secret to herself. Then, it was her and Ben's turn to order. She chose a veggie wrap while Ben went with her suggestion of the portabella mushroom wrap. Soon, they collected the to-go bags, and Daisy waved to Allison, who was still waiting for her food.

Daisy and Ben exited the restaurant, and she faced him. "They put our orders in the same bag."

Ben stared at the window of Harvest Thyme, a flyer for the play in the lower left corner. "Residents love the play, don't they?"

"It's a holiday tradition, same as the pet parade and the Snow Much Fun festival," Daisy concurred while shrugging on her gloves.

Speaking of snow, last night's accumulation had been pushed off to the side with the crisp chilly air promising it wouldn't melt. After a warmer-than-usual fall, Daisy was looking forward to everything about winter and would make the most of it until next May when spring would be a welcome change. For now, though, her thoughts centered on Ben as he'd popped up when she least expected it. Those reindeer flutters in her stomach were taking flight again. Whenever he was nearby, those feelings came roaring to life, feelings that could lead to heartbreak, as he seemed to be doing everything he could to court public approval before throwing his hat in the mayoral ring: meeting business owners, volunteering at the playhouse, endearing himself to the triplets. This wasn't about her.

It was best to cut this time with him short and return to the gift shop. At the playhouse, the triplets acted as a buffer between her and Ben. That was the way she preferred it because, for some reason, she was starting to think more and more about what it would be like to kiss him.

And there were so many reasons that would be a very bad idea. First of all, he was her opposite in every way. While he was a problem-solver, she attracted the type of situations he might find problematic but that were simply her life. She was a magnet for chaos; after all, she was the mother of impressionable and energetic triplets. And her children had already had the rug pulled out from under them once in their life. If she didn't keep her distance, Rosie, Aspen and Lily would be devastated when Ben wasn't in their lives anymore.

She wouldn't let anyone break their hearts.

Ben was a temporary inconvenience. Soon, her world would be the same as it had been before he came into her life. And yet? The harbinger of happy change had always thrilled her...but Ben disliked change, preferring the status quo. Another way they were opposites.

Her heart would be in real trouble if she didn't put some distance between them. At the theater, it was easier to keep busy in a different part of the theater than she thought it would be when she accepted the role of assistant director. Rather than forced proximity, she always found herself somewhere where he wasn't. Keeping to that arrangement suited her.

For the triplets, of course.

"See you tonight." She pointed to a nearby bench. "I'll figure out which is my lunch order and separate our containers so I can return to the Lazy River."

"But there are some logistical matters about the play we need to discuss, and I still need to tell you the real reason that I tracked you down." Ben smiled, a lightness spreading over his face that changed him from imposing to almost mischievous and nearly irresistible. "Since the meals are in one bag, instead of two, that must be a sign we're destined to eat together."

One look at his handsome face, and she threw caution to the wind. Besides, the tiny bud of curiosity as to why he was looking for her had bloomed into a full flower. She gave up resisting him. "It has to be fast. I have to get back to work."

He kept a tight hold on the bag. "When you're finished with your wrap, I'll walk you to your car."

For the first time, though, she wished Sue and Vaughn's portion sizes were smaller. "Half of my wrap. I'll save the other part for my break." Or tomorrow's lunch.

"Deal." His gaze went along the length of her. "Do you want to go back inside the restaurant? You look cold."

Her shiver had nothing to do with the temperature. "I'm okay. Come with me, and I'll introduce you to one of my favorite downtown spots during the holiday season."

He fell into step beside her, and she led him to the seating area close to the ice rink. A good number of skaters were circling the rink. Patio umbrella heaters provided enough warmth for those watching the action.

One family departed from a bench, and she and Ben claimed it for themselves. On the ground under his legs, Ben placed the bag of food next to his own reusable tote while she settled on the left side. She took off her gloves, thankful for the ambient heat. Ben launched into a series of questions before she could even extract her veggie wrap.

"Slow down." A lesson she often wanted to apply to her own hectic life, especially when the triplets clamored for her attention and there was only one of her to go around.

At that second, one of the figure skaters segued into a layback position, her elegant body curved backward in a beautiful pose, her head and shoulders facing the cerulean blue sky. Dizzy just watching the skater, Daisy held her breath. She found that she couldn't look away from the skater, entranced by her graceful movements. Something clicked, and Daisy envisioned a design for a pair of earrings. "Excuse me for a minute."

Before she could lose the thought, she extricated the notepad she kept in her purse for such occasions and started drawing a delicate pattern with curved circles, smaller on one side until the curve led to bigger discs before ending with two small discs.

Minutes later, she looked up and was surprised to see that Ben was no longer sitting with her. She looked around and found him heading toward her with two foam cups in hand, lids on each.

"Hope you like hot apple cider. You seem to like everything, though." Ben settled back on the bench and handed her a cup. "I didn't want to interrupt. Whatever you were doing seemed important."

Heat rose up her cheeks. "Sorry about that." She shoved the notepad in her purse before accepting the drink.

"Don't stop on my account." He shook his head and reached for the bag of food, extricating the first container. "What were you doing?"

She removed the lid from the cup he'd offered her, steam escaping the fragrant brew, the cinnamon and apple smells delectable. "Sketching a new pair of earrings."

"Are you a jewelry designer, too? I thought you worked at the Lazy River Dude Ranch." He opened the first take-out carrier and handed it to her while placing the second box on his lap.

She accepted it with a smile, placing the cider on the ground next to her boots. "I run the gift shop, but my real passion is designing and making jewelry out of precious metals and Western equipment like horse bits and spurs. I trained with a master silversmith."

"What type of jewelry?" He also set his cider on the ground before opening his container.

"Earrings, necklaces, belt buckles, all kinds really. When possible, I incorporate odds and ends from the ranch. Snaffle bits, horseshoes, you name it. I love working with anything metal." She especially loved turning that metal into earrings. Delicate or chunky, hoops or studs, silver or gold. It didn't matter. "When inspiration strikes, you know."

"Did you make the earrings you're wearing now?"

She was shocked and rather happy that he'd noticed them.

"Yes." She pushed away her hair so he could see today's earrings, former horse bits shaped into a snowflake. "Most of my jewelry is my own, except for some pieces that my mentor and teacher created that I cherish."

"They're beautiful."

"Thank you."

"Now about the play." Ben pulled out a notepad that mirrored her own. "Last night some of the performers were texting on their cell phones during the rehearsal."

"Rosie and Aspen don't have phones." Although some of their friends were already getting their own devices, Daisy thought that the triplets were too young. Not only that but she'd have to buy three when they were old enough.

"It's a problem with other members of the cast." Ben frowned and tapped the pencil against the top of his take-out container.

She chewed on her veggie wrap, resolved to savor the flavors from the organic ingredients, while conceding his point. How could they ask the actors to keep off their phones without causing friction?

"I've got it. Give them five minutes at the start to wrap up any texts or calls. Get a shoe organizer and ask them to put their phones in the different compartments." She'd seen a similar approach at Lily's speech pathologist's office.

"Great idea. Thanks. We make a good team."

Ben launched into a litany of other issues. She found it cute when he'd bite off a chunk of his wrap, then study his notes, his intense concentration a mark of how seriously he was taking his promise to Frank. Before she knew it, she'd eaten her whole wrap and downed her cup of cider. With her lunch break over, the gift shop beckoned.

She stood and wiped the crumbs off her coat.

"My brother will get upset if I'm late. Five new families arrived today, and two couples are checking out tomorrow. The gift shop will be busy this afternoon."

He reached into his shopping bag and pulled out the tin she recognized at once. "Then I'd best return this now so I don't forget."

"I didn't want it back." She felt offended at the gesture. "You pay it forward."

He continued holding out the tin. "To whom? Tammy bakes cookies for the ranch, and Lizzie doesn't need any cookies from me."

"You're not getting it." Daisy tucked her napkin and plastic utensils inside the container so she could recycle them. "You fill the tin with something homemade and pass it on."

"Now I do." Ben tucked the tin into his reusable shopping bag.

She reached into her coat pocket and pulled out her gloves, donning her left, then her right. "Surprises are fun, even more so during the holidays. You may not know it, but the triplets already think the world of you. For the record, Rosie, Aspen and Lily each snuck in two extra star cookies for you when the others weren't looking. See you tonight."

STANDING IN HIS KITCHEN, Ben was at a loss about what to do until it was time for rehearsal. His house was decorated for the holidays, the second tree the perfect showcase for his mother's ornaments and heirloom angel topper, gifts for his family had been ordered and he'd cleaned the house from top to bottom. He'd never encountered this problem before. First at the ranch and then in the military, there was always something to occupy his time.

That might be what he missed most about his air force days. Feeling useful to his country, to the purpose for which he was called. There was always action on the horizon. He rubbed his achy hip. Why had it suddenly started throbbing? Were those empathy pains for the dedicated men and women still serving? Most likely he was reading too much into it considering he was living near the Rocky Mountains in wintertime.

Sitting around wasn't appealing in the least. He grabbed his keys, having enough time to drive to the ranch and deliver the teddy bear he bought for the baby, when Daisy's tin called to him. The beseeching tone in her voice telling him to pass it on echoed in his mind.

That must be a signal he should bake something to take to the Holly Theater tonight for the cast and crew. But what? He snapped his fingers. His mother's homemade toffee.

Ben hadn't made it in years, but he'd come across the recipe in her totes. He consulted it and found he had all the ingredients on hand. With this type of incentive, he might stanch the loss of volunteers. Not even an hour ago, the crew member in charge of the light and sound board texted her regrets that she had to drop out, the second volunteer to quit in the past few days.

As he combined butter, sugar and salt in a saucepan, he couldn't help but miss the Stanley family. He envisioned Rosie and Aspen having a heated discussion about being the taste tester while Lily assisted him and measured ingredients. Daisy would have taken it all in stride and turned on holiday music to lighten the mood.

Ben had to stop thinking about the Stanleys. Nothing could come from this attraction to Daisy. He needed someone who would provide a haven of respite, not a beehive of activity. Besides, he'd seen too much darkness during his military maneuvers, and she was sunshine and happiness. He wouldn't do anything to obscure her light.

The silence in the house finally got to him, and he took a page from Daisy's playbook. He turned on a music streaming service, filling the air with Christmas carols. That was better. He began mixing the ingredients.

A short time later, he was breaking off the cooled toffee pieces, filling the tin to take to the Holly Theater. The doorbell rang, and he wiped his hands with a dish towel. A second peal registered as he walked to the door. Who was so impatient?

A look through the peephole provided the answer. Constance stood on his front porch, her lips thinned in a straight line, her boots tapping. It was too early for the lights to be the issue, and it wasn't laundry day. Suddenly, the full meaning behind Daisy's words hit him square in the chest. That tin wasn't destined for the cast and crew; he'd give it to Constance. He hurried back into the kitchen and retrieved it before he opened the front door.

"Mrs. Mulligan. It's always a pleasure."

Her scowl deepened, as did the lines on her forehead. His neighbor held a package in her hands. "If that's sarcasm, Mr. Irwin, I don't appreciate it."

He blew out his frustration. Constance would have intimidated some of his drill sergeants, including the toughest ones who left recruits feeling like a twisted washcloth with the moisture sucked out of it.

"I say what I mean, and I don't say anything I don't mean." His gaze went to the package in her hands. "What can I do for you this afternoon?"

"This package was delivered to my house by mistake. I don't want you thinking I stole it." She thrust the plain brown box onto the top of the tin.

He tried balancing the two, but the package

fell onto his hardwood floor. The sound of crystal shattering filled the foyer. This had to be the horse figurines he'd ordered for his sister, Lizzie, and his stepsister, Sabrina.

Wincing, he picked up the box and kept from rattling it. "I'd never do that. While you're here, though, I'll ask one more time. Why don't you volunteer at the Holly Theater? Frank and Rhonda Craddock just welcomed their first grandson and had to take leave from their positions as director and assistant director." A recent group text had shared a picture of the glowing grandparents standing in front of Noah's incubator in the NICU, along with the update he was gaining weight and doing well. "We need all hands on the flight deck so we can be ready for a smooth take-off. There are openings in wardrobe and props." And, well, in every department, but he didn't want to scare her off.

"Thank you, but no. I have other things to do." Constance turned on her scuffed and faded brown boots.

"Wait!" Ben called out, laying down the box and bustling outside to the porch, instantly regretting his move as the temperature hovered below freezing, a howling wind blowing the tops of the bare oaks and aspens. "I have something for you."

He held out the tin, and her silver eyebrow arched. "If this is a bribe to get me to volunteer..."

Ben shook his head. "It's a gift to you, my neighbor. That's all."

"Hmph." Something, though, changed in her stance, almost like she was happy with his gesture. She relieved him of the tin and shook it. "It's not pitted prunes or a twenty-year-old fruitcake, is it?"

"It's toffee. My mother's recipe." More and more, his past was catching up with him, and he was staring it right in the face.

"More like my recipe, I'll wager." She opened the box, reached for a piece and nibbled. "Yep. My recipe."

"Huh?" He always thought his mother had learned to make toffee from her mother. "How's that possible?"

"I was her babysitter way back when. I remember little Heather like it was yesterday. Russell and I would..." She closed the lid once more. "Never mind my bringing up the past. It is where it belongs."

After the shock of Constance being his mother's babysitter passed, he found his voice again. "Then you know the toffee is good."

"Don't expect me at rehearsals. You yourself said this is a gift." Constance eyed him like she was anticipating him to change his mind.

"Don't go anywhere." He ran back into the kitchen, the warm interior air thawing his cheeks. He grabbed half of the remaining star cookies from the plate and rushed back outside, tucking them on top of the toffee. "Those are from the Stanley family. Delicious, too."

Constance nodded her thanks, and a lightness he hadn't felt in a long time overcame him. Then his phone started ringing, and he excused himself to find out who was calling and get warm.

CHAPTER SEVEN

IN THE SOUND booth on the second floor of the Holly Theater, Daisy looked at the lighting control console and winced. It was as much of a mystery to her today as it was yesterday. After Rhonda gave her detailed directions about where to locate the instrument's manual, she took the booklet home and read it. Well, she tried, falling asleep on page three. Today, the challenge of operating this and the soundboard seemed insurmountable. She reached for her phone. Could there be any online tutoring clips that might make this device more comprehensible?

The makeup artist, Sally Bryant, entered the booth, and Daisy welcomed the interruption. "Hi, Daisy. I wanted to double-check with you that Rosie, Aspen and Lily don't have any skin allergies before I test the makeup on them."

"Not as far as I know." Daisy needed a break after wrestling with the console for the past hour. "Don't suppose you know about this equipment, do you?"

Sally shook her head, the dim lights of the booth picking up the silver strands in the older woman's dark hair. "You'd think I'd want to volunteer in the sound booth after working at the Think Pink salon all day, but I stick to what I know."

"Thought I'd ask." Daisy sighed.

Something was off with Sally, but what? It finally registered that the vivacious woman was wearing two different shoes. Daisy rose and patted Sally's shoulder. "Is everything okay?"

Sally gave a whisper of her usual smile. "Nothing for you to worry about. I have to go. The triplets are waiting for me in the green room."

Daisy set the instruction book next to the console and walked to the door. "I want to see their makeup."

Maybe she could also find out what was bothering Sally. Daisy followed the older woman down the narrow set of stairs that came out at the lobby and then walked alongside her. They bypassed the auditorium for the hallway that employees and volunteers used to get backstage. Daisy entered the green room, her eyes adjusting to the huge row of light bulbs located above the four mirrors on the wall, corresponding to the blue chairs where Sally transformed the actors into their characters with the assistance of cosmetics and wigs. On the other side of the room were little nooks with mannequin heads wearing a variety of hairpieces and hats. Daisy could get lost in this room if she let herself.

Sally showed her the cosmetics she would be using, and a short time later, Rosie, Aspen and Lily marched into the room in formation with Ben on their heels. Daisy was taken aback at their precise movements. Was Ben teaching them to be little soldiers? She didn't like that, and she'd best illuminate him now that she wasn't accepting this type of direction. After Sally assured her she'd be fine getting acquainted with the triplets, Daisy excused herself.

She caught sight of Ben's retreating figure and calmed those reindeer hooves playing havoc with her insides. If she were actively searching for a Christmas date, Ben wouldn't even make the cut, especially if he was trying to change her children's personalities. Childhood only came along once, and it should be full of joy without being hindered by rigid rules.

"Ben!" Daisy hurried and caught up with him, her new cranberry knit skirt, the same that was for sale at the gift shop, swishing around her legs.

He waited and held the ever-present binder to his chest. She tried ignoring how today's sweater brought out the green flecks in his eyes but failed. "How's the lighting console training coming along?" he asked.

"It's not." She dismissed that with a wave. "Why were Rosie, Aspen and Lily marching?"

He looked perplexed and then shrugged. "You'll have to ask them."

"I'm asking you. You taught them to march in formation?" She crossed her arms. "Why?"

"I didn't. Earlier they were skipping across the stage. For safety's sake, I requested they stop. Then, on the way to the green room, they started marching." He stared at her earrings. "Did you make those?"

"Yes." She touched the tiny cascading red and green bells, and their slight tinkle lifted her spirits. "But they shouldn't be marching. They should be kids enjoying their childhood."

He kept his gaze on her earrings. "Yes, I agree with you, but life presents challenges and doesn't take a person's age into account. You should know that. A little discipline never hurt anyone."

She was well aware of Dylan's loss in their lives, same as she'd lost her parents too early. "As their mother, though, I try to protect them."

"As someone who's served in the military, I've seen other mothers trying to do the same but not always succeed. We can't always control what others do, but that's not the point here." He blinked, that small tic in his jaw bulging out so slightly, perceptible to her since she was standing close to him, close enough to smell his aftershave, a most pleasant scent. "This is a theater with people milling about and a limited amount of time to rehearse. The triplets have to follow rules and procedures so everyone stays safe on the set."

"Right." Her response sounded weak as he had a genuine point about safety. More so, his subtext about the impact of his military service on him was clear. He'd seen the worst the world had to offer and chose to combat that with a rigid code of behavior. That was obviously his defense mechanism while she preferred joy and positivity as her preferred method despite her personal setbacks. "I have a lighting console to learn."

"Wait a minute!"

She made it halfway down the hall when his request stopped her in her tracks.

She faced him again. "What now, Ben?"

"Those earrings. Do you have any others like that for sale?" Ben wheedled a smile, and she realized he had a slight dimple in his right cheek.

She really wished she hadn't noticed that dimple.

"No. These are Daisy originals." She reached up for the small plastic stopper on the back but halted. "I'd give them to you, but you don't have pierced ears."

A slight red stain came over his cheeks. "They aren't for me. This afternoon, I accidentally dropped a fragile package with presents inside for my sister and stepsister. After I received an emergency call from my brother, I opened the package only to find their gifts, a pair of crystal horse figurines, were shattered. I can't replace them because they're on back order."

Her heart went out to him. This was his first Christmas back in town, and he'd obviously put some thought into their presents. He was trying and deserved credit for that.

Then all of what he said registered. "Emergency call?" She reached for his arm, his muscular presence firm and steady under the soft layer of navy cashmere. "Is everything okay?"

That red blush grew even deeper. "I mischaracterized the call. I'm my brother Jeff's Santa hotline. Now about those earrings?"

She wouldn't let him change the subject that easily. "Santa hotline? What's that?"

He blew out a breath, the blush fading from his cheeks, faintly speckled with stubble, giving him a mysterious air. "My niece, Audrey, is seven. Her brother, Zack, said something out of line to her, and Jeff told him he had a direct line to Santa." He searched the hallway as if making sure there were no children around. "This year, I'm his Santa."

This was adorable. Before she had a chance to tell him just that, one of the set designers came around the corner, running at full steam, his face bright red.

"Kenny, no running in the playhouse," Ben said, half-jokingly.

Kenny caught his breath and tugged at Ben's sleeve. "You gotta come quick. I can't believe what's happening. I don't know whether it's a Christmas miracle or not."

Daisy exchanged a quick look with Ben, who looked as bewildered as she felt on the inside. Then he faced Kenny once more. "Slow down. We're coming."

Ben followed Kenny, and Daisy followed Ben down the hallway into the theater lobby.

A crowd had gathered with almost every crew and cast member except for Sally and the triplets present. Wide eyes and mouths in the shape of an O were the predominant expression, and Daisy searched the room for what was causing the commotion.

Her gaze fell on Constance Mulligan, who stood at the entrance, her lips thinned in a straight line, her eyes taking in the scene. Ben separated from her and went over to Constance, reaching out his hand to hers.

"You took me up on my offer." Gasps came over the cast and crew until Ben faced them, his stern expression compelling them to be quiet. Then he turned toward Constance once more. "We can use the help."

The woman, whose reputation for orneriness

preceded her, arched an eyebrow. "I'm not sure whether everyone agrees with you."

Ben's jaw clenched, and that small neck vein popped out once more. "We're welcoming of everyone here, and we're behind schedule as it is."

Murmurs of agreement traveled through the crowd, and then most of the cast and crew excused themselves and hurried away. As Ben's assistant, Daisy stood rooted in place until she found her manners.

"Mrs. Mulligan, this is a pleasant surprise." She marched forward and extended her hand, giving the older woman a firm handshake. "I don't suppose you know how to run an ancient lighting console system. I'd be ever so grateful if you did."

Daisy added a winsome smile for good measure.

"Can't say I do. I work best with a sewing machine." Mrs. Mulligan unzipped her puffer coat. "I awoke from my nap needing something to do to expend all the energy from Ben's toffee."

Had Ben followed through on her suggestion to pass the tin to someone else? Maybe he was adapting to Violet Ridge after all.

"You've come to the right place. I'll introduce you to our wardrobe volunteer." Ben reached for Constance's coat and hung it on the rack with the others. "You know Daisy Stanley, don't you? She and I are directing the play while Frank and

Rhonda are in Kansas visiting their daughter and newborn grandson."

His promotion of her position was conflicting to say the least. That dimple and the way he was starting to thaw made it more difficult to insert needed distance between them. Where were the triplets when she needed them?

Daisy waved and backed away. "I have to get back to the lighting console since it won't teach itself how to operate."

In a move less than graceful, she stumbled into the ticket tower for collecting the stubs and then found herself upstairs in the operations room once more. She banged her head against the board, and the machine lit up and beeped at her.

With a start, she bolted upright in the chair. Just as she'd have to be cautious around the console, so too would she have to be careful around Ben so she wouldn't start something she couldn't control.

UNLIKE OTHER NIGHTS, Ben was ready for tonight's rehearsal to end. His head ached from fielding so many questions about how, or why, he'd persuaded Constance to volunteer. Every time, he directed the crew member to ask her.

The last chord of the musical number echoed in the auditorium, and he jumped to his feet. "Thank you. See you tomorrow evening at six."

Rubbing his jaw and wincing, Teddy waved goodbye and stepped backstage with Jessica. Other cast members mumbled their farewells and headed out through the auditorium doors. Ben massaged the back of his neck as little Lily Stanley remained behind. Her big hazel eyes, miniature replicas of her mother's luminous brown ones, locked on him.

"Mommy's not here yet." She plopped down on the stage and tucked her hands under her chin. "Where do I go?"

Out of the mouths of babes. He'd been asking himself that same question over the past few months ever since he'd been discharged from the air force. He dismissed that thought as mere exhaustion and took charge.

"Come with me." Ben reached for her hand. "Rosie and Aspen are with Sally in the green room, and your mother is learning how to operate the lighting console."

Lily didn't hesitate. She popped up from her seated position, inserting her little palm next to his. "I like singing. I practice with Winter every night while Rosie is in the bathroom."

"Repetition is key to being well rehearsed."

"Huh? Whatcha saying?" Lily scrunched her face so hard he was almost afraid it would stay in that position permanently.

"You're on the right track."

"'Kay." She hugged his waist, and all felt right in the world.

Maybe he also was on the right track. It was time to embrace Violet Ridge and accept he was home. He needed to take off the shroud of guilt over abruptly leaving the military and start enjoying this new journey. Was he on the same highway as the Stanleys? Or was he only walking alongside them until they reached the fork in the road after the play?

Daisy would tell him to concentrate on the here and now. Lean into the stories of those around him. Look for the burst of color. At this moment, though, it was his responsibility to reunite Lily with her siblings. "Let's find Sally."

Together they headed backstage and found the green room where Sally reigned over the wardrobe and makeup department. At the threshold, his mouth dropped open, his jaw slack. He surveyed the scene and released Lily's hand, the shock catching up with him.

Rosie and Aspen stared at him from their positions on the floor, an upended basket next to them. Tubes of lipstick lay open, as did pots of cream foundation. Rosie held a palette of eye shadow, applicator in hand, while Aspen possessed rouge. Rosie's lips were bright red while Aspen's cheeks were tinged with blue eye shadow.

The floor was covered in powder with glittery eye shadow mixed in for good measure.

"Uh-oh." Rosie dropped the applicator, and Lily started wailing beside him.

Ben gulped in deep breaths of air and struggled for composure. His years in the military never prepared him for this. "Rosie! Aspen! What did you do?"

He strode into the room, his boot sliding on something wet and sticky. His arms flailed out before he fell on the floor. His hip groaned at the sudden movement. The sickly sweet smell of peppermint assailed his senses. He counted to ten and took his time getting off the floor. Everything was scattered around him, and he didn't know how to begin to pick up the pieces. The empty bottle of spirit gum remover was a start.

"That's not peppermint soda, so don't try to drink it." Aspen waved his hand under his nose before a stern look from Ben quieted him.

Ben knelt beside Rosie and Aspen, his jaw locked. To his dismay, he wasn't doing a good job of controlling the consternation boiling inside him. His hip screamed at him, and the shock of finding this mess was giving way to pain. The only thing he wanted to do right now was get to the bottom of what had happened. He held up the bottle. "You two made a huge mess." Rosie started to shake her head before she met Ben's gaze and slowly nodded. "If you're going to cause mischief, I have no choice but to replace you."

At this, Lily started crying even harder, and Aspen's lip quivered. Rosie started shaking, her entire body quivering. "Miss Sally gave us mission."

Where was Sally? For the first time, it dawned on Ben that Rosie and Aspen were alone in the green room. His stomach twisted in fear for the possibility that something worse could have happened to them without adult supervision.

"Heavens above!" Speaking of Sally, that was her voice coming from behind him. He turned and found a look of horror on her face. "What happened? I was only gone for a minute."

Ben was sure Sally had been away for longer than that. While Ben wasn't condoning Rosie's and Aspen's behavior, he expected better of the adults in charge of supervising them. He'd get to the bottom of this, although it would be easier if Daisy with her positive reinforcement was here. Rosie and Aspen loved their mother, and they responded well to her steady calmness. He could do the same, thanks to his years of military training. Breathing in, he centered himself and stayed calm since that seemed the best way to handle this difficult situation. He met Sally's gaze. "Our safety precautions are clear. There are always supposed to be two adults in the room whenever children are present."

With a groan, Sally entered the room and righted the basket. "Jenny had to leave early, and I had a crucial call that couldn't wait."

"What was so important you left Rosie and Aspen alone?" Ben contained the anger simmering under the surface at the thought of either of them getting hurt on his watch.

Sally held up her phone. "My doctor just received my test results. They were benign. I don't have cancer. I didn't want to take the call in front of Rosie and Aspen in case it was the other way around, but I kept the door in my sight. I'd have seen them leave."

His anger dissipated. Here he was, the interim director, and he hadn't known that Sally, one of his crew members, was facing such a life-changing diagnosis. "I didn't know that, but I'm happy it's good news. Everyone start cleaning."

Ben froze as the time he'd spent here over the past few weeks caught up to him. Genuine surprise confronted him as he found himself caring for the cast and crew. This wasn't part of signing up as the interim director.

Sally gasped as if she was finally seeing the true extent of the mess. "My cosmetics! I put them in a basket so I could rearrange them according to the entrance of each character." She grabbed a makeup remover tissue and started rubbing Aspen's cheeks. "What did you do?"

Rosie stomped her foot. "You gave us mission."

Sally paled, and Ben could tell she hadn't given Rosie or Aspen permission to play with the cosmetics. That changed everything as far as he was concerned. A mess like this could be cleaned up, but Rosie's lie would have consequences. He'd contact Frank tomorrow about recasting the two children, three since Lily would no doubt leave the production.

And that would end his everyday contact with Daisy.

Ben knelt next to Rosie. "Do you know the difference between the truth and a lie?"

Rosie shook her head, her blond braids whipping around her face. "I didn't lie!"

Aspen also stood up, his eyes blazing. "She's telling the truth. Miss Sally said we could."

There was an easy way to settle this. Ben faced Sally and crossed his arms. "What did you say to them before you left the room?"

Sally pointed to a basket of toys. Then her face became more ashen. "I said they could play with the basket on the left side of the room. I always keep a few toys and sundries in there since so many of the productions have child actors."

Rosie's and Aspen's heads started bobbing up and down rather fast. "I know my left. It's the one with the L. See." Rosie held up four fingers and extended her thumb out until she formed an L. Then she pointed at one side of the room. "And that's left."

Sally groaned. "Rosie's telling the truth. I placed the cosmetics in a basket on what I thought was the right side so I could inventory the different shades and arrange everything at home."

Ben rubbed his temple with his fingers and then looked at everyone. He'd rushed to judgment and had been wrong. What was worse, he'd have to have a stern talk with Sally about the rules about unaccompanied minors.

A gasp came from behind him. He faced Daisy, standing in the doorway, her hand over her mouth, her eyes showing no surprise at finding Rosie and Aspen in their current predicament. That twitch at the corner of her lips said too much, although he credited her with hiding her mirth.

Lily rushed to her mother, the wailing loud and strong. "Mommy, it's awful. Rosie and Aspen are in so much trouble. They're gonna be replaced."

The humor lurking in Daisy's eyes disappeared in a flash as Aspen and Rosie also launched themselves at their mother. Lily latched onto Daisy's side with only the back of her head visible, trembling although her sniffles could be heard. Rosie held on to Daisy's arm and stared up at her mother. "I told the truth, Mommy. I want to go home."

Aspen tried comforting Rosie, but Rosie brushed him off, defiance in her eyes. Daisy opened her arms, and the trio received a loving embrace. Then she released them, and her nostrils flared when she glared at Ben. "What happened?"

"Sally had to take a call…"

"Good news. I don't have cancer," Sally interrupted.

Daisy clasped Sally's hand, genuine relief coming over her face. "That's why you're wearing two different shoes. We'll get together and celebrate soon." Daisy breathed a sigh of relief but then focused on Ben again. "Why are my children so upset?"

"While she was gone, they made a huge mess. Even if they were alone, they should know better than to upend the production's makeup supplies," Ben said. "Rosie and Aspen wrecked the room and destroyed much of the stock of cosmetics."

"We made a mess, Rosie." Aspen shuffled his feet and looked sheepish.

Daisy nudged Rosie and Aspen. "What do we do when we make messes?"

Rosie huffed before she blew out a big sigh. "We clean them up."

"Thank you for offering, but I have adrenaline from the phone call. I'll manage." Sally flicked her hands at the exit. Then she glanced at Daisy before turning toward Ben. "Now that my results are back, I'll devote my full attention to the production. I'll talk to Jenny and make sure we leave together and don't leave Aspen or Rosie alone again."

Lily broke free from her mother and gazed at Ben with big disappointed hazel eyes. That almost broke his heart. "I don't want to sing anymore. I want to go home, and I don't wanna come back."

Ben didn't know what was worse: Lily thinking badly of him or Daisy.

"Thank you, Sally. I'll take you up on that offer." Daisy shepherded the trio toward the exit, a ragamuffin crew with makeup splotches on Rosie and Aspen.

He wanted them to stay. Shocked, he found himself caring about how they felt about him as Ben, not just as the interim director. Unsure of how to set this right, he hurried to the door. "Will you be here tomorrow night?"

Lily's sniffles were his answer, and Daisy looked uncertain. "I don't know. I'll text you."

The Stanley family took their leave. Sally shook her head while reaching for the broom. If he wasn't needed here, he could use a few minutes alone to compose himself.

"I'll be in Frank's office, going over the invoices. Knock when you're ready to leave. I'll lock up and walk you to your car." He cut off her protests. "I know this is a safe town, but I'll feel better if I do. It's important you get home safe and sound."

With his production hanging in shreds around him, Ben sought refuge in Frank's office. Until tonight, he thought he could handle the chaos of the production knowing it would come together in the next few weeks leading up to Christmas Eve.

Yet the cast and crew were teaching him he had a lot to learn. His crash course, though, threatened the play itself. Daisy would have had some special insight about how to handle the mess that he'd expanded exponentially, but she was the one person he couldn't ask for insight into a diplomatic solution.

Everyone around him was getting into the holiday spirit. Even Constance arrived and had finished her first volunteer shift. Yet Ben might have just derailed the play.

He might be living up to his given name of Ebenezer after all.

CHAPTER EIGHT

A FEW HOURS LATER, Daisy shooed Pearl away from the dishwasher so she could finish loading it. To her surprise, Pearl skittered out of the kitchen. The hound normally licked the plates clean, but tonight she departed without protest.

Had Daisy also given up too easily tonight? What message would she be passing on to Rosie, Aspen and Lily if they didn't finish what they started?

At the same time, though, she didn't want them involved in the play if Ben had accused them of lying.

She longed for an hour with her silversmith tools, followed by a long, hot soak in the tub, but December brought a new set of challenges for a single mom. In addition to the normal chores, holiday preparation occupied most of her waking moments. After tonight's disastrous play rehearsal, she shouldn't work with snips. One wrong cut could damage the metal, or worse, injure herself. She'd wait until tomorrow to start on that new design she envisioned when she and Ben ate lunch together.

Ben. Last month, she thought she had figured everything out. She'd stood at her bedroom dresser and slid off her rings, saving them for Aspen or one of her daughters. She vowed she'd start dating again, believing she was past the grief surrounding Dylan's sudden passing and ready for a nice, easy relationship on the horizon. One that was laid-back and superficial. One where she wouldn't commit her whole heart. Then she met Ben, who, on the surface, fulfilled everything she wanted. He was secure and gruff to the point where she could see him and his wife sitting down to breakfast, silent except for the sounds of eating. Yet there was so much more to Ben. He turned her preconceived notions of him on end. She never expected to start caring about the military hero who, on the surface, didn't seem to have anything in common with her.

But they both loved the Christmas season. Until tonight, she thought they might continue as friends with the possibility of more after the production. The trouble was they cared about the production, and pretty much everything, in different ways. He was preoccupied with order and safety while she just wanted everyone to get along and thrive.

Then again, hadn't she set those same kinds of boundaries on her heart? Safety and security had topped her short list of attractive traits in any potential suitors. In which case, Ben, the safety expert, should be at the pinnacle.

The way he made her heart flutter, though, was anything but safe.

She banished Ben's image from her thoughts. Rosie, Aspen and Lily were quite clear about resigning before they went to sleep. They were done with the play. By extension, her tenure as assistant director also had to come to a close. Any future contact with Ben would be limited to casual hellos when they passed each other at Reichert's Supply Company or ate at the same restaurant.

In the foyer, Pearl whined and started scratching at the front door. Most unusual as she went outside via a doggy door that led to the small fenced backyard.

Daisy wiped her hands on a dish towel and went to investigate when the doorbell rang. Frustrated, she shooed Pearl away. If her brothers needed something this late at night, then Seth or Crosby should have called first. She opened the front door. "This isn't a good time…"

She stopped as Ben stood there, looking alone and against the world with his hands in his coat pockets. That attraction kicked up once more, and she stemmed it in its tide. He thought the worst of her children. She could never get involved with anyone like that.

"May I come in?" Pearl nudged her way forward and wagged her tail at Ben. Her traitorous dog jumped on him, and he petted her behind the ears.

"Since you'll freeze otherwise, be my guest." Daisy gestured at him while lunging for Pearl's harness so the dog wouldn't venture forth in the night, although she wouldn't go far in this cold.

"Thanks."

Ben shook the snowflakes off his coat and gave it a good dusting before he entered. She closed the door behind him and frowned. "You won't be staying long enough to warrant taking off your coat."

"Can't blame me too much for hoping to make amends, can you?" He gave a wry smile, the one that showed off the irresistible dimple.

Those reindeer hooves pranced in her stomach once more.

When he moved toward her, he had a pronounced limp. She motioned for him to hang his coat on the nearby rack. "Why are you limping?"

"Military injury." He did as directed while shaking his head. "I'm not here to talk about me, though."

"The kids are asleep." Finally. It had taken

some time to remove the lipstick and eye shadow from Rosie's and Aspen's faces, and then Lily wanted an extra hug. Or three. "You should come back in the morning."

He looked as if he wanted to say something else. She waited for some explanation or apology from his lips. More so, she studied him for any sign that this unexpected and inexplicable attraction to him wasn't one-sided. Nothing. That was her answer. It was wishful thinking on her part.

Ben's shoulders slumped, and he reached for his coat. "I shouldn't have bothered you."

He sounded so dejected, and she couldn't bear him going home this downtrodden. "I have some decaf green tea. That helps with bone density, and you can enlighten me about your hip injury." Oh, that was smooth. "Or I could heat up some warm milk for you."

The second attempt was even more of a disaster. She went from sounding too interested to sounding like his grandmother.

"A cup of tea sounds great. I accept. Thank you."

She led him toward the kitchen, Pearl on her heels. They were just two friends, sitting down to talk and come up with a solution that would benefit the play. If she repeated that enough, she'd believe that mantra.

She turned on the kettle and faced him. All

thoughts of the play vanished, and she turned her attention to something personal. "So, what happened to your hip?"

He rubbed the area and grimaced. "I'd much rather talk about the play or your jewelry business. Do you have any extra inventory of earrings to sell? If so, I'd like to buy a pair for my sister for a Christmas present."

Finding two bright red mugs with snowflakes on them, she set them on the counter. "Do you take milk or cream in your tea? Sugar?" He shook his head, and she dropped a tea bag in each mug. "It would be easier to create new earrings for their personalities, but we were talking about your hip."

"We really don't need to talk about that," he said and settled on a stool next to the counter.

"Talking about our pain might not eliminate the hurt, but having someone care enough to listen helps us endure." She spoke from experience as she didn't know how she would have handled Dylan's death without the support she got from the community of Violet Ridge.

For good measure, she plated several eggnog cookies from the Santa jar, then sat beside him. They reached for one at the same time, their hands brushing against each other, sparks tickling her fingers. He pulled back as if he'd felt the sensation as well. Perhaps this attraction wasn't one-sided. "Ladies first."

"Guests first," she countered, ignoring Pearl's blatant attempt at begging.

He nodded and took a bite. "Delicious." Pearl moved away from Daisy's side to his. "I don't know which I like better, these or the sugar star cookies with the icing."

"Be careful that Pearl doesn't steal it, and I don't get sidetracked easily. I'd like to know about your hip injury. The triplets should stay asleep long enough for me to hear the whole story."

His face fell. "Is Lily okay? Not that I'm playing favorites or anything." He placed the remainder of the cookie on the plate, and Daisy pushed it away from the edge so Pearl wouldn't try to steal it. "I wanted to check on them before I went home."

The teakettle whistle blew, and she hurried to switch off the burner. "That's a step in the right direction, but words and actions etch deeply into children's hearts, especially Lily's."

"What about me?" In the doorway, Lily rubbed the sleep from her droopy eyelids, dragging Winter alongside her. "The teakettle always wakes me up."

"Sorry, darling." Daisy went over and kissed the top of her daughter's warm head. Lily smelled like baby shampoo and spice and everything nice. "Ben's here."

Lily brightened and rushed over to Ben, giving him a hug. "Hi." Then her body went stiff, and she broke away. "You weren't nice to Rosie or Aspen."

She moved back toward the hallway. A shadow crossed Ben's face, and he slid off the stool, a wince of pain proving that hip was bothering him. He walked toward her, stopping before he reached her. "Two wrongs don't make a right. I came here to invite the three of you back to the play, not that you've officially left."

"Lilypad." Daisy reached for her daughter's hand. "We don't have to decide anything tonight when emotions are running high. I'll take you back to your bedroom, and you can talk to Ben tomorrow."

Something collided with her backside, and she turned only to find Aspen there, his eyes wide and bright.

"There's a monster under my bed. It wants a cookie, and then it'll leave me alone." Aspen saw Ben, and his eyes narrowed with suspicion. "What are you doing here?"

Ben met Daisy's gaze and sat on the stool once more. "Is every night like this?"

Daisy nodded and held up three fingers. "Wait for it. Three, two, one."

As if on cue, Rosie appeared in the doorway. "Is there a party down here without me?" her older daughter, by a whopping three minutes, exclaimed. Then she saw Ben and stomped her foot. "Why didn't anyone tell me Ben was here? I don't want you at my party. I didn't lie to you."

Aspen joined Rosie, and then Lily completed the group, the three of them a united front. Ben hopped off the stool and winced again as he stood upright. He limped over to Rosie, kneeling beside her, the strain on his hip showing on his face. "We all made mistakes tonight. You and Aspen made a big mess when no one was watching, and I jumped to conclusions without gathering all the evidence."

Lily and Aspen looked to Rosie as if waiting for her response. Daisy wanted to intercede, but she held back, wanting to give Ben enough room to reconcile with them.

Rosie's lower lip jutted out as if she were going to remain firm in her stance. Daisy hesitated as her family made a commitment to the play, but tension at the Holly Theater might spill over to the production. Too many in the community depended on this play to set them in the right frame of mind for the rest of the holiday. She herself had benefited from the joy it brought. She couldn't deny that to others.

Still, her children's Christmas was at stake.

Would they be happier staying in the play? Would Ben help their holiday become that much brighter?

Daisy stepped toward her triplets. Before she could say anything, Rosie bit her lip. "I'm sorry I made a big mess." Then a huge grin graced her sweet face. "But it was fun." Rosie moved toward Ben. "And so's being Noelle. I want to stay."

"Me, too. I like being Nick." Aspen joined his sister, a contrite expression replacing his normal smile. "I'm sorry we caused trouble."

Rosie and Aspen were easier to forgive and move on than Lily, who wore her heart on her sleeve. A little like her, and a direct contrast to Ben's tight hold on his emotions. How could one have a future with someone who didn't talk about the past?

They didn't.

Daisy stood, rooted to her spot, willing away this unsettling attraction so she could move on and find someone safer than Ben, someone who didn't make her heart pitter-patter.

Lily held back as Rosie and Aspen crowded around Ben, peppering him with questions about whether they were truly welcome back on the set. Pearl joined in on the fun and licked the stubble on Ben's face, obviously looking for crumbs. He waited patiently and then reached out his hand to Lily. "How about it? Are you coming back?"

"You didn't say sorry. Mommy always makes me say sorry when I hurt Rosie or Aspen's feelings." Lily kept her distance and hugged Winter tight to her chest.

That small vein on the side of his neck popped out, and she feared they'd be waiting forever for his apology. To her surprise, it wasn't a long wait. "I apologize for saying you lied. You told the truth, and you stood up for yourselves."

Lily threw herself into the group hug, and Daisy felt as if she was on the outside looking in. She'd done a good job inserting the triplets between her and Ben. Too good of a job.

Now he cared about them, and she was their mother—that was how he saw her. That was why he was there.

At least the play was back on track. She'd have been disappointed in herself if she'd broken her promise to Frank.

"Time for bed." She clapped her hands.

"But I'm thirsty." Rosie offered up an excuse to stay awake for a few extra minutes.

"And the monsters are still under my bed." Aspen screwed his face in a tight look of determination.

"And Winter wants to hug Ben, too." Lily wrapped her doll around Ben's arm while Pearl barked her reason for prolonging bedtime.

After a few more complaints and filling cups

of water, she ushered the triplets back to bed and escorted Pearl to Daisy's bedroom.

When she finally returned to the foyer, she found Ben buttoning his coat. "Going already? What happened to the story about what happened to your hip over a cup of tea?"

"It's getting late, and I'd best make sure my Christmas lights turned off." He reached into his pocket and then wound a red plaid scarf around his neck. "Is it always like this?"

She fingered her Christmas tree earrings. This was the season of their life where Rosie, Aspen and Lily wanted reassurance she was there. She wasn't much older when her parents passed away, and she and Crosby would go into Grandma Bridget's room every night for an extra hug. Just to make sure some part of their world hadn't changed.

It wouldn't last forever, and then she'd return to her silversmithing work bench. "Some nights it's monsters, others it's a bad dream. There's always something."

His gaze flickered to her earrings. "If I come over tomorrow night and make sure they stay in bed, will you help me with a one-of-a-kind Daisy creation for my sister?"

She laughed. "That's a tall order on your part." Then she grew serious. "Are you going to fashion a first-grade boot camp? I'm not sure I'm on board with that."

Just as she was no longer all right standing in the cramped foyer with Ben. He might only have noticed the triplets, but she noticed him. His woodsy smell. That slight layer of stubble showing off his strong jaw. The softness of his navy cashmere sweater that she was longing to touch. He was definitely not the safe, solid man she thought him to be. She moved toward the door and turned the knob.

"No military moves, just a little ingenuity that my older brother taught me." He frowned. "By the way, there's nothing wrong with discipline and routine. My father instilled my work ethic that got me through twenty years in the air force."

"And left you without a willingness to talk about your hip," she fired back without a second's hesitation. "They're only seven once, and they've already lost their father. If they need their mother after a bad dream or want a glass of water, there's nothing wrong with seeking love and affection to make everything better. I think you know what I'm talking about. After all, you followed your heart and did the right thing by apologizing even though it was hard."

The foyer never seemed smaller, the electricity in the air strong enough to light up the entire

Violet Ridge downtown district. She'd dreamed of moving on, finding someone else to share her life with. The first man who sent sparks running through her veins was also the most obstinate man she ever met. Worse yet, they were talking about her children, rather than acknowledging whatever was happening between them.

She was ready to shake off her grief and get on with her life, but she wanted someone who cherished her and treated her as an equal. Sparks with a sense of humor. Chemistry with compassion. She wasn't just the triplets' mom. She was Daisy.

He didn't avert his gaze, and he seemed at odds about something. She didn't know him well enough to know what that was, and he didn't seem ready to let her in to discover the real Ben Irwin under the cashmere and stiff oxford shirt.

"How old were you when your parents died?" Ben raised his hand as if he wanted to touch her but quickly lowered it again.

"Eight. Seth, Crosby and I were spending the night with Grandma Bridget and Grandpa Martin at the main house at the Lazy River Dude Ranch. Jase was sick so Mom and Dad were taking him home. We lived in a cabin on the other side of the ranch. He was asleep in the back seat when they hit a deer, and that was probably what saved him."

"I'm sorry," he said. He seemed to lose whatever battle he was fighting with himself and his green eyes moved down her face. He reached out his hand. "Do you mind?"

If he kissed her?

"Not at all."

She closed her eyes, and then she felt his fingers skim her hair and land on her earring. "My plan has nothing to do with discipline."

She opened her eyes and cleared her throat, feeling her face redden. "Why don't you want me to know about your hip?" she asked pointedly. This was the key to him. She was sure of it.

He stopped touching her earring. Withdrawing his hand, he said, "I'm proud of my military service, but there are nights I wake up covered in sweat. I've seen the best of people, but I've also seen the worst. You don't need that in your life."

"That's my decision to make, not yours. I want to know more about you."

When he didn't respond right away, she took a step toward the front door and opened it. A frosty, almost arctic, gust of wind chilled the air. He crossed the threshold and turned around. "I'll meet you here tomorrow night?" He hesitated and shoved his hands in his pockets. "After play rehearsal with the triplets?"

Of course he mentioned Rosie, Aspen and Lily again. He made it clear where his concern lay. She nodded and rushed to close the door, shutting him out and, by extension, eliminating any possibility of a kiss, and more.

Sighing loudly, she leaned against the door until her bottom collided with the hard wood. She'd done exactly what she'd set out to do. She'd proved to herself that she was ready to face the world of dating and relationships once more.

But then, when the most stubborn, obstinate, intriguing man came into her life, she had thwarted herself by using the triplets as a buffer. That worked too well as Ben was now enamored with them, and not her. She felt as though she'd awakened to find a stocking full of coal and nothing else.

CHAPTER NINE

ANOTHER PLAY REHEARSAL was in the books, and Ben was only too happy to take off his coat in Daisy's foyer. Just as he and Daisy were opposites, so too were their homes different. Every time he crossed her threshold, he was struck with how this was a true home. His house was a peaceful sanctuary, but the silence that pervaded his dining room every morning, the same oppressive quietness that gnawed at him as his parents sat stony-faced at opposite ends of the table, was now a gaping hole.

Rosie and Aspen clamored to put Ben's coat on the rack while Lily sat by the crackling fire, reading to Winter. Pearl made her presence known, nudging Ben's hand until he acknowledged her. The hound wagged her tail with appreciation.

The coziness of the evening drew him like a moth to a lamppost, the impact stronger than he'd have liked. Too many nights on the ranch had been wrought with reminders that his parents had nothing in common, his father an outdoorsman who loved his mustang, his mother a social butterfly who sought the theater and other town events.

Had he used his parents as a way to avoid the messiness of relationships? Excuses were simply words without heft.

If he wanted to act on this inexplicable bond growing between him and Daisy, he'd have to ask her on a date.

His mouth grew dry. If he did anything like that, he'd have to conclude his duties as interim director. He wouldn't risk anything between them ending and adversely affecting the play.

No. He would just enjoy her company tonight as she crafted gifts for his family and he watched the triplets.

It was the Christmas season, though, and anything was possible. Daisy's optimism was already brushing off on him and becoming a guiding force in his life. He watched as she pushed a strand of damp curly brown hair off her forehead with the back of her hand. She still wore the same long skirt and oversize chunky yellow sweater from earlier, but he would never tire of seeing the way the fabric swirled around her legs or the way the color brought out the amber in her eyes.

"You arrived in time for dessert. It's peppermint trifle," she said.

Rosie pulled at his sweater and endowed a

crooked smile. "Aspen and me crushed the candy canes, and I used the mixer for the first time."

Aspen rushed over, his head nodding at an incredible rate of speed, similar to the jets Ben had piloted before his hip injury ruled him out of the cockpit. "It makes a great big sound like an airplane." Then Aspen spread his arms out wide and ran around the living room, whirring as he navigated around the tree, and then Lily, before circling around Ben and coming to a full stop.

Lily carefully placed her bookmark inside her book and headed their way. "I put the brownies at the bottom of the bowl."

Then the trio looked at him with expectant eyes as if his presence was the only thing they wanted at Christmas, causing his stomach to do a funny flip. In return, he locked into Daisy's gaze. One time when he was flying a jet, he'd climbed too high in altitude with hypoxia and tunnel vision setting in for a flicker of a second before he reached for his oxygen mask. After a few seconds, he recovered enough to descend to a safer altitude. This tailspin was altogether different, and he didn't think he'd ever be able to pull out of it.

That might not be a bad thing.

He wasn't sure how long of a time elapsed when Rosie yanked harder on his sweater. "I'm hungry."

Ben blinked and pulled himself together. As the independent middle brother, he'd never been prone to flights of fancy. In his professional career, he'd risen to the rank of colonel. Whenever Daisy was around, his whole world flipped upside down.

"I've never had peppermint trifle before." Then he remembered why he was here. "Are you inviting me for dessert? I thought we were just starting the earrings for my sister and stepsister."

"It'll get done, but probably not tonight." She nibbled at her fingernail. "Remember how it's always something? We stopped on the way home to get the ingredients for the trifle, and we ran into Zelda Baker, who asked about you."

"And Uncle Crosby!" Lily's eyes sparkled. "He was buying cereal and milk. He got so excited about his new project he stayed up all night and slept all day. He just woke up."

Aspen's head started bobbing again. "I want to be just like Uncle Crosby and stay up all night."

Pearl gave a bark for good measure, and Ben couldn't tell if the bloodhound agreed with Aspen or was trying to talk him out of it.

Daisy ushered everyone to the kitchen as she glanced at Ben and scooped trifle into bowls. "Crosby's my youngest brother in case you didn't know. He's a regular absent-minded professor." She started to hand over Aspen's dessert and paused. "No staying up late tonight. It's a school night, and it's not healthy for you."

"How come Uncle Crosby gets to do it then?" Her son jutted out his lip and crossed his arms. "He has all the fun."

"It's not healthy for him either. I expect you to go to bed and sleep all night." Daisy waited until Aspen gave a slow nod of agreement before handing him his share of the trifle. "After school, Tatum is taking you to the Lazy River since Uncle Seth said you can go riding with the group that's heading out to sled near the ice pond."

Cheers erupted before everyone dug into their portion of the delicious dessert. Ben complimented the triplets on helping Daisy. After everyone finished their trifle, the trio invented ways to delay bath time. Ben checked his phone, set it on the table and counted down two minutes until his surprise was set to arrive. With as much nonchalance as he could muster, enough that Teddy Krengle would be proud of Ben's acting skills, Ben pushed his cell phone so it would be in Rosie's line of sight. Right on cue, a video of Santa's sleigh filled the screen with the sound of jingle bells announcing a call from Kris Kringle himself.

Rosie oohed. "Do you know Santa?" Her eyes were starstruck.

"Doesn't everyone?" Ben stuck as close to the truth as possible before reaching for his phone and placing it on speaker. "Hello, Santa."

"Merry Christmas from the North Pole!" A booming voice that sounded rather like his own rang out in Daisy's dining room. "I don't have much time because everyone's busy getting everything ready for Christmas Eve, but I had to call my good friends Rosie, Aspen and Lily."

Lily gasped and clutched Winter close to her chest. "Santa knows my name!"

"You're coming in…" Rosie held up her fingers and used both hands to count "…eight days, right?"

"Of course. Hold on." Santa shouted some orders to Rudolph and the other reindeer while Aspen's eyes grew as large as the bowl that had held his trifle. "I'm making my list and checking it twice and making sure you're not naughty but nice."

The triplets chimed in with how they'd helped Daisy make dessert. Then Aspen started to look rather skeptical. "Is this Uncle Seth?"

Daisy's phone rang, and she held it up for everyone to see. "It's Seth. I have to take this in the other room."

Ben couldn't have planned that better. Aspen started backpedaling. "Wow, Santa. It's really you." That skepticism changed into wonder.

"I forgot to make my bed this morning, but I'm trying," Rosie admitted.

"That's a good start. Don't forget to wash behind your ears and go to bed on time. Sleep is important," Santa said in his jolliest voice. "I'm afraid Mrs. Claus and the elves need me, but leave out a plate of cookies for me and carrots for the reindeer on Christmas Eve, would you? Ho-ho-ho!"

The triplets sat in stunned silence, a happy one, the type that held the promise of a full stocking on Christmas morning, not the harsh or cynical silence from Ben's childhood.

Then Rosie gasped and reached for Aspen and Lily, squeezing their hands. "You heard Santa. We have to take our baths and go to sleep. Come on."

"This is the best Christmas ever!" Aspen declared, balling his fist and pulling it toward his body in a victory sign.

Ben had been putting off a family for so long that he'd never experienced moments like these. This must have been what Daisy wanted for them. Together they made a good team, and yet what he was beginning to feel for the attractive brunette was anything but a friendly colleague vibe.

The three rushed out of the room and almost collided with Daisy, who appeared at the threshold, her pretty face the picture of bemusement. "So Santa called?"

Footsteps sounded on the staircase with Pearl trotting after them. Rosie's voice could be heard in the distance. "I get first bath."

Daisy crossed her arms and leaned against the side of the archway. "You didn't think of consulting me first?"

Her gaze went from side to side and then focused on him. She approached until she was so close he could smell peppermint and chocolate, sweetness he didn't want to taint with his nightmares.

That didn't mean he was ready to leave just yet, but he might have crossed the line by arranging for his brother to make the call without asking Daisy first.

"Jeff was returning the favor. I've done the same for my niece and nephew." It went deeper than that. For a long time, he'd used his physical distance as an excuse for putting emotional distance between him and his siblings.

Daisy was making him confront his past and those pesky excuses. When he called Jeff for the favor, they'd spent a good two hours catching up and becoming acquainted all over again.

Then a smile broke out on her face. "They loved it, you know." Her eyes drifted to the ceiling and she pointed at a sprig of mistletoe hanging there. "May I?"

He braced himself but nodded as she stood on

her tiptoes. Daisy had such a presence about her that he hadn't realized, until she was in her bare feet, that he was a good six inches taller than her. Her warm lips brushed his cheek near a slight scar on his jawline. Tingles radiated across his face from the contact. Then she stepped back and traced the scar with her finger. "Did you get that in the air force?"

He shook his head with some reluctance. He wanted to feel her touch for longer, and the movement ended the pleasant sensation. "From my brother, Jeff, when we were learning how to lasso cattle."

She smiled, the softness touching some part of him he thought he'd locked away forever. "Sharing one piece of personal information about yourself wasn't so hard, was it?"

No, it wasn't. That had been easy. The problem was she made everything seem so simple. Peppermint trifle. Making time for snow angels. Holiday cheer. Returning to his quiet shell of a home was the hard part.

She waited for his response, so he admitted the truth. "You're making everything much too easy."

For it would be the joy of his life to let everything tumble out of him right here, right now. His concerns, his career, his dreams. And yet he couldn't risk the triplets hearing him thrash from the final accident that made retirement mandatory and ended any possibility of returning to the cockpit for any stretch of time longer than fifteen minutes. He knew that he was fortunate in his ability to walk and run—others had sacrificed far more than he did—but he could no longer fly, and that had upended his life to a greater degree than he cared to let on.

She narrowed her eyes as though she could sense his retreating into himself. "Then let's do something you might not find so easy, shall we? I'll check on the triplets and then be back with the tools we'll need tonight to start those earrings." She paused at the threshold, twisting her face enough so he could see her smile. "But don't think you're off the hook that easily. Everyone has a story. It's finding someone to listen, someone who cares. That's what makes the difference in life. Our type of connection doesn't come along every day. We need to cherish that and not take it for granted."

With that, she left the room. His heart seemed to beat overtime as he digested her words. *Someone who cares.* What would it be like to have Daisy in his corner? What would it be like to kiss her, a real kiss, slow and tender, full of the positivity she was introducing back into his life?

Pearl skittered into the dining room, her nails clicking across the hardwood floor, as she nudged her head under his hand, wanting some affection. "You have it good here with Daisy and the triplets." She thumped her tail as if agreeing with him. He settled in a chair, lavishing attention on the hound. "If I tell her my story, though…"

He let his words trail off. Maybe Daisy wouldn't run off. Maybe she'd listen and still care. His stomach clenched in the same manner as that long-ago night when he looked out at the Holly Theater audience and found himself standing on logs instead of legs, the cotton in his mouth absorbing the moisture and making it impossible to speak.

Pearl rested her head on his leg, her presence almost as calming as Daisy's. For now, he'd enjoy this evening and then beat a hasty retreat before his heart could become entrenched in Daisy's life.

FROM HER BEDROOM CLOSET, Daisy lifted the boxes with her silversmithing tools, relieved for the heft of the containers. What had possessed her to kiss Ben on the cheek? Since she left the dining room, she'd only been able to think about what a real kiss on the lips would feel like. Strong and forceful, he'd sweep her off her feet.

But then where would her heart be? She couldn't get involved with someone who held back whole areas of his life from her. And yet? She was already in too deep with Ben. For so long, she believed she would date again and find a way to have her candy cane and eat it too. She'd get involved with someone but hold back the piece of her heart that was scared of opening the door to a police officer in the same manner as two years ago when she received the news of Dylan's accident.

She should have known that wasn't who she was on the inside. When she committed to something, she gave it her all, no half measures for her. Even the tools inside these boxes weren't in everyday use because she didn't want to rush the process and deliver anything less than her best to a customer. A necklace should enhance a person's full potential and add beauty, making a statement about individuality and presence. Earrings could be delicate or emphatic, communicating the personality of the person wearing them. Her jewelry was an expression of herself, same as her heart was the living, beating epitome of her true center.

As much as she longed to share her heart with Ben, he was holding himself back. Even tonight when she kissed his cheek, he'd turned aside and stiffened, corralling his defenses in front of her so she couldn't see the man within.

Somehow, tonight, she'd find the fortitude to

ignore the mistletoe and the crackling fire and the cozy parts of her home. Instead, she'd focus on the work in front of her. Fashioning a gift for someone Ben did care about.

With that in mind, she watched Pearl enter Daisy's bedroom and circle her dog bed three times before settling in place. Daisy wished Pearl good-night and sailed into the dining room, where she found Ben texting on his phone, a concerned look deepening those faint lines on his forehead.

"Is everything okay?" Daisy asked as she placed the first box with tools and implements on her table.

Ben jumped to attention and reached for the other box, setting it alongside the first. "You should have asked. I'd have helped."

"These aren't heavy, just bulky." Besides, she'd needed the time to pull herself together. With that, she began unloading her tools and some of the materials, asking him questions about the personalities of the gift recipients.

"Why does that matter?" he asked.

"I'll use the triplets to explain why. Rosie's an extrovert. She likes to be in charge and chooses bolder colors than Lily, so I'd choose something like this." Daisy found her portfolio and opened it to a picture of a chunky turquoise necklace that she'd made for her grandmother's seventieth birthday. "Lily's my dreamer and sweetheart who loves animals, so I'd make her a heart necklace from spur buttons or something with a more delicate feel. You said you wanted a gift for your sister. Does she have pierced ears?"

Ben turned his phone over and flipped through the pages of her portfolio. "Yes. She wore our mother's ruby earrings that matched her engagement ring at her wedding. You did all of this? It's amazing." She nodded while he continued, "What made you start working with silver?"

She selected sheet metal that would turn red upon being heated with the blowtorch. "When I was thirteen, my grandfather invited a friend of his who'd just lost his wife to stay at the dude ranch. Gray ended up living with us for ten years and became our resident silversmith. He was a master and taught me the tools of our trade, becoming more like an uncle to me than anything."

"Does he still live here in Violet Springs?"

"He passed away when I was twenty-three." Daisy felt a twinge of sadness for her teacher and mentor before a smile came over her at the lessons he'd passed on to her. "Before then, though, he taught me how to weld, how to grind metal and how to make the best chicken potpie you've ever tasted."

"No, Tammy's is. She tried to teach Jeff and me, but mine's not as delicious." Ben picked up two pairs of wire cutters. "What's the difference between these?"

"Those are my hard wire cutters for cutting steel binding wire while those flat-nose pliers help me bend the metal." She pointed to the ones in his left hand, then his right. "Why did you go into the military instead of following Jeff to college or staying on the ranch?"

Ben almost looked trapped, and he placed the two pairs of snips on the table while she prepared herself for the excuse he'd use to leave.

But he didn't.

"It took my father twenty years to ask that same question. Same as it took him that long to accept Lizzie's the only one of us siblings to love the land with the same passion and commitment he has. Jeff's tenacious, and he always had his head buried in his books. He met his wife in law school, and they settled in Boston."

That might be the most he'd ever told her about himself at one time. Her heart soared as a design for Lizzie's earrings cemented in her brain. She reached for her sketch pad and pencil. "Keep talking. I'll listen while I draw the initial concept."

After she finished, she showed him two sketches. He picked the pair where circles formed the shape of a horse. They settled down, working on the first earring for his sister, using a disc cutter for the circles. Even so, she braced herself for the inevitable disruptions. By now, Rosie had usually asked for at least one glass of water, and Aspen wanted an extra squirt of monster spray to ward off whatever was lurking under his bed.

"What's the matter?" Ben covered her hand with his strong capable one, tingles shooting through her body.

She couldn't help herself. He might not be forthcoming with her, but that wasn't the way she operated. Maybe by sharing with him, he'd feel more comfortable around her and do likewise. "I keep expecting someone, more like three little someones, to interrupt us." Then comprehension dawned on her as she reached for her blowtorch. "You asked your brother to call so they'd stay asleep."

He frowned. "That makes me sound calculating. Discipline and schedules go a long way in promoting a healthy lifestyle and increasing concentration and productivity."

She returned his scowl with a patient smile. "They're children. They learn from their mistakes."

She flicked on the blowtorch, coloring the steel circles from the bottom up, waiting for the dull color to come alive in a glorious red for the horse's mane.

"Even adults benefit from a set schedule." He

continued flipping through her portfolio until he reached her signature rings. "These are beautiful. When do you have time to create such exquisite work?"

"Right now, I don't." Satisfied with the color, she turned off the blowtorch and set it alongside her other tools, none of which were safe for an energetic group of seven-year-olds. "When they're older, I'll find the time."

He closed her portfolio and tapped on its cover. "Don't put it off. Sometimes it's easy to think you'll do something when the time's right and never get around to it."

His terseness was exactly what she expected of him, but she was no longer fooled that was his entire self. "That sounds almost personal." She leaned forward in her chair, letting the picture of Ben sink into her permanent memory. The way that single strand of his dark hair fell across his forehead, the intensity that always brought a fire to his green eyes, his navy cable sweater stretching across his broad shoulders. The man was too attractive. She wondered about his marital status. After all, he was handsome and good with children. "Why are you still single?"

Ben picked up one of the circles and rubbed the outer edge with his index finger. "What happens next? It just looks like a mess of circles without any rhyme or reason."

"Ah, but that's where you're wrong." She searched the box for the thin wire that would bring everything together. "What looks disorganized and messy will become a beautiful piece of art."

Her nimble fingers worked with the circles until they formed the design of the horse she'd envisioned in the original drawing. Then she snipped the wire, added a hook and handed him the first earring.

He held it in his palm, his eyes reflecting his appreciation. "I'm impressed. Lizzie will love this. Thank you."

It would be easy to lose herself in his gaze, but she wanted to finish this pair of earrings.

For herself as well as Ben and Lizzie.

"While I work on its match, why don't you answer my earlier questions? Were you talking about yourself? Why are you still single?" Daisy selected the materials she needed but set about at a slower pace, hoping that would encourage him to share some insight about himself.

"That's a lot at once, but yes, I was talking about me. I stayed single by choice. Considering my profession, remaining unattached seemed like the right path. When others count on you, that split second of doubt or indecision can be the difference between life and death." Ben set the earring beside her. "I never wanted any distractions to hinder my response time."

"Life is more than a series of decisions. It's the everyday moments. It's the people who surround us and support us. I don't know where I'd have been without Seth and Crosby and my grandparents after Dylan died." She reached for a glass of water only to realize neither of them had anything to drink.

Excusing herself, she went into the kitchen and pulled herself together. She didn't have to look behind her to know Ben followed her. He didn't say anything, but he didn't need to, the silence between them comfortable like her grandma Bridget's shawl. Besides, she already knew the way he smelled, the way he forged into a room, no hesitation, no holding back. She found herself taking her time when she reached for two glasses from the cabinet and filled them with water.

If he wouldn't share about himself, that eliminated any possibility she could be happy with him. She'd have to settle for friendship.

Only when she was composed did she turn around and hand him one glass.

He accepted it with a nod of thanks. "How did your husband die?"

She leaned back against the cold cabinet, wishing for her grandmother's shawl now. "It was the weekend after Thanksgiving." She traced the rim of the glass with her finger, avoiding his gaze out of fear that if he showed understanding, she'd never want to look away from him again. Yet, for the umpteenth time, she was sharing something personal about herself without any reciprocation on his part. Whatever attraction was rearing up between them wasn't sustainable without him giving of himself. Still, she forged forward. "A group of our high school friends invited us to go skiing, but I wasn't sure if I was coming down with a cold. The triplets were already sick, so I insisted he go for the both of us. The authorities said the avalanche took him right away."

Only then did she look into his eyes, the compassion stronger than she'd hoped. She forced herself to stay where she was. She might regret not acting on whatever was pulling them together, a force she couldn't control, but she couldn't take that step toward him, seeking comfort in his arms, acting on an impulse. She deserved more.

"I'm sorry for your loss." He leaned toward her and then pulled back. "I've said it to military families too many times, and that phrase always sounds cliché and cold."

"Being empathetic is never cold." She sipped the water, the coolness quenching her dry throat. "Dylan's death was an accident. He loved me and the triplets and left nothing behind to regret."

"Sometimes, regrets center around something that never was as much as the way things are."

Ben's faraway gaze left her no doubt he was talking about himself for once.

"What's your regret?"

His chest rose and fell. Then he traced the rim of his glass with his finger. "I regret spending too much time pondering if it would be unfair to leave a family behind if I was killed. Even the thought of asking someone to move constantly or having them stay behind when I deployed weighed on me. In the end, I didn't drum up the courage to even try. But then I consider my life in the present, and I understand why better. I've grown accustomed to being by myself. It's easier that way. I'm not one for change."

With a steady hand, she placed her glass of water on the counter and stepped toward him. "Why? Change can be wonderful, a hint of new possibility on the horizon, a step toward hope beyond our dreams."

"Innovation has merit, but change?" That small vein on his neck popped out, and he stood resolute. "What's wrong with something staying constant? If something's within your control, it's best to stay a steady course."

"Where's the fun in that? Change can be scary but exciting at the same time."

She licked her lips and narrowed the distance between them until only Lily, the most petite of the triplets, could fit in the space. She banned the triplets from her mind for the present moment. There was no mistletoe, no reason for her to kiss him except for the sheer rightness of what she was feeling inside her, the inner calm that always guided her in moments like these.

Something vibrated in his front pocket, followed by a reveille ringtone, the trumpet notes that accompanied a new dawn. He reached for his phone, and his eyes widened. "It's my brother-in-law. He and Lizzie just arrived at the hospital. I have to go."

With a tinge of something bordering on regret, she reached for his hand and squeezed it. "See what I mean? The baby will be a change for your family, and it will be wonderful."

Daisy escorted him out the front door. Closing it behind him, she leaned against it. She'd been so close to kissing him, the harbinger of change in any relationship, the moment of no return where two people face what's in front of them.

A knock startled her, and she found Ben on her doorstep with a sheepish smile. "I forgot my keys." He brushed past her and was back in less than a minute, jangling them. "I guess I'm flustered."

"Welcome home to Violet Ridge, Ben. It's a nice place to live, especially when you lose yourself in what's going on around you." Daisy shivered as much from the precipice of the unknown as the chilly wind blowing inside.

He hesitated as if deciding whether or not to kiss her, but perhaps that was wishful thinking on her part. He gave a brief nod and disappeared down her steps into the darkness of the night. She flipped on her porch lights, and he turned and graced her with one of his rare smiles.

For the first time, he looked at her like she was his future.

And, for the first time, she understood what scared Ben about change.

CHAPTER TEN

THREE DAYS LATER, Ben sat in the middle of the auditorium and signaled for the actors to begin their lines. This evening, they were rehearsing the scene where Santa arrives at Nicky and Noelle's house to deliver presents and bumps his head, waking up to find them standing above him without any memory of who he is.

Teddy Krengle, the actor who played Santa, knew his part backward and forward. Ben scanned the script and moved his lips with Teddy's delivery, pausing when Aspen delivered his line.

Except Ben had trouble hearing the mumbled words. From his position in the sixth row, Ben stood and clapped his hands. "I like the energy and forcefulness in your hand gestures, Aspen. Now, let's project that same energy in your voice so I can hear you."

Ben's phone vibrated, and he checked who was calling. Frank Craddock. Ben announced a ten-minute break and tried to call him back from the theater office, but his call went straight to voice mail. He swiveled in the desk chair and found Daisy at the doorway. He'd done a good job of avoiding her, as if that would make it easier to resist another kiss and confronting what was between them. But how had he stayed away from her so long? This evening, she was looking particularly beautiful in a long swishy burgundy skirt paired with a gray beaded sweater. Delicate snowflake earrings dangled next to those light brown curls that cascaded to her shoulders.

Yet her beauty was more than skin-deep. Even though Frank required parents of the child actors to volunteer, Daisy was going above and beyond by learning the logistics of the complicated light board that was almost as old as she was.

He reached for any question that would prevent him from talking about them, more specifically about that kiss. "How's the light board training coming along?"

"Long and arduous. Teddy sent out a message to the group about the ten-minute break. Thought you might like a bag of crackers." She held up two packages of cheese crackers and threw one to his desk. "How's Lizzie?"

Daisy crunched a cracker and then popped another in her mouth.

"Two bouts of false labor have her feeling like this pregnancy will never end. She can't wait to meet her baby and introduce him or her to the horses in the Double I stable." He opened the package and devoured a cracker. "Thank you."

His phone rang, and he mouthed the words "Frank Craddock" to Daisy. Ben shifted in his chair and repositioned his phone to his ear so he could hear Frank, who was probably checking in on everything from Topeka. With any luck he'd confirm he was coming home tomorrow night, too.

Daisy waited in the doorway while finishing her crackers as Ben listened to Frank, his stomach dropping at the owner's news. Daisy must have noticed his distress because she came over and placed her hand on his forearm, inches away from where he'd rolled up the sleeves of his blue oxford shirt. "Is everything okay with Noah?"

Ben relished her touch and didn't want it to end, but he broke the contact and pocketed his phone. "Noah's fine, but Frank is staying in Topeka until the twenty-third. Rhonda's not coming back until after the holidays." He finished the package and threw away the plastic wrapping. "Can you help me round up the cast and crew so I can update them?"

This was a wrench in the play for sure. Operating on a skeleton-thin crew as it was, the production was behind, according to the schedule Frank left in the binder. With a week to go, the set wasn't ready, the actors weren't projecting and the light board was so old as to be obsolete. And the weather forecasters were talking about a storm system that might arrive tomorrow. If it was as severe as expected, it would wreak havoc on the remaining rehearsals.

Ben groaned. If he couldn't produce the town's beloved play, how could he convince voters to elect him mayor?

He pushed that aside and corralled everyone to the auditorium, where he delivered his announcement to hushed murmurs of concern. Most of the crew scurried away to work on the sets or costumes although a few people remained behind, including Daisy.

Constance marched up to him and popped her hands on her hips. "This is not a sustainable enterprise, Mr. Irwin."

Frustrated at having to remind her once more to call him Ben, he contained his emotions. "We're a few days behind, but it's my experience people step up and perform beyond expectations when there's something at stake."

"I was referring to the concession stand. Are we behind schedule?" She pursed her lips together, and her eyebrow rose a fraction of an inch, enough for her disdain to be noticeable. "My parents would never have tolerated that."

"Never mind about the schedule, what's the problem with the concession stand?"

Constance cleared her throat. "Frank and Rhonda's ordering system is in disarray. They have five years' worth of straws but no napkins. A case of juice boxes arrived today, but no water or soda."

Constance elaborated on other issues involving snacks and equipment until Ben's head felt ready to explode.

Sally came over and pushed herself between Constance and Ben. "I'm a vegan, and there are no healthy options. I think you should add something nutritious and fortifying. Healthy snacks like kale chips or edamame."

Constance and Sally began arguing over the merits of that idea with Constance emphasizing the cost and Sally standing her ground about variety. Ben looked over their heads and found Daisy observing the matter, her steady presence giving Ben peace of mind to step into the fray.

"Thank you both for bringing up valid concerns." He'd handled generals and privates in the military, so he could manage this situation. "Constance, go ahead and inventory the supplies on hand. Tomorrow, I'll consult with the vendor on file to ensure we have everything for Christmas Eve. I like the idea of adding a couple of low-cost, season-specific snacks to the concession stand for variety, including one healthy alternative. I'll talk to Oren Hoffman about the possibility of selling his chestnuts for those who want something other than popcorn or candy."

The two older women walked away, and Ben couldn't tell whether or not they approved of his solution. Daisy came over, and that rush from being around her exploded inside him. Why did he have a feeling that long silences at the breakfast table would never happen with Daisy around?

A bemused smile lurked on the edges of her lips. "You handled that well. I can see why you're running for mayor."

"Now to convince the residents of Violet Ridge of that."

"You will."

The one resident of Violet Ridge whom he wanted to offer his heart was standing in front of him. Yet this was hardly the time or the place with the play at stake. "We both have major New Year's resolutions. I'm running for mayor and maybe you should consider expanding your jewelry business? Your silversmithing skills are incredible."

That smile faded. "Someday, when the triplets are older and settled, I'll get around to resuming my hobby."

"Don't discount yourself. That's no mere hobby. Your designs are a work of art." He reached over and admired her long earring before yanking his hand away. "You made those, didn't you? Why aren't you doing this full-time?"

"I have a commitment to my family to run the gift shop, especially after Grandma Bridget's stroke." Daisy twisted the ring on her right finger, a huge daisy she must have created to honor her name. "I can't leave my family high and dry for a hobby."

"What you do isn't just a hobby, Daisy. You have talent, and you love working with those tools. I can see it in your eyes." One of the set designers brushed by him, and he pulled Daisy aside to the corner of the stage.

"Thank you for that vote of confidence."

That smile was back, and darned if he had to keep from reaching for an oxygen mask to combat the hypoxia that was causing his breath to come out in short spurts.

After the production was over and he'd proved to the residents of Violet Ridge that he could manage a successful play, he might act on his feelings. "We're behind. I have to direct the play. Aspen and Rosie are probably raring to go."

Daisy's intake of breath surprised him. "And I only have a short time to figure out that light board. Excuse me."

She hurried away, and he watched her leave. It would be even harder to do so on Christmas Eve when the curtain came down on the production.

DAISY RUSHED INTO the sound booth and closed the door behind her, flipping on the switch so everything was bathed in a bright light. She blinked away spots from the sudden change as her eyes adjusted to the intensity. The light board sat on the table, looming large in its very existence, the silence of the booth as charged as every fiber in Ben's body. While the silence hadn't bothered her over the past few days, a welcome way to concentrate on learning the complicated machine, tonight it bore down on her like a stampede of bison.

She needed noise, and lots of it. Helping Ben and the cast run their lines was out. Ben was exactly what she didn't need as he was the cause of her imbalance. So she hurried downstairs, headed for the sewing room and marveled at the progress. Colorful fabric was transformed into costumes that would immerse the audience in the story world where Nicky and Noelle helped Santa reconnect with the innocence of Christmas. She couldn't help but hope that her family was helping Ben do the same.

Daisy entered the room, surprised to find Constance Mulligan the sole occupant.

"Don't just stand there if you're good with a needle." Constance didn't take her eyes off Mrs. Claus's costume.

"What if I'm not?" Daisy asked.

Constance harrumphed. "I've known Bridget Virtue since we were in kindergarten. Dollars to doughnuts she taught you and your three siblings how to sew and then took you down to the river and demonstrated how to cast a rod."

"If you knew the answer, why'd you ask?" Daisy came over and settled next to her. "And yes, Grandma Bridget did teach me how to use a sewing machine and fish, as well as lasso a steer."

"You've got spunk. I like that." Constance handed her the costume Rosie would change into for the second act when she and Aspen visited the North Pole as Santa's helpers. "I've basted the hem, but it'd be a task off my list if you can finish the seam for me."

Daisy settled herself at the sewing machine, the rhythmic tap-tap breaking through the silence, which didn't feel as ominous as it had in the light booth. She finished one pant leg when Rosie barged into the room. "Ben sent me to get you, Mrs. Potter. He wants to talk to you."

Daisy gasped at her daughter getting Constance's name wrong. "Rosie, this is Mrs. Mulligan, not Mrs. Potter."

Rosie scrunched her nose and tilted her head. "Huh? Then why does everyone call her Mrs. Potter?"

Daisy's cheeks warmed although she had also

heard the crew refer to Constance as the female version of Mr. Potter, the banker character in *It's a Wonderful Life*. She hurried over to Rosie, placing her hands on her daughter's shoulders, before sending a glance back to Constance. "I'm sorry about this. I'll talk to Ben and report back to you."

"I'll come with you." Constance rested the costume she was altering on the table and rose from the ergonomic chair. "And, to answer your question, Rosie, they think I'm like a movie character."

"That's neat! Mommy won't let me go by my favorite character's name. She says I have to be myself. Rosie."

Constance sighed. "The problem is, Mr. Potter isn't a nice character."

Rosie went over and hugged Constance. "You are nice! I like you."

"Thank you." The older woman returned the hug and then broke off the contact. "You may call me Constance."

"'Kay. Can I tell Aspen and Lily that? That's easier to say than Mrs. Mulligan 'cause Lily sometimes has trouble with her words, but Aspen and me help her out so Lily doesn't feel bad. Maybe everyone should call you Constance so you don't feel bad either."

Daisy saw a fine sheen of moisture pooling in

Constance's eyes as she gripped Rosie's hand in a firm squeeze before releasing her. "That's very sweet. You remind me of me when I was your age and running around this theater."

"Were you the first Noelle?" Rosie asked.

Constance shook her head. "My parents used to own this theater. They sold it to the Craddocks a long time ago."

"'Kay. I'm gonna tell Ben you're coming and tell everyone to call you Constance." Rosie smiled and skipped out of the room.

Daisy moved toward the hallway. "I'll be back to finish the costume."

"Hold on," Constance said. Daisy halted at Constance's request and turned toward the older woman, who was dabbing at her eyes with a handkerchief. "I know what people say about me behind my back. There's a note of truth in it as I own quite a few downtown buildings and stay isolated."

Stunned at the confession and unsure of why Constance was confiding in her, Daisy stayed rooted in place. "I had no idea you owned real estate."

"Of course you didn't. I don't go around broadcasting my business, just like you don't go around complaining about your lot in life. You have a sensible head on your shoulders, just like your grandma Bridget, and I see you're trying your best with those three. They're a real blessing. Russell and I wanted a passel of kids, but we never had a baby." Constance held her chin high and stuffed the handkerchief in the sewing apron tied at her waist. "We were thinking about adopting when he passed away suddenly. He'd had rheumatic fever as a kid, and his heart was bigger than it was strong."

Daisy's heart went out to the crotchety older woman, something she never imagined would happen. "How long were you and Russell married?"

"Only six years, but they were glorious." Constance dabbed the corner of her eyes again.

Six years. "That's the same amount of time Dylan and I were married before he died in the avalanche. I can tell you loved Russell very much."

"With all my heart. He crafted stained glass windows and had the soul of an artist." Her gaze softened as she twisted the cotton square in her hands. "My parents didn't like him because he worked with his hands."

Daisy felt a connection with Russell Mulligan. Neither of them worked in traditional art forms, but there was something about stained glass and jewelry that made the world more colorful and beautiful. "Is any of his work still around?"

Constance nodded. "That stained glass window at the Violet Ridge library? That's Russell's work. In my bedroom, there's his lovely piece of a sunset that I see every day."

That explained why Constance was known for yelling at anyone who played baseball near her house. "It sounds lovely."

"He said I was his inspiration." She sniffled and wiped her nose with the hanky, then she blinked as if she realized she'd been talking to someone who wasn't much more than an acquaintance. "You must think I'm a foolish old woman to be telling you this."

Daisy's heart went out to the woman. It was never too late to seek out friendship. "Not a bit. Sometimes we just feel a natural kinship with someone and find it easy to talk to them."

Daisy stepped toward Constance, enveloping the woman in a quick embrace.

"Thank you, Daisy." Constance patted Daisy's shoulder. "If Russell and I had had a daughter, I hope she would have been like you."

"That's quite a compliment." Daisy kept her voice soft and low.

Before Constance could respond, their phones started vibrating and blasted a weather alert.

Daisy reached for her phone at the same time Constance whipped hers out of her sewing apron pocket. A winter storm warning flashed across the screen, along with the news it was imminent with fifteen to eighteen inches of snow and ice forecast in the next forty-eight hours.

They looked at each other. "Ben." Daisy uttered his name as shouts were heard from the hallway. Everyone else must have received the same alert. "This is why he's calling a meeting."

Daisy followed Constance out of the room, unsure of what concerned her more. Finding the strength to love again or being isolated in a house with three seven-year-olds while the fierce blizzard raged outside.

With a generator and a closetful of games back home, the answer was clear when she spotted Ben, looking cool, calm and devastatingly handsome as he took center stage. Daisy sat in the auditorium while Ben gathered everyone together.

The triplets joined her, and she listened while Ben reviewed safety procedures, his face a picture of steadfast resolve, his body a tense coil ready to spring into action for the good of everyone in his circle.

"This storm is expected to be intense, which is saying something since most of us hail from this area. Use the group chat to let me know that you arrive home. Your safety is my priority. I'm canceling rehearsals until further notice." Ben went through a list of activities each cast member could do until the crews managed to clear the roads and OK'd travel once more. "I'll use the chat to let you know the date and time of our next rehearsal as well as our revised schedule. Stay safe."

"One question." Teddy motioned for everyone to remain in place. "We're already behind on the sets. The window frame still needs to be installed as does the hearth. And the North Pole set is in even worse shape. We're in real trouble, Ben. The cast is still missing cues left and right. From the looks of this storm, we'll be missing our first dress rehearsal."

Ben held his folder close to his chest. "When the storm subsides, we'll finish the sets and see how many dress rehearsals we can reschedule."

Dismay lined Teddy's forehead, and it was like Santa himself was frowning. "Will we be ready for our Christmas Eve performance?"

The triplets gasped with Lily clutching Daisy's side. Rosie stomped up the stage toward Ben, her miniature heart-shaped face fierce with determination as she tugged on his shirtsleeve. "We'll be ready, Ben. Won't we?"

"Without sets and rehearsals…" Ben glanced at her, the conflict clear in his eyes. "We'll do our best, Rosie, and reevaluate after the storm."

He didn't promise the show would happen on Christmas Eve. The world spun around her. Daisy grasped the armrest of her chair.

Part of Christmas was the anticipation of the

community coming together at the theater, with residents greeting one another by name and laughing at the familiar punch lines. Then everyone went home and celebrated the holiday with a light heart. Without the play, how would she make this Christmas memorable and meaningful for Rosie, Lily and Aspen?

CHAPTER ELEVEN

TWO DAYS LATER ONSTAGE, Ben hammered the last stocking in place, taking care with the delicate plywood that formed the fireplace mantel. While others waited out the storm at home, Ben hadn't left the theater. Instead, he utilized his childhood carpentry lessons from the ranch's foreman to good use by finishing the set. He even tested the carousel device, ensuring there'd be enough time at intermission to swap out the set that served as Nicky and Noelle's living room for the North Pole scenery.

He jumped off the stage and ate the final handful of popcorn that served as breakfast. Concession stand food was getting rather tiresome. There were only so many nachos and buckets of popcorn a guy could tolerate. However, the snow was tapering off and the weather radar showed blue skies ahead. The crews had eighteen inches of snow to move off roads and walkways, but they were experts. He checked an app and found welcome news that they had, in fact, begun the arduous task of clearing the roads. With a bit of good fortune, the Smokehouse would be open for business this afternoon, and he'd tuck away a hot meal. He sniffed the air around him. Before he ventured out into public, he'd shower in the bathroom adjacent to Frank's office.

His hip would especially appreciate going home to his bed, the throbbing after sleeping on the small couch in Frank's office particularly achy.

The show must go on. Rosie, Aspen and Lily were counting on that. With clear roads, rehearsals could recommence tomorrow. He sent out a group text and then set out to conquer his morning's list of tasks without anyone to interrupt him before the cast and crew would be bustling around the theater once more. He retrieved the small pail of paint and touched up the window frame. Perfect. Now it was ready for Teddy to make his entrance as Santa. His stomach grumbled, catching him off guard. It was already lunchtime. After a check of local restaurants confirmed they were still closed, he set his phone on the sawhorse. Then he visited the concession stand, where one last hot dog was warming on the roller. After depositing the cost of his lunch in the register, he jotted a note to order more relish packets. Rummaging through the cabinets for hot dog buns, he came up empty. That didn't matter as he had survived worse meals in the air force. He took his repast to Frank's office and wolfed down the frankfurter along with a bag of potato chips. Fresh vegetables at his next meal would be as welcome as they'd been in previous times after enduring a month of MREs during his tours of duty.

Ben crumpled the hot dog wrapper inside the bag and guzzled half a bottle of water before heading back to the auditorium. His eyelids grew heavy. A little nap sounded good after that lunch. There were worse places to sleep than a theater seat, and Ben ought to know.

In his dreams, Ben visited the North Pole where Daisy was dressed as Mrs. Claus. To his surprise, he found himself wearing a Santa suit with the big black boots. She waggled her finger at him. "Christmas Eve is only five days away. We have to do our best to have everything ready as so many children are depending on you."

Then Constance made her appearance, dressed as Scrooge. She mumbled something about Christmas. Hard as he tried, though, he couldn't understand her. Ben shifted in his chair, willing the voices to go away so he could finish his nap. Then his hip might stop hurting.

"Ben!" The concern in Daisy's voice forced Ben to open his eyes.

Daisy and Constance were standing in the

aisle, and he rubbed away the sleepiness. Then he ran his hand through his hair. Sure enough, it was sticking up in every direction. He smoothed it as best he could without a mirror.

Unlike him, Daisy was a drink of water. Her curls surrounded her shoulders, showing off her earrings, snowflakes sitting atop green cowgirl boots with crystals forming a star in the middle. He glanced past the hem of her emerald green and teal skirt and saw the tips of her green boots. She was even more beautiful than in his dream.

"What are you doing here? Rehearsals aren't until tomorrow."

"Your lights have been on around the clock." Constance pursed her lips in a straight line. "When I knocked on your door last night, you didn't answer. This morning, same thing. Since I've seen you two together, I called Daisy, and when she didn't know where you were either, we began to worry."

Ben bolted upright and groaned. "I broke my promise to you. I'm sorry. The timer must have broken during that power surge. At least, there was a surge here. Did you have one, too?"

Daisy gasped and then narrowed her eyes.

"Are those the same clothes you were wearing at rehearsal the other day?" Daisy sniffed and then waved her hand under her nose. "Have you been here the whole time?"

"Rosie's depending on me." The inside of his mouth tasted like wet cotton, and he sipped the last drops from his water bottle. Then he rose and stretched, the cramped quarters not helping the ache in his hip. "Besides, Frank's still in Topeka. Someone had to watch over the theater during the storm. How did you two get here? I thought the roads were closed."

"I have a snowmobile in my garage. When you're my age, you can't rely on others during an emergency." Constance jangled her keys in front of him and then walked to the stage. "You finished everything by yourself?"

He squirmed, and it took all of his willpower not to rub his hip, sore from the extra lifting. "I didn't have to be anywhere else."

Daisy bumped his arm, a scowl overtaking her pretty features. "That's not true, Ben. The triplets would have been more than happy to have you stay with us. For the past few days, it's been Ben this and Ben that." A small hint of a smile lightened her expression. "And I could have used your muscle to help me dig dog tunnels for Pearl."

Speaking of Rosie, Aspen and Lily, they were nowhere in sight. "Where are they?"

"With my next-door neighbors, the Delgados. Tatum is breaking the news to the triplets that she has enough saved to start college a semester early. They're going to miss her so much." Daisy bit her lip and then shrugged. "When Constance called me asking if I knew where you were, I panicked and contacted Lizzie, who, by the way, is still on baby watch. She said you weren't at the Double I, which is doing fine, and she wants you to text her."

Guilt about leaving his sister out of the loop descended on him. For too long, it was a matter of national security and his career not to share information about his whereabouts or actions. Habits were hard to break even with the best of intentions. Real change needed more than intent.

Change. He shuddered at the concept, yet it swirled around him. The Smokehouse had added new items to their menu. Lizzie was in charge at the Double I. Chestnut carts added a spicy smell to the air and made it feel like Christmas.

Change was happening all around him whether or not he liked it. Buying a house was the first step in laying down roots. Now, it was time to build relationships. The concern on Daisy's face was evident, and she and Constance revved up a snowmobile to find him. That alone proved how much they cared.

He let them know he'd be right back. After he retrieved his phone from the sawhorse, he returned to the auditorium. Surprised, he found a number of texts from almost every Irwin in Colorado along with his stepsister and her husband, who had started a local rodeo academy. Jeff was threatening to take the next plane to Colorado if Ben didn't return his text, and Zelda had also inquired about his whereabouts. Ben's heart expanded as his fingers flew over the small keyboard, alerting his family and friends to his well-being.

Constance rejoined them and gave a swift nod. "Daisy, your brother Crosby is meeting you here in half an hour to take you home, right?" Daisy nodded, so Constance faced Ben. "I expect those lights turned off tonight by eleven, and not a minute later."

Ben watched her leave the auditorium, his mouth ajar at the change in his neighbor. Christmas miracles were real. He snapped his jaw shut and faced Daisy.

Nerves swept over him. "You dropped everything to make sure I was okay?"

"As soon as I texted Lizzie, I had a feeling where you were. I needed to see for myself." Daisy blinked and faced the stage. "How did you do all this by yourself?"

"Most of it was already in place. I just came along at the right time." He wasn't being modest. Everyone else had already contributed so much, and he provided the extra touch. Anyone would have done the same.

Daisy nodded. "Well, now that everything's

in place, I want to check the lighting," Daisy said. She started down the aisle and then stopped. Suddenly, she was running back toward him, her face scrunched up in fury.

She pointed a finger at him. "Don't you dare ever do anything like that again! Have you forgotten how dangerous Colorado weather can be? You have to let someone know where you are when there's a blizzard!"

Was she offering to be that someone? Then he remembered how her husband had died, and guilt overtook him. "You have my word. I wasn't thinking that anyone would miss me."

"Well, start thinking." Her brown eyes blazed at him, and she poked his chest with her index finger, the one with the daisy ring. "It's time you wake up. You're a stubborn, infuriating man who should be thankful for what you've got."

"Maybe I'm learning to care for a stubborn, creative person who brings sunshine into every room she enters."

Lightning hitting a propeller was something he could handle, being trained for such emergencies. Nothing had ever prepared him for Daisy Stanley. He stepped toward her, wanting to reach out and touch her.

She closed the gap between them, so that her sweater touched his wrinkled, paint-splattered shirt. "I'm not made of sunbeams and moon dust.

I'm real. I won't shatter," she said quietly, gazing up at him.

He peeled his eyes away from her face for a moment to cast them upward. "There's no mistletoe."

"All the better. We'll kiss because it's what we both want." She clutched his arms and pulled him toward her.

A kiss on the cheek had seared him, but a kiss on the lips branded him. Her softness was in direct contrast to his hardness, their differences sparking something deep inside him. Her light floral scent overpowered the fumes from the paint and varnish. He cupped her face with his hands, her smooth skin creamy and delicate under his rough fingers. Although they were in a theater, where performances transported audiences to other worlds for a short time, there was nothing ephemeral about this kiss. Instead, there was only something life-changing and different.

For once, he didn't mind the prospect of change. In fact, he relished it, reveled in it as much as the taste of her, peppermint and vanilla rolled into the essence of her. He moved his hand, coming in contact with her earrings until he tangled his hands in the silky curls that fell to her shoulders.

His lips left hers, trailing a series of little kisses all the way to her ear, where he pressed his cheek against her skin, marveling at the wonders of home and the sheer delight of Daisy.

"How about we skip the light board and go spend some time with Rosie, Lily and Aspen? Should we tell the triplets about us now or after the play?"

She stiffened under his touch and pulled back. "We're a package set, but that's hardly what I wanted to hear after our first kiss."

What did she want him to say? "I'm not one for casual relationships. When I'm in, I'm all in."

Her eyes grew wide as she sidestepped out of his reach. "This is new, and I'd like to keep it between us for a while. The triplets already think you walk on air, and I don't want them getting their hopes up."

He was coming to care for her, and he couldn't fathom why she wanted to keep this as classified intel. "I don't understand."

She scowled, a most unusual sight. "What if it doesn't work out? What if…"

"What if this is something that caught us both by surprise but is wonderful?" Did he, former air force colonel Ben Irwin, really say that aloud? He didn't know who was more astonished by his pronouncement, him or her.

"It's too soon. There are consequences and adjustments. A relationship takes time…"

"Discipline." He finished her sentence for her,

keeping the distance that seemed to be growing with every second.

She wrinkled her nose. "I was going to say trust and communication. You still haven't shared any personal details about your hip injury."

They were at an impasse, and he didn't know how to close the gap.

"You're right on both counts. I'll check the light board with you. I haven't been in the sound booth since the snowstorm."

She looked as if she was about to add something but merely nodded and turned on her heels, heading upstairs to the booth. He followed and brushed by her, reaching for the keys to unlock the room. Unsure of why he'd locked it when a blizzard was swirling around the theater, he relished the second to pull himself together.

He opened the door and allowed her to pass, trying not to inhale her fresh scent but losing that battle. She sailed into the booth and touched the switch on the wall. Nothing. She tried again, but the lights didn't operate.

"A fuse must have blown. Wait here." He found his way to the operations room where the circuit breaker was located.

Sure enough, the breaker was thrown. Ben flipped the switch and returned to the booth, which was now flooded with light. Too bad he couldn't say the same about the look on Daisy's face.

"The light board won't operate."

The problem didn't lie with the fuse box, as the overhead lights were proof that the circuit was now in the correct position.

That left one answer, and he didn't like it any more than he liked Daisy's response to their first kiss. The snowstorm must have overloaded the light board.

Without that piece of integral equipment, he wasn't sure the show could go on as planned.

FROM THE SOUND BOOTH, Daisy texted Tatum and let her know the theater emergency would push back her arrival time. Within seconds, Tatum let her know everything was fine. The triplets were relishing a change of scenery after several days trapped in their house. If only Tatum had such an easy solution to everything else in Daisy's life. How was she going to afford alternative child-care next year? She couldn't have the bus drop them off at the dude ranch after school as her grandmother was still recovering from the stroke she'd experienced earlier this year. The employ-ees had their own duties, and Seth was preoccu-pied with the rumor of a new luxury dude ranch, opening in early spring.

And that concern paled next to the issue of her and Ben's first kiss—an earth-shattering, real kiss. That was no mere press of lips to the cheek under the mistletoe; it was intense and intentional…everything she'd come to expect from Ben and more.

She'd never expected to experience these kinds of flutters over someone again. All she wanted was someone safe and surface-level so she'd never go through that same devastating moment when the police officer broke the news about Dylan.

Daisy felt anything but secure around Ben Irwin.

He made her alive again. She wanted to kiss him over and over and build a relationship where they shared their lives, past, present and future. And that was the problem. Ben had closed himself off.

Daisy found herself standing on the precipice. If she didn't hold back now, she'd find herself falling once more, and with someone like Ben in her life, she didn't think she'd ever land on solid ground in one piece.

She just needed to toe this delicate line until the final bows were taken and life returned to normal. So, why did that sound boring and awful?

Ben entered the booth, his large frame taking up as much space as his personality. "I just got off the phone with Frank. The light board and sound controls are on the same fuse box. He said there's no backup equipment."

He checked the power on the sound equipment with the same result. He banged his hands on the board, but nothing happened. Both the light and sound boards were destroyed in the power surge.

No lights. No sound amplification or sound effects or music. Without these, the play wouldn't soar.

Without trust, her and Ben's relationship would never get off the ground either.

But that type of defeatism wasn't her style. She could accept this disaster, or she could do something to fix it. Well, she could do something to save the play. That was the easier problem.

She started with the obvious. "Did he give you the name of his repairman?" The dress rehearsals could still go on while the equipment was being fixed.

Ben frowned. "I asked him about that. Frank fixes everything here at the Holly. He's checking flights, but Noah's not out of the NICU yet." A ping from his phone alerted Ben to an incoming text. "Excuse me."

She watched Ben disappear, and her heart went out to Frank, who was now faced with a difficult choice. Leave his family behind or come back and save his livelihood.

Daisy let out a deep breath and stared at the equipment.

It was Christmastime. Everything should be

straightforward in this season of cheer. Instead, her issues seemed insurmountable with no ready solutions.

Her phone chimed, and she read Crosby's incoming text and laughed. Once again, he was running late as he'd fallen asleep while burning the midnight candle on his dissertation. He had just started eating breakfast. Typical Crosby. She updated Tatum on the delay. In return, Tatum sent her a picture of the triplets having a wonderful time stringing popcorn.

One more chuckle escaped before a middle-aged cowboy with a toolbox opened the door. "Howdy, you must be Daisy." He tipped his Stetson her way, his boots loud against the tiled acoustic floor, echoing in the small chamber. "Ben's making some calls in Frank's office but said you can join him while I fix the sound-board."

"Oh, did he?" Her ire rankled at Ben's sending orders through someone rather than delivering them himself. "He should have had the manners to tell me that himself."

The cowboy's face broke into a wide smile. "We're going to get along just fine."

"Who are you? And how do you know Ben?" Daisy folded her arms and stepped in front of the sound and light boards although the toolbox was enough confirmation Ben had sent him upstairs.

"I'm JR, the foreman at the Double I. Lizzie sent me to check on Ben." He removed his Stetson and placed it over his chest before laying it on the soundboard. "Tammy and I have known your grandparents for years."

Even though Violet Ridge was small and she knew most of the residents, especially those that lived in town, she hadn't met everyone who worked on the Irwin ranch. After chatting for a minute, she excused herself and went in search of Ben.

She didn't have far to go as he was exactly where he said he'd be, talking on the phone in Frank's office. His eyes seemed to light up when he waved her in and mouthed "high school drama teacher."

So he was looking for a backup light and soundboard. She waited until Ben was done. As soon as he hung up Frank's landline phone, she didn't waste time or pretense, knowing that was the way he preferred to operate. "Next time you can introduce me to someone who's important in your life."

Ben leaned back in Frank's chair, dark circles lining his eyes from having spent the past few nights at the Holly. She immediately regretted her brusque tone.

"You're right." He sat up. The chair snapped into position, surprising them both. "But since you've lived in Violet Ridge your whole life, I thought you knew JR."

"I've met Tammy but never JR." She softened her voice. "Who was on the phone?"

"The high school drama department can't help us out. If it can be fixed, JR's the person to do it, but if he can't, we need a backup and we're running out of time." He tapped the phone, his gaze distant, as if he was trying to come up with solutions before they found out the true condition of the sound and light boards.

That type of conscientious behavior, the same that led him to stay and finish the set, went a long way in Daisy's book.

"Then you're forgiven for not introducing me to JR." She kept her tone lighter than she felt inside, those hooves working overtime. "How can I help?"

Ben rose and scooted the chair under the desk. "Isn't your brother coming to pick you up?"

"Not for another hour." She hesitated, deciding on how to describe her youngest brother in a positive light. "Crosby gets caught up in his work to the detriment of the rest of the world."

"Nothing wrong with a strong work ethic." Ben brushed past her and paused at the entryway. "I'm going to finish the work on the North Pole set if you want to help."

She should just walk home. Constance had

guided the snowmobile past the road crews, who were clearing the streets and were probably done by now. Still, she was his assistant, and he needed her help whether or not he wanted to admit it. "Of course I do. Tatum and her mother are taking good care of the triplets so I have time."

She and Ben settled into a rhythm of working on the North Pole set design until JR joined them, his face grim.

"What's the verdict?" Ben asked, popping up from under the elves' workbench.

JR simply shook his head. "The power surge fried both of them."

At that point, Crosby entered the auditorium. "Hey, Daisy." Crosby tugged at the sides of his beanie. "Ready to go?"

This might be a first. Crosby showing up on time. She held up a finger so he'd give her a minute.

She faced JR and Ben, who were huddled together.

"Where do we go from here?" She almost hastened to add the words *about the play*. Then she stopped. She wasn't sure she and Ben had anywhere to go after the play.

"Have a spare light and sound board in your attic?" Ben laughed yet there was no trace of humor in his tone. "Without those, there will be no music or sound effects or lights."

"Doesn't your father own the Irwin Arena? And isn't your stepmother a famous singer?" she challenged him. "Reaching out to them for help would be a start."

"I'll text Frank first, then try my connections." Ben's fingers began flying across his phone screen.

"My wife, Tammy, bought tickets to the play." JR faced Daisy with a smile. His low chuckle echoed with goodwill. "You two are a good team."

Daisy's insides burned. *A team?* That implied there was a Ben and Daisy when there wasn't. She'd tried everything to propel them skyward and—to put it in a way that Ben would understand—there had been no liftoff.

Somehow, she had to find a way to salvage Christmas.

Crosby climbed the steps to the stage, and Daisy knew it was time to leave. Her brother ran his hand over the elves' workbench. "I love this theater." Then he brushed the velvet of the scarlet curtains. "If only these walls and curtains could talk, they'd have some great stories for my dissertation. There's even a story of this building having its roots in the era of bootleggers and gin joints."

Daisy knew that if Crosby got on a roll, they'd be here a while. "I'm ready," she said, turning to face Ben. "Unless you need me to stay."

Ben scrubbed his chin and then shook his head. "Thanks, but I'd rather spend time with the triplets if I had the chance. Go home. I'll schedule a rehearsal for tomorrow."

They departed the stage, and Daisy looked back at Ben. "Do you want the triplets here tomorrow or does Crosby need to babysit them?"

Ben nodded. "If they weren't here, that would be for the best."

Daisy returned the gesture, waiting for some move on his part to follow up on the earlier kiss. When Ben didn't make a move, Daisy girded her heart and walked alongside Crosby to the exit.

CHAPTER TWELVE

THE NEXT AFTERNOON, Daisy entered the theater and hung her coat and scarf on the packed lobby rack. She must have been the last to arrive. She hurried into the auditorium, where Ben stood at the front of the seating area, holding a clipboard, with everyone else milling about, oohing over the living room set, which looked perfect.

Ben held the clipboard up to quickly scan it and called the group together. "Everyone gather round for the latest update."

With that official voice, he commanded the room. Daisy found a spot toward the back next to Constance, who turned toward her with a curt nod before paying attention to Ben. Since yesterday, he'd shaved and showered, but it was obvious he was still favoring his left hip.

He didn't mince words. "There's a new soundboard on the way and thanks to my stepmom for finding it and to Frank, who's offered to cover the cost of the shipping. Frank will find more sponsors to offset other costs when he returns."

Constance raised her hand, and he called on her. "If we need sponsors to defray costs, why are you still here?"

Ben blinked. "Huh?"

Constance repeated her question and then reached for Daisy's arm. "Everyone here knows what to do as far as their volunteer duties. Take Daisy with you to solicit sponsorships. There's no soundboard for her to operate yet, and everyone in town loves her. She'll soften your edges."

This time it was Daisy's turn to sound like Ben. "Huh?"

"You're wasting time." Constance tapped her watch. "The stores and businesses will be busy, but you can make that work in your favor. Explain you'll be out the door faster if they agree to sponsor the theater on the spot."

Ben stepped backward and shook his head. "I need time to prepare a presentation with facts and figures."

"You need to strike while the iron is hot. It's business. Besides, storeowners would run if they saw me coming." Constance moved away from Daisy's side and joined Ben, taking his clipboard. "You two will do fine. I'll take over here. Now scoot."

Before Daisy knew it, she and Ben were in the lobby, collecting their coats. Ben pulled on his wool cap. "The military lost out when she didn't enlist."

Daisy agreed and zipped her coat. Then she pulled on her gloves. "Do you want to divide and conquer?"

If she could cross her fingers inside her thick waterproof gloves, she would.

"No. Constance is right. You get along with everyone, and everyone likes you. I need you."

She reached into her pocket and wrapped her favorite holiday scarf with gingerbread people around her neck while his scarf was standard black wool that contrasted with his red cheeks. "Oh, okay." She'd take the compliment as he opened the door for her.

Two hours later, they'd collected several sponsors as Emma from the Rocky Mountain Chocolatiers had pledged her support as had Regina Dunne-Sullivan at the Over and Dunne Feed and Seed. Daisy could see Ben's rising frustration at how much time she was taking with each proprietor, asking after their personal lives. But Daisy had gone to school with Emma, and Violet Ridge residents had cheered when Regina reconnected with the love of her life, Barry, a few years ago around the same time as his nephew Will had fallen for a local wind sales representative, who'd left her company, EverWind, and started a consignment store at the Feed and Seed.

Now, Ben and Daisy found themselves walking toward Lavender and Lace, an upscale women's boutique.

"Maybe we should spend a little less time at each business," Ben said.

Daisy huffed, a puff of white air wisping away into nothingness. "Ben." She placed her gloved hand on his strong muscular forearm and then pulled away. "This is more than just about sponsorships. We're a community. We've grown up together and care for each other. When I ask Emma about her daughter, it's more than just casual conversation."

"And asking about the goats at the Silver Horseshoe?" With some mirth beginning to register in those green eyes, Ben named the ranch where Regina now lived with her husband and his family.

"Snow and Flake are rather famous in these parts." Daisy laughed. Rosie, Lily and Aspen had recently enjoyed an afternoon at the Silver Horseshoe, which was home to a menagerie of animals. She had tried to convince Seth that a petting zoo at the Lazy River Dude Ranch would attract families with young children, but so far he hadn't gotten on board. Speaking of her family's business… "The Lazy River will be more than happy to buy a platinum sponsorship, so that makes three sponsors. The play is about more than just the Holly Theater. It brings people together on Christmas Eve."

Ben gazed at her in wonder. "Thanks for the reminder about why we're doing this. Some mayor I'd be. I've never felt more like my namesake."

Confused, she stopped in front of the elegant boutique's holiday display. "I'm missing something. What does the name *Benjamin* have to do with anything?"

He stood next to her, an imposing figure in his plain navy peacoat, his back ramrod straight. "My name's not Benjamin," he mumbled.

It just went to show how little she really knew the guy even though he'd kissed her like the existence of the sun and moon depended on it.

"What's your name?" Then it dawned on her, and a giggle escaped. "Don't tell me…"

"Ebenezer is a family name." Ben stared at the window display as if the answer to all of life's mysteries resided within it.

"Well, hello, Ebenezer." She held out her gloved hand. "Very nice to meet you, Ebenezer. Does this make Aspen or Lily Tiny Tim?"

He faced her and rolled his eyes. "I've heard all the Scrooge jokes." Still, he obliged her with a handshake. "But I'd have to say Lily would be Tiny Tim."

Even with thick gloves separating them, the jolt that went through her body alarmed her. She withdrew and pointed toward the entrance. "It's getting cold. Let's go inside."

The heat from the store enveloped her in a cushion of warmth and delight, but she knew it wasn't because of the furnace and had everything to do with the man who was accompanying her today. Shoppers lingered at the various displays. One older man was shifting his weight from side to side as his wife dropped hints about a shawl she wanted under the tree. Daisy glanced around for Valerie Kaminski, the owner, and finally spotted her near a line of customers at the register. Valerie headed their way, her white blond hair fashioned into a French twist, her tasteful white pantsuit the same as the one on the mannequin in the display.

"Ben, Daisy. I've been expecting you." She came forward and clutched their hands before bestowing her refined smile at them. "Ben, I'll be a gold-level sponsor."

Daisy blushed. She should have known the Violet Ridge business chain would have been buzzing with their sponsorship project.

"Thank you. That's very generous." Ben reached for his phone. From her vantage point, Daisy saw him entering information into a spreadsheet. "You've put us that much closer to our goal."

A customer approached, and Valerie motioned

for one of her employees to be of assistance. "My first job was at the Holly. Some days, I still smell the popcorn when I wake up." She turned away from Ben and focused her attention on Daisy, her gaze going straight to Daisy's pink Christmas tree earrings, topped with a gold star. "I've been meaning to contact you."

Suddenly self-conscious, Daisy reached up until her gloves brushed against her earrings. "Why?"

Valerie tapped her own tasteful silver hoop earrings, and Daisy recognized them as ones she made out of horse bits. "Every time I wear these, I have at least five customers asking me where I found them. A couple of years ago, your rings and earrings were my best jewelry sales, and I was wondering if you'd consider commissioning custom orders again. I'd give you top placement on a rack near the register and your own display."

A few years ago, she'd have jumped at this type of offer. Even now, her fingers itched to start on a series of rings, each unique, each tying to the beauty found in the springtime meadows at the Lazy River Dude Ranch. And yet? She barely found time for sleep. Her head ached at the thought of handling everything once Tatum left for college.

She ignored the voice that told her she could

afford more lessons and childcare if she took Valerie up on her offer.

"That's generous, but the triplets are an active crew." Regret laced her voice. Here was the offer that could put her jewelry design business on the map, more so than if she just sold her line at the dude ranch gift shop, and she had to refuse.

"I understand, but if you reconsider, I'd be most grateful." Valerie walked over to the register and handed her business card to Daisy. "I'm expanding my store and adding two new locations, one in Gunny and one at a nearby ski lodge. Having you as an exclusive designer would benefit us both."

Daisy thanked her for the card and stuck it in her purse. "If anything changes, I'll let you know."

Valerie smiled and escorted them to the door. "I've heard the Smokehouse is most amenable to a sponsorship, Ben, as well as catering your mayoral kickoff campaign. You might want to head there next."

Ben's jaw dropped open. "How did you know I'm running for mayor? I haven't made anything official."

Valerie laughed. "This is Violet Ridge." As if that explained everything, which to Daisy it did.

A customer entered, and Valerie excused herself. Ben's mouth closed, and Daisy patted his arm. "Ready for the next stop?"

Ben nodded, looking rather shocked, same as her.

If Valerie was serious, this could be a nice income stream for her. Better yet, she'd be returning to the craft she loved, the feel of the metal under her hands as it changed from something utilitarian into something unique. There was nothing else like it.

Well, there was one thing, and that was what she felt for Ben. Whether or not she wanted him in her heart was no longer in doubt. She cared about him, that was a given, but was that as far as she could take this?

Her heart seemed ready to take a chance.

Could she let the rest of her follow?

As THE AFTERNOON gave way to early evening, Gregson Park hummed with activity. Kids and tweens alike slid down the snowy hill in the last of the daylight. From his side of the bench, Ben crumpled the hamburger wrapper, his stomach full, his mind racing with the offers of sponsorship pouring in from all over Violet Ridge.

The new owner of the Smokehouse had pledged at the platinum level and thrown in two free dinners for Daisy and Ben. She suggested they eat outside and enjoy the lovely weather.

Ben wouldn't go so far as to call this freezing air lovely, but he had to admit that after the last few days of ice, wind and snow, being able sit outside was an acceptable change of pace.

"That's quite a serious face for someone who set out to do something today and accomplished it." Daisy waggled a potato crisp in front of his face before popping it into his mouth. After he swallowed it, he laughed and she smiled. "That's better. You should laugh more."

With everything he'd seen and witnessed, he sometimes lost sight of the reason why he served in the first place. Yet he'd also experienced many good times in the past twenty years. The sunrises where the morning dawn glowed with the promise of hope on the horizon, the camaraderie of his fellow troops, the friendships that lasted. Just yesterday he'd received a baby announcement from an officer who received her honorable discharge last year.

Daisy helped him reconnect with that. She was a caring woman who brought a calm ease and underlying positivity to everything around her. Even if he wasn't her boyfriend, he wanted to help her in any way he could. "You should take Valerie up on her offer."

She chomped on a raspberry. "There are only twenty-four hours in the day."

"Seems as though we both have challenges in

the year ahead. You need to find time for your business, and you told me I need to find time to laugh." It wasn't lost on him that those were also two reasons why it wouldn't be smart to pursue a relationship. Love was hard enough when you lived under the same roof and committed to each other. What about when he was running for mayor and she was working two jobs and raising three children? Were they doomed to fail before he had taken her out on a date?

Daisy tsked from her side of the bench. "Those lines on your forehead will be etched there forever if you don't laugh more."

His phone alerted him to an incoming text. "Hold that thought."

He whooped with joy while reading his stepmother's offer. She and his father were in Los Angeles, where she was preparing for her guest role in a holiday edition of a singing competition show, but she pledged her support for the Holly Theater along with a generous and anonymous donation. Evie had also arranged for a top-of-the-line sound and light board to be delivered tonight!

"Daisy!" Ben couldn't wait to share the good news with her.

He looked around, and she wasn't there. His heart sank as he realized something. He wanted to share all his good news with her first. She had imprinted herself onto his heart, and now she was nowhere in sight.

Pow! A snowball hit him square in the chest, and Daisy popped out from behind a bare silver aspen. "Here I am."

Her eyes glowed with amusement and the satisfaction of catching him off guard. "Just for that, you'll have to wait to find out what was in that text," he said.

Daisy bent over and packed another snowball. "Good, because in case you haven't noticed, Mr. Ebenezer Irwin, now is not the time to talk about business. This is your time to have fun and laugh."

Her next snowball caught him right above the heart. In that instant, he knew. His heart was hers forever.

He threw away the rest of the dinner containers and nodded in her direction. "Challenge accepted."

He judged the layout of the land and formed a winning strategy. In a matter of minutes, they were lobbing snowballs at each other, and his coat was covered with ice and snow. Her giggles echoed in the air while a snowball pelted her, one he hadn't thrown as several residents now joined in the melee.

Soon, more people stopped sledding to take part in the snowball fight. A group of middle-school youth were shouting and claiming sides while whooping with joy. Everywhere around the park, people started scooping up snow and throwing it at the closest target.

Ben's gaze surveyed the scene. Once again, he'd lost sight of Daisy. Where was she?

Someone clutched his coat and pulled back his collar. A whiff of Daisy's light floral scent caught him off guard, leaving him powerless to respond. Before he could react, cold snow traveled down his back.

"Gotcha!" she yelled triumphantly. "I am the queen of the snowball fights!"

He faced her, dancing on the snow, joy written all over her face. It was time to think about what he had to offer. Other than himself, it might not be much, but he had to be honest with her about what she was getting into before they had a chance to go forward.

"Yes, you are." He watched as she continued her victory dance in front of him, so much so she didn't see the snowball in his right hand. He approached her and held out his spoil. "What will you give me not to put this down your back?"

"You wouldn't." She tried to retreat, only to come in contact with the siding of the public use facility.

One look into her trusting, triumphant eyes and he knew he wouldn't do anything except fall more in love with her every day. Until they talked and he laid out his past, though, he wanted to keep this moment light. As she said, there was a time to have fun, and after a day like they'd had, this was a celebration.

"Maybe I will, maybe I won't." He waggled his eyebrows, connecting with his light side that he didn't even know existed. Until her.

"I don't like ice on my back." Daisy eyed him with suspicion. "Name your price."

"One kiss?" He let the snowball escape from his hand. "There's no mistletoe, nothing hanging over us."

"Seems like I'm a double winner. I can't believe you bought my performance." She grinned. "Made you stop."

He laughed. "You said that on purpose?"

"Of course. All's fair in love and snowball fights." Her breath hitched, and she caught herself. "I mean, all's fair..."

"I understand." He lowered his head toward hers, his lips coming in contact with her soft mouth.

She gripped the sides of his coat, bringing him closer, her skin smooth and soft. Their second kiss was even better than the first, the peppermint from her dessert almost as sweet as her. He wrapped his arms around her waist, no distance separating them, as the noise and busyness of the park faded away and there was only the two of them.

The kiss felt like home, like her, like forever.

Her hands loosened their grip as she broke contact. "If you kiss like that, why are you still single?"

Her eyes no longer showed signs of mirth. Interest and emotion lurked in their depths, reflecting that she cared about him, the real him that was more than a ranch owner's son or a military colonel or a future politician. Suddenly, he stood before her, humbled she wanted to be a part of his life.

He tugged off his gloves and traced the curly strand of her hair peeking out of her beanie, slightly damp from the snow and ice. "That's a complicated question."

"You're a complicated man on the outside—" she leaned into his touch "—but I think you're hiding what's inside. Someone with a great capacity for attention to detail, not to mention a whole lotta love. You shouldn't conceal that. You're a good man, Ebenezer Irwin."

"Sometimes." The nightmares disagreed with her, but he resisted the urge to run and hide. Sharing began with one morsel of truth, just as a snowball began with a few snowflakes coming together in one larger orb. "You know, my mother died when I was twelve."

"I remember." She reached out and hugged him. "Have you made a snow angel lately?"

He nodded his reply. "Two days ago during the blizzard, on the sidewalk in front of the Holly, but there's more to my story. My parents were verging on divorce when the doctor diagnosed her with cancer. They only stayed together because she was dying."

"Oh, Ben. That must have been awful for you." Her voice was laced with sympathy, and she entwined her gloved hand in his.

"From when I was little until she passed away, she and my father had this icy silence at the breakfast table." There was something about Daisy that allowed the details to flow out of him, her rare sense of composure speaking to him in a way that transcended silence or words. "For a long time, I didn't want to risk turning out the same way. It was easier to just get involved for a short time and then end things at the first hint the relationship was going south."

"Things like those silent moments. You know those can be a sign you're becoming more comfortable with each other. Silence can be healthy and beneficial." Daisy's slight challenge was more proof that she was the one he wanted in his life after the play.

He tilted his head to one side and blew out a slow breath, the wisp of fog evaporating in the slight breeze. "Then time sped up, and I was commemorating my tenth year in the military. After that, it seemed as if the bachelor life was here to stay." He gazed at the snowy ground, the white layer captivating and bright. "It was easier to keep everything I'd seen in combat to myself."

"You must have seen a side of life that is beyond my understanding, but it doesn't mean that you should keep that bottled and inside of you." She wrapped her arm around his waist. "You don't have to walk on shattered glass around me. I might not have seen what you have, but everybody endures a different lot. I'm stronger than I look."

He met her gaze, electricity passing between them. Then he lowered his head for another kiss when something hit his midsection. Another snowball, but one not thrown by Daisy.

"Hey, Ben!" Aspen's voice came out clear. "Whatcha doing here? Oh, hi, Mommy."

Ben backed away from Daisy and found Aspen heading his way. Soon Rosie and Lily came into sight, followed by Crosby, hauling a large backpack and a sled. Ben hurried over to help Daisy's brother. "Let me help."

"Thanks. I didn't know you were here. Thought you were looking for sponsors." Crosby handed the rope connected to the sled to Ben.

"We just finished dinner and were heading home next." Ben pulled it in Daisy's direction.

Lily pulled on Ben's coat. "Want to go sledding with us?"

Ben looked at Daisy, who was pulling down her beanie to cover her ears, tinged pink from the cold. She mouthed the words, "We're not finished yet."

That was what he was counting on. "I accept that kind invitation." Ben reached for Lily's gloved hand as the group headed for the top of the hill.

At this moment, Ben felt like he'd reached the peak of Mount Everest. For the first time in a long time, anything was possible.

CHAPTER THIRTEEN

WITH CHRISTMAS EVE in three short days, Ben's stepmother had come through on her promise of pulling a few strings, and the new sound system and light board had been delivered this morning. At this afternoon's rehearsal, Daisy was receiving a crash course about its operation. Ben stepped into the limelight, giving her a thumbs-up that she could hopefully see from her vantage point in the sound booth. However, Daisy's learning curve wasn't his only problem right now. He'd introduced a new staging direction for the actors, which was causing trouble.

"Teddy, this is the new spot for your monologue." Ben held up his hand. "I know you've delivered the same speech from Santa's bench for years, but Constance couldn't see Rosie put her hand in yours so I've switched you to stand over here."

Teddy rubbed his jaw until it popped. Then he winced. "Sorry. I'm having a hard time concentrating on account of this tooth. I have an appointment with my dentist the week after Christmas."

"Okay, but let's try it one more time. I'll dem-onstrate the scene first." Ben nodded at Rosie.

On cue, she came over and reached for his hand. "I believe in you, Santa."

Then Aspen hit his mark and clasped Ben's other hand. "We all believe in you, Santa."

Ben glanced at Rosie's pleading face, then As-pen's, before launching into Santa's monologue. He'd heard the lines so many times he didn't have to glance at the script anymore. Then he turned to Teddy. "It's your turn."

The pro that he was, Teddy did an even better job with the part, and Ben clapped. Then he called for a huddle and thanked the cast for a great job, calling for tomorrow's rehearsal to begin an hour earlier. He led the triplets to Daisy's booth and waited for her signal to enter.

Daisy looked rather disheveled but beautiful in her green cardigan set that paired perfectly with her long floral skirt. "Wait a minute." She flipped to the next page of a thick instruction manual. "I'm still reading through this. I really need another couple hours to familiarize myself with the new system."

Lily tugged on Rosie's arm and leaned over, whispering something in her sister's ear. "Yes!" Rosie exclaimed. "That's a great idea!"

Rosie enlightened Aspen in the same manner,

and he fisted his hand and pulled it toward his chest in a victory motion.

"Yeah," Aspen said. "That would be epic!"

Uh-oh. Ben was already learning that when the three of them agreed on an idea, it was probably a doozy.

Rosie nudged Lily and pushed her toward Ben. "Do it! He'll say yes if you ask him."

Ben frowned. Was he really that much of a pushover? He rubbed his hip, still recovering from sleeping in close quarters. "I don't think I'm up to sledding."

Lily shook her head and held up her purse. "We want you to take us Christmas shopping." She wiggled her finger until he lowered his head to her level. "I need to buy Mommy a present."

Shopping? With the triplets? This couldn't end well. Ben started to protest, "Your uncle Crosby or uncle Seth would…" He looked into Lily's large expressive eyes, and his insides went to mush. Colonel Ebenezer Irwin *was* a pushover for these four Stanleys. "If it's okay with your mom."

Rosie, Lily and Aspen surrounded her and pleaded their case. Daisy glanced at Ben. "It's your call."

Part of him worried about keeping up with three active seven-year-olds. What if he lost one of them? Knowing the triplets as well as he did, he'd most likely lose Aspen. Daisy wouldn't like him nearly as much if he only returned two of her children.

And yet? She needed this time to acquaint herself with the new system. He could handle this.

"How much time do you need?" His voice croaked at the end and he cleared his throat, taking a more forceful approach. "Take your time. We'll be fine."

Boastful words, he thought to himself an hour later in the busy confines of Reichert Supply Company, a general store that carried a little of everything. Aspen had already sprinted out of Ben's sight once, and Ben promised he'd take them all home if Aspen did that again. Rosie now contemplated a display of stuffed animals. "Do you think Mommy would like this one?" She thrust a sparkly, tie-dyed unicorn toward him, followed by a pink koala with impossibly large black eyes. "Or this one better?"

Ben sighed and sent a pointed look in her direction. "I think you want those for Christmas."

"But I get her a stuffed animal every year." Rosie returned both to the shelf. "It's a tedition."

"A tradition." Ben corrected her mispronunciation and stifled a laugh. "Sometimes it's nice to think about what will make the gift recipient happy. What makes your mom happy?"

Rosie tapped her chin as if giving his question

hefty consideration. Aspen chimed in, "When Pearl howls that she wants to go outside."

That gave Ben pause. "How does that make her happy?"

"Because then she doesn't have to clean up the carpet." The little boy grinned and then snapped his fingers. "She always tells us not to yell in the house, so I have the perfect present for her." He started for the end of the aisle and then returned. "I 'member."

Ben sent him a thumbs-up. "Good job, Aspen."

The boy reveled in Ben's praise and tapped his foot with some impatience. Lily whispered something in Rosie's ear, and Rosie brightened. "You're right. Mommy does like it when Pearl keeps her feet warm."

"I really want to look for my present." Aspen squirmed and wiggled. "And I saw one earlier. I don't want them to run out."

After that kind of buildup, Ben steered Rosie and Lily in Aspen's direction. The little boy led the way to the dollar section. There he held up his prize with aplomb. "A kazoo. That way we can let Mommy know when we're going outside."

Ben opened his mouth to argue with that logic but nothing came forth. Instead, he remembered his mother's advice that it was the thought that counts. In that respect, Aspen's gift was given with the best intentions. He held out the shopping basket, empty after an hour's time. "At last we have one winner."

Aspen's grin said everything as the boy deposited four in the basket. "One for each of us, and one so Mommy can call for us to come inside."

Then Rosie tugged on Ben's arm and yanked him to another part of the store. He wasn't sure where he was anymore until he found himself in front of a big display of cozy socks. Ben glanced at Lily, knowing she gave her holiday present idea to her sister. He sidled over to her. "That's a sweet gesture sharing your Christmas plan with Rosie. Your mom can always use two pairs of socks."

Lily gave him a forlorn little smile. "Don't tell Mommy Rosie used my idea. Rosie loves being the center of attention, and I like it when people aren't watching me. I'll buy Mommy something else."

Ben's heart went out to her, but it was a strong person who kept the peace by being true to their nature. "Do you have something else in mind?"

Lily shrugged. "I'll know it when I see it."

Rosie settled on a pair of yellow socks with smiley faces on them, and Ben approved. For the next thirty minutes, Ben held his breath as Lily had, so far, stopped in front of a kayak, a large insulated cooler and a cast-iron camping Dutch oven. He noticed a definite theme as Lily loved nature, same as her mother. Finally, they found themselves in the jewelry section.

"Mommy can make all of this, and better." Rosie's pronouncement brought a look of disapproval from the employee stocking the shelves.

Ben shrugged while internally agreeing with Rosie. He placed his hands on Lily's shoulders. "You could draw her a picture or read her a book. Moms love those things."

"I 'member about your mommy." Lily squeezed his hand. "I'm sorry. You can borrow mine since yours died."

His heart clenched at the caring sweetness in Lily's eyes. "Thank you, sweetheart."

His voice cracked, so much so he barely recognized himself. He even felt a tear forming at the corner of his eye.

Lily let go of his hand and darted toward something. "What does BOGO mean?" She faced him with her nose scrunched up. "Does that mean I gotta pay extra?"

Ben cleared away that boulder in his throat and shook his head. "It means buy one, get one free."

"Epic." Lily perked up and reached for two friendship bracelets, one with pastel shades of yellow and gold while the other was bold blue and red. Each circle was made of twisted skeins of thread braided together with a connector, a daisy for the yellow and a flag for the red. She placed them in the basket. "I'm done."

The four of them made their way to the long line

at checkout. The triplets taught Ben an alphabetical game pairing a first name with a food item and occupation. "Annie the artist loves asparagus!" Rosie giggled as she came up with an example.

The trio continued with the game until it was their time to pay. Ben extracted his wallet, and Lily shook her head. "Uncle Seth paid us for collecting the eggs this month."

She retrieved three wallets out of her purse and handed a blue one to Aspen and a teal one to Rosie. After they paid, they headed back to Daisy's house where a wonderful aroma of beef stew in the slow cooker greeted them. The triplets headed upstairs to hide their presents. Ben let Pearl outside and turned to find Lily standing there.

"You scared me." Ben placed his hands over his chest.

"Sorry." Lily held her doll Winter in one hand and the red-and-blue friendship bracelet with the other. "I don't know if I'll see you on Christmas so I'm giving you your present now. It's not wrapped or anything."

"I thought that was for one of your uncles." He wiped away a pesky tear before Lily could notice.

"I want you to have it. We're friends." She held it out for him. "And at Christmas, you and Mommy will match."

Ben accepted it without words, although there were none that needed to be said aloud. He knew

Lily was an old soul. She was Daisy's daughter all right.

How had the four of them done it? Somehow, they thawed his heart, an organ he thought was frozen in time forever.

IN SPITE OF the brisk night air surrounding her, Daisy yawned as she slipped inside her house. She unwrapped her wool scarf patterned with gingerbread people and hung it on the stand along with her coat. The smell of hearty beef stew filled her with appreciation that a hot dinner would soon be on the table. After she cooked some egg noodles, she and the triplets would sit down for a meal together, then she'd finish her preparations for the best Christmas ever.

Wait! Something was wrong. Daisy blinked, her senses on high alert. Pearl hadn't greeted her at the door, and the house was eerily silent. No Rosie laughter, no Aspen shouts and no Lily hugs. She extricated her phone from her coat pocket when the back door squeaked. Pearl traipsed over and sat in front of Daisy, who rubbed behind her ears.

"Where is everyone?" Daisy laughed as she realized Pearl wasn't giving away the secret.

Daisy started for the back door when something in the dining room caught her attention. Her mouth dropped as she found a chain of paper snowflakes near the ceiling extending around the room. A poinsettia tablecloth covered her table, and four plates rested on matching red place mats. Two candy-cane amaryllis flowers in a crystal vase served as a centerpiece. If Pearl wasn't by her side, she'd have thought she entered the wrong house.

Shouts of enthusiasm came from the kitchen with Rosie bounding into the dining room first. "Hi, Mommy," she said, spreading out her arms for a big hug.

Rosie was wearing her coat so she'd obviously been outside in the backyard. Daisy obliged before Aspen ran in and launched himself on her other side.

"Do you like it, Mommy?" Aspen broke away with a big grin. "We taught Ben how to make a snowflake chain. He hung it for us, then taught us how to set the table. We waited for you, and I'm so hungry."

As Aspen rubbed his stomach, Lily entered with a bowl of rice and Ben followed with a tureen, no doubt full of stew. She hadn't come home to dinner served to her in so long.

Ben glanced her way, his green eyes meeting hers. Her palms grew sweaty at the softness she found lurking in those depths. He'd swapped out his usual navy sweater for an emerald green Irish knit one that showed off his wide shoulders. A slight five-o'clock shadow drew attention to his strong jawline. She'd miss him something fierce once the play was over.

"Rosie wanted to surprise you, so we decorated your dining room. Then Rosie and Aspen fed Pearl while Lily helped me with the rice." Ben stopped when Rosie and Aspen surrounded him with a big hug.

"Divide and conquer." Aspen gazed at Ben with something close to hero worship.

"Absolutely." Ben extended his hand, and Aspen delivered a high five.

"This is beautiful." Daisy reached up and fingered the chain of paper snowflakes held together with white twine before she looked at Ben once more. "Thank you."

He gave a cursory nod and waved. "See you tomorrow at rehearsal."

"You're staying for dinner, aren't you? Especially since you and Lily made the rice." She hesitated. "Unless you have somewhere else you need to be."

The triplets chimed in with their pleas for him to stay. He looked fondly at each of them in return. "Since the three of you insist."

Daisy wobbled for a second. It wasn't her request to stay that he accepted; it was the triplets'.

In no time, Aspen set another plate at the table while Lily folded a napkin and Rosie retrieved silverware from the kitchen. Daisy placed aside her misgivings and enjoyed dinner. Rosie kept everyone laughing with her stories, and the meal was over too soon. Even better, Ben built a fire while the triplets cleared off the table.

Her children surrounded Ben in the living room, and he tapped his watch. "Rehearsal starts early tomorrow."

"Bedtime. Maybe Mommy will call Santa and tell him who's first in bed." Rosie rushed out of the room, beating her siblings to the stairs.

Lily hung back and brought Ben a bag. "Don't forget this."

Her younger daughter gave him a hug before heading upstairs. Curiosity got the better of Daisy. "What's in there?"

Ben crossed the room and showed her. "Rosie insisted on making me a snowflake chain for my tree. Aspen and Lily helped."

How long had she stayed at the theater? The triplets were her responsibility. Heat flooded her face, and her cheeks must have been a brilliant red. "The new light and sound board is much simpler than the last one, but there's still a learning curve. I didn't mean to take so long."

Ben frowned. "You don't have to make excuses. The triplets and I had a great time shopping." He chuckled, a deep rich sound that filled the room. "Words I never thought I'd hear from my mouth."

She smiled at him. "I'm glad. Thank you."

Flustered at how she was feeling at his mere presence, Daisy reached for the poker and poked at the log until small sparks popped, releasing a burst of heat.

"I might have an ulterior motive," he said.

Daisy held her breath at Ben's words, her heart beating faster, her breath coming in short spurts. Feelings she never anticipated experiencing again roared to life even stronger than the flames. She licked her lips, waiting for him to kiss her. He might have stayed for dinner for the triplets, but he was still here for her. She delighted in the heady emotion of anticipation, something she thought she'd lost forever.

"Yes?" She faced him, her word of encouragement as much for her as him.

"Jeff and his family are coming to Violet Ridge for Christmas. They want to meet Lizzie's baby and celebrate the holidays here. I'd like your help for a gift for my niece and sister-in-law." Ben looked at her with expectation.

For the second time that night, disappointment trickled through her. He'd spent his afternoon with the triplets, and then stayed behind to ask for a favor. He wasn't here in a romantic way.

She nodded, her throat dry and her limbs heavy. "I'll be right back."

Collecting her tools, she swiped at the corner

of her eye. Anticipation was tricky like that, and she pushed away the blow to her psyche.

Thankfully, Rosie asked to be tucked into bed. Then Aspen wanted her to spray monster spray, which was actually glitter water, to ward off the monsters. Finally, she could prolong her time upstairs no longer and placed her tools on her dining room table. She and Ben settled into a rhythm with lively conversation. Ben elaborated on his sister-in-law's and niece's unique characteristics so she could personalize something special for them. Soon she was lost in the joy of fashioning a pair of sophisticated earrings for his sister-in-law while designing a cute ring for his niece.

She sketched two different ideas for the earrings, and he chose the simpler pair. "Those look like her."

"Good choice." Daisy laid out the tools they'd need.

While she unwrapped the black velvet bag containing her planishing hammer, he leaned forward in his chair. "Did you give more thought to Valerie's offer?"

She shrugged and concentrated on her work. "Seth called an employee meeting today. A development corporation bought a thousand acres south of Violet Ridge. There are rumors they're opening a luxury guest ranch."

"I can ask my father if he's heard any rumblings," Ben said.

"Thanks. The word about town is they intend to focus on the high-end tourist side. Our clientele is geared more to families and repeat customers." At least she hoped the Virtue family didn't have anything to fear from the new lodge. Grandma Bridget and Grandpa Martin had raised two families at the Lazy River, first their son and then her and her three brothers.

"From everything I've heard, you have many repeat customers." Ben kept a controlled tone while concentrating intently on the task at hand.

"Our guests are the best." Even though she wasn't as involved at the Lazy River as Seth, she took pride in her family's operation.

"Same as your jewelry is the best. Valerie would be fortunate to sell your line." Ben didn't avert his gaze from the metal.

"I just have to wait until everything is at an even keel to accept her offer, but I'm so thankful for everything you did today. The shopping, dinner, everything. I haven't had anyone spoil me since Dylan died." Her voice came out garbled, most unlike her usual cheerful tone. Ben had that effect on her.

"It was nothing. Glad to help." If anything, he was concentrating even harder on his task. "Others would be happy to do the same so you can get your business off the ground again. Zelda Baker or her twin sister, Nelda. Even Constance."

She noticed he didn't include himself on that list. His point made, she changed the subject to Christmas presents, elaborating on what Santa was bringing the triplets. He received the message. The log in the living room fireplace was a stub by the time they finished the earrings. His whistle complimenting them was low enough not to wake up the triplets. Pearl, however, ambled into the dining room and stopped in front of Ben. She circled three times and curled up at his feet, closing her eyes as she did so.

Ben fingered the earrings, and she thought she saw a hint of a smile on the corners of his lips. "My sister-in-law will love these. Thank you." He glanced at his watch and blew out a breath. "It's late. I should go."

Before she knew it, Ben had taken his leave, and she stood alone in her foyer. Pearl padded over to her, her tail thumping twice on the hardwood floor. "Is it your bedtime?" Daisy glanced at her watch. Tomorrow was her day off from the dude ranch. "It's not mine yet. I'm staying up to finish the ring for Ben's niece."

With that in mind, she went back into the dining room, a new design surging through her. She reached for the pliers with renewed focus and determination.

CHAPTER FOURTEEN

THE NEXT DAY at the Holly Theater, Ben knocked on the sound booth door and waited. As soon as he heard Daisy's request to come in, he took a deep breath.

Last night, he'd come close to making a huge mistake. Just when he'd been on the verge of admitting his feelings and asking her on a date, her voice grew husky when she mentioned Dylan. There was no way he could take Dylan's place, especially since she still harbored feelings for her late husband. Her tone and facial expression had proved that.

Even now, as he entered, it took every bit of his self-control to hold back from revealing how fast his heart was beating and how she caused him to dig deep and confront the good and the bad of his past. Instead, he soaked in the sight of her sitting there, looking beautiful in her burgundy sweater. He pasted on what he hoped was a convincing smile and forged forward. "We're done with the rehearsal. The triplets are waiting with Constance in the green room."

"Already?" Daisy picked up her phone and grimaced. "That went faster than usual. I keep finding new features on the soundboard. I actually think I'm hooked on volunteering at the theater. Who'd have guessed?"

Her frown turned into a smile that filled his chest with lightness. In the past month, she steered him toward a new path, one where he could grasp hope again.

"Sometimes life takes us by surprise." This was now the second day in a row that he said something out of character.

"Why, Ben Irwin." Her grin grew even wider. "That's positively positive."

"That's the first time I've noticed that," he said, pointing toward a door on the other side of the sound booth. If he judged correctly, it might be a shortcut to the green room.

"After looking at that curtain for the past few weeks, my curiosity finally got the best of me. When I pulled it aside, I discovered the door. I haven't checked to see whether it's a closet or if it goes somewhere." Daisy winked at him. "Want to go on an adventure with me?"

Always, but her heart was closed to that possibility so he'd settle for the time they'd spend together during this production. "I'm game."

Daisy rose and jiggled the knob. "Argh, it's locked. Oh, well."

From his pocket, he held up the set of keys Frank had given him. Since Frank hadn't declared anything off-limits, Ben had no qualms about finding out what was behind the door. "I have a master key."

Daisy moved out of the way, and Ben tried every key until he heard a click. The last one was indeed the charm. He opened the door a crack in case it was an overloaded closet. It appeared to be some sort of stairwell.

"Ooh, I wonder where it goes." Excitement laced her voice.

He searched the wall in the narrow dank chamber for a light switch but didn't feel anything. Instead, he turned on his phone's flashlight. "Let's find out. I'll go first."

The stairs spiraled in a circle, the passageway narrow. Stale air surrounded them, and her floral scent was more comforting than ever. He focused his flashlight on the walls, a dark dingy gray, the texture grainy and rough. With a steady hand, he shined the light to the ceiling where cobwebs proved this stairwell wasn't used on a regular basis. Then he concentrated the beam on the stairs, testing each step to make sure it was safe for human use. No creaks. No buckling, He had a good feeling about this.

"This is so cool," Daisy said.

Her hand brushed his shoulder, and he savored the moment. Then, he carefully crept down the spiral staircase, the narrowness more confining and restrictive than he anticipated. A claw clutched at his chest. He stopped to catch his breath, as the world became a pinpoint of black.

"Ben?" The earlier note of excitement in her voice gave way to concern. "Are you okay?"

It was as if all the oxygen was sucked out of the stairwell. He clutched at the metal rail for support. His hip screamed at the tight confines, and he was back in the cockpit the minute before he pressed the eject button.

Daisy rubbed his arm, a comforting touch, one that eased his breathing. She repeated his name. Slowly, the tunnel vision faded. "Is there someone I should call? Lizzie? Jeff? Your dad?"

He could hear the fear in her voice.

"No, don't worry them."

"Share the details with me, then?"

He wanted to keep his anxiety to himself, the fear of bringing the past into her world pressing on him. And yet, she'd experienced tragedy at an early age, first losing her parents and then her husband. Those events molded her into the strong woman she was. He could confide in her even as a mere friend who was obviously still in love with her late husband.

"Have a seat." He reached the first landing and waited until they were sitting side by side. Then he continued, "I was two months away from retirement, but the military had extended an invitation to reenlist. I intended on accepting, especially as Lizzie had everything in control at the ranch. Then, on a routine test flight, the plane went into a nosedive, and the copilot and I both ejected."

Daisy placed her hand over her mouth. "Did your copilot survive?"

"Yes, and with minimal injuries. However, I broke my hip. I can run and swim, but I can't sit in the same place for long periods of time. No more flying for me." Before he had arrived in Violet Ridge, he experienced the loss with an acute sense of despondency. Yet since he'd talked to Zelda and had started volunteering here at the playhouse, that sensation had dissipated. Now, it was the people around him who filled him with a sense of purpose.

And at the top of that list was Daisy. Perhaps they were helping each other find their way after losses that rocked their worlds.

He wasn't the best when it came to handling change, but with Daisy? Maybe constant change wouldn't be so bad.

"I used to love skiing and haven't been for two years." Longing for the sport came through, but

he knew why she hadn't returned to the slopes—
Dylan. "But I think it's time, just like it was time
for you to find your way home."

His new house was where he lived, but it wasn't
filled with the same love and energy that made
Daisy's small abode a home.

"After the play…" Ben screwed up his courage.
"Would you like to go skiing with me?"

"Can you ski with your hip?" His phone's flashlight caught the deepening pink in her cheeks, a
sweet flush he anticipated seeing more in the future.

"It's fine when I'm active. It's inactivity that
makes it ache." Hence the reason he could still
run and commit to most athletic activities.

"I'd say that's true about most things in life."
She pointed downstairs. "It's time we find out
where this goes, I think. Don't you agree?"

He noticed she didn't say yes or set a date for
the ski trip. With a pang of regret, he reached
out and found a locked door blocking any forward progress.

SHE ALMOST BUMPED into Ben while he jiggled the
antique silver knob of the door. More than anything, she wanted to kiss him before he opened
that door and they ventured forth into the great
unknown. For the first time, he'd opened up to
her about his past, giving her hope about their

future, one filled with unexpected adventures and kisses that made her toes curl.

Considering her life was as busy as it was, did Daisy need to go skiing to prove she was over Dylan? Maybe she did, maybe she didn't. The important part as far as she was concerned was living again.

Now that Ben was opening up and talking about his past, she intended to act on whatever was happening between them. And yet, talking about his past was only half the problem. The flip side of the past was the future. Did he only see her as his friend, the mother of the cute triplets who had ingratiated themselves into his life?

Or did he see her in the same romantic way she saw him, a partner with whom to experience life's joys, someone to share the ups and downs while cuddling next to a fire or exploring the many outdoor trails around Violet Ridge?

She was about to ask when Ben twisted a key and turned the knob. On the other side of the door was a black curtain. Ben pushed it aside, and they laid eyes on the green room where Constance had her hands full with the triplets. Daisy brushed past Ben and hurried over to help.

To her surprise, Constance didn't seem surprised to see them. "So you found the bootlegger's stairwell."

Daisy found herself surrounded by the triplets, who hugged her. "The what?" Daisy asked Constance over their heads.

"It was a secret passageway in the 1920s when the theater opened. Have you found the floor safe where they stowed alcohol during Prohibition?" Constance wiggled her finger until Rosie returned to the older woman's side.

Daisy made a note to tell Crosby about this. This unknown piece of Violet Ridge history would keep her brother fascinated for days. Then again, she'd best wait until after Christmas, or he might forget to show up at the Lazy River for the festivities.

"A secret passage? How cool!" Aspen started for the doorway, but Ben shook his head.

Ben locked the door before the triplets reached the passageway. "I couldn't find a light switch, and I don't want you to get hurt."

Rosie, Aspen and Lily put up a few murmurs of protest before Constance reminded them she needed to time their costume change.

Ben tapped his watch. "I have to go to a meeting with Oren Hoffman about supplying the concession stand with chestnuts." He smiled at the triplets, crinkling the fine wrinkles on the sides of his eyes. Those faint lines brought out the strength in his face. "As well as a few other surprises. Excuse me."

Daisy watched as he left the room without a

backward glance. Once again, he'd addressed the triplets without clarifying the status of what was, or wasn't, happening between them. She kept from sighing and helped Lily with her costume.

"Stand still, Aspen." Constance whipped out a tape measure and held it against his leg. "You've grown this month. I'll let out the pants an inch tonight."

Aspen wrinkled his nose at Rosie. "Told you I was taller." Then he glanced at Constance once more. "How come you know so much? Do you have a little boy?"

"Aspen!" Daisy exclaimed, heat rushing up her neck.

Constance shrugged and pressed the button so the tape measure contracted back into its container. "Not many people in Violet Ridge have the gumption to ask me about me, so I'll share my story with you. I loved my husband, Russell, very much. He had mumps as a teenager. That left him with a bad ticker, and he died too early. We weren't blessed with children."

"What's a ticker?" Rosie asked, her hands holding up her chin.

"His heart." Constance motioned for Aspen to go behind the tall screen in the corner to change.

Lily went over and gave the older woman a hug. Surprised but happy, judging from the look on her face, Constance returned the embrace.

"Thank you, Lily. You and your siblings will have to come see the stained glass window Russell made." Constance separated from Lily. "He was very talented. The window is fragile, and it can't be replaced. That's why I make sure no one plays in my yard."

So many actions had an explanation when you sought out the inner meaning. Daisy nodded in understanding.

Sally ducked her head into the green room. "Oren brought samples. Can the triplets have some?"

The three rushed over to Daisy, locking their hands together entreating their mom to agree, which she did. They disappeared with Sally while Daisy stayed behind. "Can I help with anything?"

Constance came over and laid her gnarled hand on Daisy's, the age spots standing out against Daisy's pale skin. "I've seen you around town your whole life, but I've been reclusive for the past few years. I used to be good friends with your grandma Bridget. She was so happy moving to the Lazy River Ranch after she married Martin Virtue."

"Grandma tried to get me to move back there a few years ago." After Dylan's death, she'd chosen to stay in her house, as much for constancy for the triplets as for herself.

Constance started tidying the table strewn with

sewing odds and ends. "My parents wanted me to move back in with them after Russell passed away, but I didn't. They ended up selling the theater to the Craddocks and moving to be closer to my older brother."

"If you had to do it all over again, would you have gone with them?" Daisy handed her a pair of scissors, which Constance placed in a caddy while shaking her head.

"No, but I might have accepted Marshall Bayne's offer to date him." Constance closed the caddy and reached for the spray bottle of cleaner.

Everyone in Violet Ridge knew Marshall, the town auctioneer who was the cheerful half of the Bayne brothers. The brothers now resided at the Silver Horseshoe bunkhouse with their friend and former town veterinarian, Doc Jenkins. "It's never too late. Why don't you ask him to the play?"

"We'll see." Constance shrugged. "What's happening between you and our director?"

Daisy ripped off some paper towel from the roll and wiped the tables. "Ben cares about the triplets. I'm just the mom who was assigned to be his assistant."

Constance shook her head while pushing the chairs into place. "Oh, honey. You can believe that, but there's something between you and Ben."

Before Daisy could protest, Sally led the triplets back into the room with Rosie and Aspen carrying small boxes of chestnuts. Aspen handed one to Constance while Rosie delivered hers to Daisy.

"They are so yummy." Rosie patted her tummy and licked her lips, a smattering of cinnamon sugar at the corner.

Daisy expressed her thanks while Constance arched an eyebrow in her direction that Daisy knew had nothing to do with the snack. Then the older woman chimed her appreciation to Aspen.

Taking a hesitant bite, Daisy ate one of the chestnuts coated with cinnamon sugar while glancing at the door that led to the sound booth. Ben had opened up to her. Was that a sign he thought of her as more than just the triplets' mother? Anticipation tasted as sweet as the unexpected treat. The future stared right at her, starting with the play followed by a delicious step into the unknown.

CHAPTER FIFTEEN

THE NEXT DAY, Ben arrived at the Holly Theater for the final dress rehearsal. Tomorrow was Christmas Eve, the day the cast and crew had been anticipating. Violet Ridge was ready and looking its best, with the sidewalks cleared of snow that had been piled on the other side of the road. The town almost preened. Ben pocketed the keys and then patted his inside coat pocket with two tickets for the local lodge's ski lift, his Christmas gift to Daisy. After the rehearsal, he intended to ask her out on their first official date. Even better, last night, he'd talked to his stepsister, Sabrina, and her husband, Ty, who promised to babysit the triplets.

He felt as though he'd arrived home. Everything was now on the upswing.

On a nearby sidewalk, a stranger operated a 3D scanner and a theodolite, tools used for surveying. Ben remembered too well engineers taking measurements of an airplane debris field or using the same tools at the beginning stages of a jet hangar. Ben narrowed his eyes looking around for a city truck. Failing to find one, he zeroed in on the man's neck, searching for a lanyard. Without seeing any identification, Ben sidled over to the man.

"I'm Ben Irwin, the interim director of the Holly Theater. I haven't seen you around Violet Ridge before. What are you doing with the surveying equipment?" Ben asked, while the middle-aged man jotted notes with a stylus on a tablet.

The man kept at his measurements. "If you'll excuse me, I have to finish my job."

Ben wasn't put off that easily. "What job? I'd like to see some identification, or else I'm contacting the authorities."

The man sized up Ben and showed him his identification. "Look, I just want to finish this and return home to Gunny so I can celebrate Christmas Eve with my family tomorrow. I'm the construction supervisor for the Wilshire Development Corporation. My boss is anxious to begin work on our newest sales facility, opening in the spring."

Ben searched the area, unsure of where the facility would be located. Maple Valley Drive was packed solid with the theater, restaurants and other town businesses. Before Ben could inquire further, a long black Cadillac pulled up to the curb. An older man in a wool overcoat and plaid scarf emerged from the back seat, followed by, of all people, Frank Craddock, whose arm was encased in a red sling.

"Ben! Good to see you." Frank came over and patted him on the shoulder with his left hand while the other man consulted the surveyor.

In spite of his curiosity about the newcomers, Ben focused his attention on Frank. "How's Noah? And the rest of your family? What happened to your arm?" The questions sounded like those Zelda would have asked, but Ben found himself caring about the details.

"Just a little accident while I was blowing off Cheyenne's driveway. Nothing serious, but I can't do anything with it for the next week. Get tired easily, but I should be as good as new in no time. My family's doing great. Rhonda's arriving on the twenty-sixth, and then we'll start saying our goodbyes and packing up our house."

Flabbergasted at Frank's news, Ben gasped. "You're moving to Topeka?"

Frank nodded. "Noah's gained a pound already, and he should be discharged around New Year's. Rhonda and I agreed it's time to leave Violet Ridge. We want to be closer to our family."

Ben connected the pieces. The engineer was surveying the theater. But this was the heart of the entertainment district of Violet Ridge. Plays, recitals and movies provided families with needed joy and laughter, get-togethers and memories. Without the theater?

Violet Ridge wouldn't be the same.

"What's going to happen to the Holly?" Ben turned around and soaked in the ambience of the stately building, even more meaningful to him now than a mere month ago.

"It's grown obsolete." Frank sighed and swiped at his eye with his good hand. "As you know, the Irwin Arena is a state-of-the-art facility for bigger concerts. Then there's the drive-in, and the new high school will have an auditorium. The Holly Theater needs too much updating for a viable offer. The sound equipment is proof of that. Killian Wilshire has been after this location for the past few years."

As if on cue, the older stately man joined them. "You must be Ben Irwin." Ben nodded, and the man reached into his inner pocket and handed Ben a business card. "I'm Killian Wilshire, the CEO of Wilshire Development. I own several ski lodges throughout Colorado and Wyoming, and I'm expanding into luxury hotels here in Violet Ridge. We've purchased a tract of land for our new luxury guest ranch. This property is ideal for our sales headquarters. Both enterprises will add several hundred jobs to the area. Frank and I talked about you and your upcoming mayoral bid, and I know your father. He's a sound businessman, and we have much in common. That's good enough for me. We'll talk more after the holidays about my organization's support for your campaign."

Ben fingered the card, the triplex cardstock high end, the gold foil of equal quality. "Is the sale final?"

Frank exhaled and stepped back. "Pretty much. I came to deliver the news that this will be the last production of *The Santa Who Forgot Christmas*. From here, we're heading over to the attorney's office to sign the contract."

Then Ben still had a little time. Pocketing the card, he evolved a plan so the play could happen in the theater next year and the year after. He'd text Zelda and also alert Daisy's brother Crosby, the town historian. That bootlegger staircase and the history of the theater might qualify the Holly for historical preservation.

"Production? I thought we agreed you would cancel that." Killian's brows creased, and he frowned. "Time is of the essence. I plan to open the lodge in April. My sales hub has to be ready by then. With Colorado weather, we need to proceed with the destruction immediately."

"I didn't agree to that." Frank's body tensed, and then he let out a sigh. "Rhonda and I have our eye on a house in Cheyenne's subdivision. We need the money from the sale for our down payment. Everything we have is tied up in this building, but the show's happening tomorrow. Surely one day won't make a difference."

Wilshire's face was unreadable. "I'll have to consult with my engineer about the time frame while you deliver your announcement."

Wilshire strode in the other direction, ice chips flying under his thick black boots. Ben shivered, the cold seeping into his bones having nothing to do with the chilly December air and everything to do with Wilshire. Ben considered waiting outside for the verdict from the surveyor, but he had texts to send and not much time to set everything in motion.

He opened the door to the lobby and waved at Frank. "After you."

IN THE GREEN room before the final dress rehearsal, Daisy pressed her hand against her chest, her maternal pride almost bursting out of her. Only two years ago, she brought the triplets to this very playhouse so they could cherish one happy memory from their worst holiday season. Today, in their costumes for Nicky and Noelle, Aspen and Rosie looked so grown up. Lily was adorable in the elf costume she wore as an extra in the play's second act at the North Pole.

Daisy shivered with delight. Despite the many obstacles, this play was really happening tomorrow, and she had even more to look forward to after this production. The future was within her grasp, especially after signing a contract this morning with Valerie after extracting promises from Crosby and Seth to babysit the triplets. She'd also contacted other parents for a rotating set of playdates. Until the wee hours of the morning, she sketched designs for rings utilizing equestrian snaffle bits and horseshoe motifs. Everything was coming together, and she intended to relish each minute.

Yet the one person she wanted to share this with the most was Ben. He'd brought so much into her life over the past month. His gruff outside belied the kind and thoughtful man he was on the inside. He'd taken the triplets on a shopping excursion—no small task. And those kisses? For a man who epitomized safety and order, his kisses left her breathless with anticipation.

Here she'd told herself to find someone safe, someone who would keep her sheltered and protected. Someone who wouldn't touch her heart. While she found the ultimate man who treasured security and order, his presence radiating consistency and solidity, the feelings he stirred in her were anything but calm and steady. When she was around him, she soared to new heights, even higher than Pikes Peak in northern Colorado.

The one man who was the perfect solution to

keeping her feelings in check ended up being the man who rattled her the most. He forced her to confront her need to design and mold intricate pieces of jewelry while he confronted his own battles. Yesterday, he'd shared himself with her. That was their breakthrough.

The Daisy of the past two years was satisfied with the status quo, and yet that wasn't the real her. Ben helped her reconnect with herself, and she liked to think she did the same for him.

Her legs almost gave out from under her. She reached out to steady herself as she faced the truth.

She was falling in love with Ben Irwin.

What was she going to do about it?

Better yet, when? As much as she wanted to scour the halls of the theater until she found him, she'd wait until tomorrow. She wanted him to bask in the production, the promise of a month of hard work coming to a culmination of joy and love.

What could be better than sharing her feelings with him after the play? The triplets had worked so hard, as had Ben. They all deserved a moment in the spotlight before she bared her heart to him.

"Sally, Constance." Daisy's voice wobbled, the emotion of the day catching up to her. She started over. "Thank you for all your work with the makeup and costumes. Everything looks wonderful."

Sally grabbed her new portable cosmetic lockbox while the triplets beamed. "I'm heading to Teddy's dressing room to finish his makeup. I'll be in the audience for the rehearsal."

"Jot down any notes about the lighting or sound issues, okay?" Daisy called out in time for Sally to smile her agreement. Then she faced the small group. "I'd best head to the booth."

Constance tapped her watch. "Can you help me affix Lily's elf ears before you go upstairs?"

Daisy accepted one of the ears and used a bit of spirit gum to affix the prosthetic in place.

"I'm an official elf!" Lily was ecstatic. "I wish Winter could see this."

"I wish your uncle Jase could see you." Daisy pulled out her phone and snapped a picture.

Her younger brother Jase was a detective in Denver. Constantly on the go, he rarely came back to Violet Ridge. Ever since he graduated, he'd done his best to avoid the area. While she knew why, it was still hard not seeing him more often.

More than anything, she longed for Jase to meet Ben and give her his opinion, although Daisy knew that wouldn't change her newfound feelings.

Daisy placed her phone back in her pocket and hugged Lily. "Break a leg, Lilypad."

Lily gasped, her big eyes widening in horror. She jerked away. "Mommy! That would hurt so-o-o much."

Constance reassured Lily. "It's a stage expression that people say to wish each other well."

Lily knit her brows together and tapped her chin. "I don't get it, but 'kay." She hugged Daisy again. "Break a leg in the sound booth, Mommy."

Daisy stifled her laugh but didn't correct Lily. "Thanks, darling."

"Miss Constance, will we see you again?" Daisy was almost out the door when Lily's question stopped her in her tracks. "Or will you stop being our friend after the play?"

Lily's voice quavered, and Daisy rushed back into the room but stopped short when Constance gave her a nod that Daisy understood. She wanted to speak to Lily. Constance lowered herself to a kneeling position, staring straight into Lily's eyes.

"I cherish your friendship, Lily. The future can be scary at times with change we have to face, but now we have each other to lean on." She reached out and pulled Lily into a sweet embrace before they separated. Then she smiled at Rosie and Aspen, who hugged her as well. "The three of you are very special. You're always welcome in my home."

"And likewise." Daisy watched her Violet Ridge family expand, with Constance adding a new dimension to the mix.

Would Ben be next?

Sally rushed inside, her hands on her hips. She struggled to catch her breath. "Frank's back."

Daisy relaxed. Perhaps she could talk to Ben after the rehearsal since the weight of the production was off his shoulders. "That's great."

Sally shook her head. "No, something's wrong. Ben is calling an emergency meeting."

Whatever it was must be important considering the look of panic on Sally's face.

Rosie and Aspen pulled Daisy out of the room, and she turned back to see Lily holding Constance's hand. Whatever it was, they'd face it together. Then she'd talk to Ben.

At least she hoped she would.

BEN PACED ALONG the small rectangular path in front of the first row and below the raised stage while people were filing into the auditorium. He spared a glance toward Frank, who was talking with Killian Wilshire and the engineer. Frank shook his head and looked distraught, his jaw clenching, but Wilshire kept talking.

Soon, the cast and crew assembled, including Rosie, Lily and Aspen. He should have texted Daisy and warned her to make other arrangements for the triplets, who might not understand what was coming.

Here he was, thirty-eight years old, and he didn't fully understand the urgency behind Wilshire's offer. Wasn't it better to take your time and do something right rather than rush and pay the consequences later?

As with anything in life, it depended on the circumstances. He turned until he connected with Daisy. She was one of the best things to happen to him. Although they'd only known each other for a short time, he was positive she had changed his life forever. Her kindness, her love of animals, her abundance of creativity and love. All of that was her, and so innately wonderful. He'd arrived in Violet Ridge, fighting change tooth and nail, yet she was part of the change that engulfed him and left him a better man.

Daisy was motion in action, a force of nature, a creative whirlwind who was in the middle of everything going on in his life.

And he wanted to spend every morning at the breakfast table with her. Whether or not they talked wasn't as important as her mere presence and inner glow.

Chills ran down his body.

He was falling in love with Daisy Stanley.

Now to tell her that. He patted the tickets in the inner pocket of his jacket, ready to part the crowd and ask her how soon they could go skiing, but he knew that now wasn't the time. He glanced at Frank arguing with Killian Wilshire and he realized he had a choice: either he'd come out in support of tearing down the town's beloved theater to add needed jobs to the community or he'd disappoint Killian Wilshire, a wealthy and influential business owner who would support whoever helped his cause. For the past few weeks, Ben had become more and more certain he'd find a way to become the next mayor of Violet Ridge, preferably with Daisy at his side. Now, that was in jeopardy as he and Frank were about to announce this year's production of *The Santa Who Forgot Christmas* might very well be the last.

While he'd already texted Daisy's brother about whether the theater qualified for historical preservation, he hadn't heard back yet. Neither had he received a reply from Zelda.

Without the prospect of becoming mayor, what would he do in Violet Ridge?

Ben scrubbed his face, the stubble prickly against the blisters formed from building the set. With everyone's gazes upon him, there was no longer any reason to delay the inevitable. He clapped his hands and called for attention.

Frank and Wilshire joined him, while many chimed in their welcomes to the theater owner, along with questions about Rhonda's absence and his family's health. Everyone was talking at once before Frank motioned with his one good hand for silence.

"This theater has been part of my family since

the seventies when we purchased it from the Sims family." Frank cradled his sling next to his chest. "But all good things must end."

Frank explained everything he'd already told Ben, stopping at one point to accept a tissue from Sally. He then canceled the final dress rehearsal while everyone buzzed about his and Rhonda's decision to move.

Killian Wilshire introduced himself and explained how his new facility would bring jobs and tourists to the area.

Gasps and grunts of disapproval greeted Wilshire's announcement, and Ben didn't blame anyone for their shock.

Rosie Stanley stepped forward, hurt etched over her face. "I'm seven, and I don't think that's very nice. This is a happy place, and I like it here." Several of the cast and crew clapped while others patted her on the shoulder. Aspen and Lily moved to flank their sister in support. Then Rosie faced Ben. "Will we all break legs tomorrow?"

Ben blinked, not understanding the question. He sought out Daisy, who evidently understood her daughter. "I told them to break a leg for the rehearsal. She's asking if the play will go on as scheduled."

Wilshire moved aside and consulted with his engineer before returning. "It depends on how everything goes at the attorney's office this afternoon. We'll keep in touch." Some cast and crew expressed their displeasure, and Wilshire continued, "I promise we're going to bring tourists and jobs to Violet Ridge, which will benefit everyone in the long run. Ben, here, agrees with me. Good day."

Wilshire and the engineer strode to the back of the auditorium before the businessman searched for Frank. "Ride with us to the attorney's office?"

Frank's jaw clenched, and he shook his head. "I'll meet you there."

As soon as the door slammed, indicating the departure of Wilshire and the engineer, everyone peppered Frank and Ben with questions. Ben stopped listening, though, when Daisy ushered Rosie, Lily and Aspen to the side, each of them quivering and sniffling.

He joined the Stanley family. Daisy stared at Ben. "Who are you supporting? Are you on Wilshire's side? You want the Holly to be turned into a sales complex?"

She cut straight to the chase, something he appreciated, but the sadness in her eyes reflected too much. The ski lift tickets burned in his pocket, next to his heart. He had a bad feeling he'd never use them. "I want what's best for Violet Ridge."

And for Daisy. Yet right now, he couldn't tell her how he felt. Not with people's eyes drilling holes in the back of his head, not with the fate of the theater hanging in the balance, not with the triplets turning from her to him, their big eyes expecting him to save the day.

"Killian Wilshire." Daisy connected the pieces. "He owns the Wilshire Development Corporation that's bringing the luxury dude ranch to Violet Ridge, isn't he?"

Ben gave a slow calculated nod. "Yes."

Daisy's throat bobbed. "New jobs will probably be a great mayoral pitch, more so than future productions at the Holly."

Rosie came over and pulled at Ben's coat. "You're going to save the Holly, aren't you?"

Was this building what was best for Violet Ridge? Could emotion win out over cold, hard numbers? He wanted the Holly Theater to stick around for years to come, yet Wilshire promised jobs, and paychecks put food on the table. Could Ben support the alternative?

Daisy's eyebrows knitted together, and she pulled her three children together. "I know we've talked about change, but sometimes, it's the traditions and love that counts. I no longer take either for granted. This theater is the heart of Violet Ridge. Goodbye, Ben."

She ushered her family out of the theater, and Ben felt their absence down to his toes.

CHAPTER SIXTEEN

WITH THE PINK rays of dawn beginning to break over the craggy, snow-peaked mountains, Ben slammed his SUV door and headed for the sidewalk that led to his house. It was Christmas Eve, and he hadn't even awakened in his own bed. Instead, he'd fallen asleep sometime during the night in the back offices at the historical society. He gave Daisy's brother Crosby credit. Together they were trying to find a legal way to stop the sale from going through. Frank Craddock had thrown out a lifeline by declaring he wouldn't sign any papers until after the play, even though it was Christmas Eve.

Ben had until the curtain closed to craft a compromise that would leave both sides happy. However, that wasn't the holiday miracle he wanted the most. That involved a certain brunette and her three children. The look on Daisy's face when she believed he'd choose tearing down the theater to further his career devastated him. He didn't know what was worse: her believing he'd do such a thing or his hesitation about the Holly Theater's future.

Taking care on the sidewalk covered with crusted ice and windswept snow, Ben kept his head down until something prickled at his spine. For the first time since he'd pulled into his driveway, he looked at his surroundings. His jaw dropped.

A genuine holiday miracle had come to Violet Ridge. Constance Mulligan's house was covered with Christmas lights, the glow almost blinding at the brink of daybreak.

Anything was possible after all.

At that moment, his neighbor emerged from her home with a big basket of laundry. Ben hurried over and heralded her. "Your lights are perfect. Merry Christmas Eve, Constance."

"Same to you, Ben." She set the basket on the ground and reached for clothespins from the holder attached to the clothesline, a task made more difficult with her gloved hands.

"Why don't you use my dryer?"

"If I did that, my sheets wouldn't have the smell of fresh air. What would be the good of sleeping in a bed that didn't smell like the mountains I love so much?" Constance grunted while spreading out a flannel fitted sheet on the line and attaching clothespins.

"Then you're not doing this to save money?"

He winced at how cold and insensitive he sounded. Constance shot him an arched look. "Of course not. I own half the town thanks to my parents and their investments. How many times do I have to repeat myself? I like the smell of fresh linen."

Would wonders never cease?

"Good to know." Ben rubbed the sleeves of his coat.

She stared at him and arched her eyebrow. "You've been out all night."

Ben nodded. "Crosby Virtue and I are working together to save the theater, including scouting out other locations for Wilshire's flagship sales center." They hadn't succeeded yet, and they were running out of time.

"What about you and Daisy?" Constance kept pinning her sheets to the clothesline.

Those ski lift tickets lay heavy in his pocket next to his heart. At this point, he wasn't sure she'd accept his offer to go skiing with him, not after yesterday. "What about us? We both have too much baggage. She's in love with her late husband, and I thought a relationship with someone would turn this house into a home. Turns out relationships require trust, and I blew it with Daisy."

Confiding in Constance might be the second holiday miracle. Dare he hope for more?

She finished her task and reached for the basket. "I have a large pot of coffee already brewed, too much for one person. Come on over, and I'll discuss an idea with you."

This wasn't how he envisioned his first Christmas Eve back in Violet Ridge, but then again, maybe that was the beauty of coming home.

IN THE SOLITARY moments before the triplets awoke, Daisy cupped her hands around her mug of cinnamon tea, the aroma filling her senses with the realization that Christmas Eve had, indeed, dawned. For the past month, she'd been concentrating her efforts on ensuring this was a holiday to remember for Rosie, Lily and Aspen. And yet? She had overblown expectations, trying to turn this holiday into something impossible, a perfect day with no problems. Rosie, Aspen and Lily would love today because of who they were and their resilience.

There was something to be said for resilience. Ben was the epitome of that. He'd carved out his own path with purpose and determination. Both would help him be a great mayor.

Looking at the snowcapped mountains from her kitchen window, she sipped her tea and remembered the day she had encouraged Ben to make snow angels for the sheer joy of it.

Ben. Her heart twisted at the way she callously

walked away from him without giving him a chance to explain himself. She ached at ending any possibility of them.

For yesterday felt like an ending, not a beginning.

But while she thought she was protecting the triplets, that wasn't the truth. She was protecting herself.

"Mommy?" Lily's voice startled her, and tea sloshed out of the top of the mug.

Daisy faced Lily, who was standing in the doorway, looking adorable in her footed pajamas covered with reindeer. To Daisy's surprise, Lily wasn't holding Winter but a wrapped gift. Daisy placed her tea on the counter and hugged her younger daughter, the warmth of her slumber still clinging to her. "Merry Christmas Eve, Lilypad."

Lily returned the embrace and then separated from her, thrusting out the present. "This is for you."

In spite of her heart being shattered in pieces over Ben, Daisy's love for her daughter expanded. "That's so sweet of you, but I can wait until tomorrow."

Lily shook her head, her long braids moving around her. "It has to be today."

"Aspen and Rosie are still sleeping." Daisy

didn't want them feeling left out. "We should wait for them to open presents."

"I'm awake." Rosie came in and hugged her sister.

"Me, too." Aspen emerged from behind her, trudging every step of the way. "Everyone needs to learn to sleep longer."

He'd always been a better sleeper than his sisters. "Are you ready for breakfast?" Daisy asked with a smile in spite of the giant ache inside her.

"Are we going to act in the play tonight?" Rosie asked.

Daisy should have had coffee rather than tea. With a glance at her phone, she exhaled a deep breath. "I haven't heard otherwise, so I think the answer is yes."

Rosie and Aspen lifted a loud cheer of victory while Lily embraced Daisy's side and then held out the present once more. "For you."

Everyone encouraged her to open the present. Daisy accepted the package that Lily had obviously wrapped herself. "You three still have to wait until tomorrow."

She ripped off the gift wrap and opened the rectangular box. Nestled on soft cotton was a friendship bracelet in various shades of yellow, Daisy's favorite color. Without missing a beat, she rolled the bracelet onto her wrist and then kissed Lily's cheek. "Thank you, Lilypad. It's beautiful, and I love it."

Lily beamed. "Now you and Ben will match."

"What do you mean?" Daisy asked.

"I already gave Ben his bracelet. He loved it." Lily beamed, the joy of Christmas captured in her cute face.

Her daughter never failed to surprise her. Generous and loving, she'd gone out of her way to make her and Ben feel cherished.

Daisy rubbed the threads that wove together to make a circle. She and Ben did match in what mattered. They both loved Violet Ridge and wanted what was best for the town. They loved this holiday and what it represented about hope. And, perhaps most important, they spurred each other to be a better person.

He'd been a holiday miracle when she least expected one.

Even the best miracles, though, could fall flat if one didn't take full advantage of what had been gifted to them. She'd received so many precious gifts this season, the best of which was hope.

Now she hoped that Ben would be open to her apology and something more: the promise of her heart.

CHAPTER SEVENTEEN

AT THE HOLLY THEATER, Daisy greeted the crew members who'd already gathered. But several key players, including Teddy, Frank and Ben, were nowhere in sight. How the play could happen without Santa or either of the directors, she wasn't quite sure, but there was still plenty of time for everything to come together.

At least for today. After the holidays? She wasn't sure of what would happen, but that was part of the joy of life. Having Ben by her side to uncover all of the little surprises would be like uncovering something in the boot of a stocking, an extra gift you weren't expecting but the one that ended up as the favorite.

Daisy walked to the lighting booth and checked on the equipment. Once everything was in order and operational, she opened the door to the not-so-secret stairwell, intending to go downstairs and see if everyone had arrived. Especially one person in particular.

She needed to see Ben and ask him if he felt

the same way about her. That was, after she confided that she supported his mayoral campaign, because she knew he had Violet Ridge's best interest at heart, whether that meant razing the theater or not. She trusted him.

Still, worry bit at her fingertips. At this point, she just hoped the absence of the major players didn't herald the worst: that the play was, in fact, canceled. Nope. She wouldn't give in to negativity. Instead, she clung to the expectation the show would go on as scheduled.

She reached the bottom of the stairwell, where, to her surprise, Aspen was sitting on the bottom step, dressed in his costume with his stage makeup intact. Maternal pride burst into full bloom until she saw a look of pure dejection on his face.

"Aspen?" She motioned for him to move over, and she sat beside him. "Is everything okay?"

He plopped his face onto his hands, his elbows resting on his thighs. "Everyone's talking about this being the last play. That's not right, Mommy. I like being Nicky. I want other kids to be Nicky, too. I want to come back here and watch more plays." He glanced her way, misery written there. "I don't want them to tear down the theater."

Her heart went out to her son.

She wound her arm around his shoulders, taking care of his costume. "It will be hard for the town to go on without the Holly Theater. But no matter what happens, Violet Ridge will survive. If I know Ben, he'll make sure there's a production of this play somewhere next year, and the year after. The story will live on, no matter where it takes place."

Just like Dylan would live on in the triplets. Just like he'd have wanted her to grasp happiness with both hands. Her feelings for Dylan had evolved, so that she could love someone else. And not just anyone. She had fallen for Ben, who brought those reindeer to full flight inside her.

A rock lodged in her throat as this was a long-overdue conversation with Aspen, one that paralleled their lives. Maybe he'd read more into her meaning, but most likely it would go over his head. That was okay. She was saying this for herself as much as for him. The Stanley family had survived. She gulped away the rock and pulled herself together.

Aspen frowned. "But I like this place."

"So do I. It's beautiful and familiar, and so many people have good memories here, but the play will continue, even if it takes place somewhere else." More than ever, she wanted to say all of this, and more, to Ben. "That type of community support will ensure the play keeps happening for years to come."

Aspen scrunched his face. "Then where is everyone? There are already people sitting in the chairs."

Daisy tapped his chin. "I don't know, but Teddy and Ben will be here. They wouldn't miss it. The show will go on, and you'll do great."

"You're saying that 'cause you're my mom and you have to say junk like that." Aspen pressed his lips together.

"I love you because you're my son, but I've also been in that booth for rehearsals. You're a natural."

Suddenly, a figure walked into the stairwell, and Daisy's breath caught. It was Ben.

How much of her conversation with Aspen had he overheard?

"Your mom is right. You're a natural on the stage, much more than I was when I froze up there all those years ago. You and Rosie love acting. You're going to break a leg." Ben nodded, and Aspen jumped up and launched himself at the stoic veteran.

Then Aspen moved his head while he stayed connected to Ben's waist. "Thanks, Ben."

Ben stepped back and tapped Aspen's shoulder. "It's almost time for the final cast meeting. Can I talk to your mother first?"

"Sure." Aspen separated from Ben's side and stopped at the threshold. "Hey, you're wearing Lily's bracelet. Now you and Mommy match."

Aspen departed, and Daisy felt as self-conscious as Ben must have all those years ago on the stage when he couldn't overcome his nerves.

Collecting herself, she rolled up her sleeve and placed her wrist next to Ben's. Sure enough, their bracelets matched. Leave it to Lily to discern the rightness of this relationship before her mother had. "I know you don't have much time before the play starts…" She stopped and bit her lip, too aware she needed to apologize. First, though, there was something she needed to know. "The play will go on, right?"

"Frank didn't sign the papers yesterday. He told Wilshire he'd wait until after the show since Christmas Eve wouldn't be the same without the production kicking off the holiday." Ben scrunched his eyebrows together as if he wanted to say something else, and Daisy worried she might have cut their connection for good.

She neared his side. "You were just as surprised as everyone else. I should have given you a chance to explain, especially after I kept asking you to open up to me. I'm sorry, Ben." She pressed her hand to his heart. "I believe you'll do what's best for Violet Ridge. I believe in you."

He grasped her hand in his and kept them both close enough so she could feel his heartbeat, fast and steady. Their gazes met. He might not say everything in a romantic way, but his gaze said it all. In it, she saw today, tomorrow and the day after that.

"Daisy." Her name had never sounded as sweet.

He closed the distance between them, his head bending toward hers. Her pulse accelerated as the scent of lime and pine trees and Ben flooded her senses. He cupped her face with his hands. Before his lips connected with hers, a flash of movement caught her eye.

Sally entered the stairwell. "Thank goodness I found you. It's a calamity of the first kind. There hasn't been anything this awful since Ben froze on that stage all those years ago." The light from the green room illuminated her red cheeks. "Sorry, Ben."

"No offense taken." Ben moved away from Daisy. "But it must be pretty bad if it's worse than yesterday's announcement about the sale of the theater."

Daisy's maternal instincts reared up as did the hairs on the back of her neck. "Rosie and Lily! Are they okay?"

Sally waved away her concerns. "They're fine, but come quick! This news is awful. The play's canceled!"

IF YESTERDAY WAS a bad omen, today's tidings were an unmitigated catastrophe. Ben wanted to look away from Teddy but couldn't. Instead of wearing his Santa costume, Teddy was wearing a red plaid flannel shirt and blue jeans, his usual jovial appearance replaced with a look of misery.

His wife, Jessica, did the talking. This morning he dislodged his dental bridge and couldn't talk. His dentist had opened his office, but the news was grim. The bridge couldn't be reattached today, and Teddy risked permanent damage to his mouth if he performed. Everyone went over and hugged Teddy.

As soon as Jessica finished talking, Ben hurried to the front. "That's why we have an understudy." Then his stomach clenched as his gaze landed on Frank, his broken arm still in a sling.

Frank joined Ben, his face grim. "I'm Teddy's understudy, and I can't perform, not with a broken arm. What's important is neither of us have permanent injuries. It's just that we're the only ones who know the lines, so the play is officially over."

"No, it's not." Rosie's voice came out strong and emphatic.

Everyone moved to the side while the Stanley triplets rushed to Ben. Aspen pulled on Ben's coat and looked at him with those big eyes. "You know the lines. You don't even look at your script."

Ben's blood ran cold. Twenty years of military service was nothing compared with the thought of getting up on that stage in front of an auditorium full of people.

As if to confirm this, he peeked out through the curtain from his spot offstage. The residents of Violet Ridge had arrived en masse. He saw Lucky escorting a full-term Lizzie to her seat beside his stepsister and her husband. Jeff, his wife and their children were laughing with their father and stepmother. Ben's breathing came out shallow and erratic as his stomach twisted into a tight knot. His hip ached with an intensity he'd never experienced before. This was exactly like the tunnel vision on that long-ago flight when he survived hypoxia.

Someone patted his shoulder, and Ben snapped out of his reverie. Frank stood there, his head shaking. "You're paler than Casper in our Halloween play. It's okay. I'll make the announcement."

Ben's gaze fell on Daisy, who came forward. She grasped his hands as if channeling her calm inner strength into him. "No matter what happens, I believe in you, Ebenezer Irwin."

He let her words of belief and love sink into him, along with the training he'd received during his military career. The knot unraveled, and he could breathe again. Daisy was part of it, but so was the dedication that had served him through his military career as well as the thought that he was providing joy for Lizzie and everyone else out there. The play wasn't only about him. He was going to perform for the people whom he loved and who loved him in return. For the first time, he understood Zelda and why everyone stopped at their table at the Smokehouse. She served this community because she cared for every resident.

He would do no less.

"What are we waiting for? I need help changing into my Santa costume." Ben found his voice and there was no trembling, no hesitation. "The show must go on."

CHAPTER EIGHTEEN

DAISY THANKED THE usher for the program and started toward her brothers to say hello before she traveled to the sound booth for her last volunteer shift. Then she returned to the usher and asked for an extra for her brother Jase. Even though he was working in Denver over the holidays, she wanted to send him a physical copy rather than a mere digital file. She held out hope he'd come home to Violet Ridge someday.

Then, she located Seth and Crosby in the audience. The brothers were night and day in appearance with Seth's darker olive complexion like their father's and Crosby's lighter skin tone so much like their mom's. Their personalities were also different, with Seth more intense while Crosby was everyone's best friend.

Seth stared at her when she greeted them from the aisle. "I heard a rumor Killian Wilshire's behind the new lodge. That man's legendary for his real estate ruthlessness," Seth said.

That was her older brother. No beating around

the bush. Daisy accepted a hug from Crosby and waited for them to settle in their seats before answering. "Yes, and he wants to buy the theater. From what I heard, Frank isn't signing the contract until after the play." She longed to give her older brother more reassurance that Wilshire wouldn't impact their livelihood, but she couldn't. "I have to head up to the sound booth."

Crosby reached over and squeezed her hand, a string tied around his right middle finger. "I'm so proud of Rosie, Aspen and Lily."

She ruffled her younger brother's hair. "And I'm proud you remembered the play. The string's working, then?"

Crosby laughed and plucked off the twine. "Nope. It didn't work for Uncle Billy in *It's a Wonderful Life*, and it didn't work for me either. I forgot a date last night."

"You didn't miss anything," Seth interrupted. "Your date showed up at the ranch and was quite irritated. She was belligerent and rude to Grandma Bridget. You're better off without her. Besides, who needs love anyway?"

Daisy laughed, hoping Seth would find love someday, preferably sooner rather than later. More so, though, she was thankful her brothers were distracting her from the nerves just now starting to quell in her stomach. The past twenty-four hours had been a cyclone of emotions, but she held out hope the future was bright.

With a deep breath, she entered the sound booth and switched on the equipment. Sally knocked and gave a ten-minute countdown. Daisy finished going through the meticulous checklist that she and Ben had created while preparing for the production.

He cared for her, Daisy Virtue Stanley. She was sure of it, and it was time to stop dancing around that.

With only a few minutes to spare, she opened her program, smiling at the cast photos of Rosie and Aspen next to their bios. Rosie dedicated her performance to her grandparents, Pearl, her siblings, Daisy and Dylan. Her throat clenched for a second. She would have expected that of Lily, but it touched her innermost core that Rosie hadn't forgotten Dylan.

Life changed, but there were some truths that just stayed with you forever. Daisy had loved Dylan, and she'd always cherish their time together. While she thought she'd play it safe and seek out someone who wouldn't occupy space in her heart, sometimes love snuck up and blossomed as bright as the Christmas star.

If she wasn't mistaken, and she wasn't, Ben's gaze in the stairwell reflected how much she meant to him. If only Sally hadn't interrupted them. If only Ben had given her some indication of how he felt about her.

Wiping away a tear, she read Aspen's bio, laughing as he dedicated his performance to Pearl and his new pal Ben.

Rosie recognized the past and Aspen had hit upon what Daisy hoped would be their future.

Then she read Ben's bio, quite impressive with his military honors listed. She skimmed ahead to his dedication.

I dedicate this performance to my codirector who encourages me to see the beauty in the simple things in life. Daisy Virtue Stanley, I owe you a snow angel, and I intend to make one with you every winter from here on.

She brought her hand to her mouth, her gaze going to the side door. As she rose from her seat, the curtains rustled, and Frank appeared, giving Daisy a cue to start a spotlight and the music. Only her responsibility to the production kept her from running down the stairwell to Ben. This dedication was everything. It was his way of telling her how much she meant to him.

Her hands shaking, she operated the soundboard as if she'd been doing this all her life. Hard to believe she'd originally protested when Frank insisted on her volunteering for the play. She wouldn't have missed this for the world. The thought that this would be the last production to take place at the Holly brought tears streaming down her cheeks. She brushed them away and focused the spotlight on Frank.

"Thank you for coming to this year's production of *The Santa Who Forgot Christmas*." He paused, clutching his sling to his chest. "The Craddock family has been proud to be a part of your family's Christmas Eve tradition since the 1980s, but the time has come to start a new chapter of our lives in another state. To this end, we've sold the theater."

Daisy heard the intense buzzing from the audience, and she longed to be near the triplets and Ben.

Frank held his hand over the microphone and waited a minute for the noise to fade away. Then he continued, "Now, I'd like to introduce you to the next owner."

Daisy waited for Killian Wilshire to make his appearance, her heart going out to Seth and all of Violet Ridge. How Wilshire's real estate holdings would impact the Lazy River Dude Ranch was unclear going forward, but her brother was resilient. Seth would find a way to succeed, just like Violet Ridge would come together and find a new venue for the play.

Instead of Killian, though, Constance Mulligan walked onstage. Confusion trilled through Daisy, but she stayed where she was. What was going on? Was there yet another delay in the start of the play?

The older woman accepted the microphone from Frank. "Today I've come full circle, returning the Holly Theater to the Sims family once more. For those who don't know, my full name is Constance Sims Mulligan. This theater was like a second home to me growing up, and I've finally come home. I trust you will continue to enjoy many plays here. I'll be adding new events and performances while keeping true to the historic integrity of this old girl. The Holly Theater will remain a Violet Ridge treasure, same as it was in the 1920s."

Constance bought the theater? Daisy rushed over to the window in time and found the audience jumping to their feet. Constance received a standing ovation with cheers and whistles. The older woman was soaking in the love, if the sheepish smile and glow in her eyes was any indication. Then she introduced a new sponsor for the following year's schedule.

Killian Wilshire walked onstage, and Daisy returned to the soundboard while he discussed his new luxury dude ranch along with his proposed sales facility to be located near the Over and Dunne Feed and Seed. "This was made possible through the ingenuity of two people who deserve the credit, Crosby Virtue and Ben Irwin.

This is the beginning of a prosperous relationship bridging Violet Ridge's past and future. I look forward to being part of your community. Thank you."

Constance then announced the play would start in five minutes. That should be just enough time for Daisy to tell Ben to break a leg.

And so much more. There was no time like the present to make this Christmas her best one yet.

BACKSTAGE IN THE wide expanse of the green room with the rest of the cast already in place for their cues, Sally applied one more stroke of rouge to Ben's cheeks. "There, now you're Santa."

Ben nodded, his palms sweaty. He tried to remember Santa's first line. Nothing. Everything was a complete blank. The entire script had gone out of his head. As hard as he tried, none of the lines came to him.

Constance, Frank and Wilshire joined him while Frank eyed him with suspicion. "Do I need to change into costume?"

Ben wiped his palms on his red Santa pants. No longer was he the young seven-year-old with the weight of his father's expectations upon him. He had served in the military and retired after surviving a plane crash, ejecting in time for him to begin a new chapter of his life, one that included Daisy. Coming home brought him something surprising and oh so right.

He could do this. He was born to play Santa.

Daisy emerged from the secret passageway, and his lines flooded back. Ben faced Frank. "I've got this."

Daisy's gaze met his. In her eyes sparkled the promise of the present and future entwined into one. He joined her. "Merry Christmas Eve, Daisy."

Her red cheeks glowed with something more than holiday goodwill. "You've been busy."

He shrugged. "I like to stay busy."

"I have a feeling life's about to get much more hectic for you," she teased and reached out to touch his fake beard. "This is real, isn't it?"

She wasn't talking about the beard, and he knew it. "I couldn't have done this without my codirector. You're the most genuine person I've ever met." He leaned into her touch. "The triplets are a bonus."

Before he could tell Daisy how he felt about her, Constance came over and cleared her throat. "Bah, humbug. Save the sentiment for after the play."

Ben faced Constance, her tough exterior not fooling him for a minute. "Thank you for buying the theater."

"It's good business sense." Constance's shoulders relaxed as her gaze traveled around the room. "And this place will give me something to do. Russell would be happy that I'm finally getting in touch with my hometown again."

Ben turned back to Daisy, who clutched his hands. "I signed the contract with Valerie."

He stepped even closer to her when Rosie rushed into the green room. "The crowd and Aspen are getting restless." She waved at Daisy. "Hi, Mommy. Shouldn't you be in the sound booth?"

"On my way there." She squeezed Ben's hand. "Break a leg."

She disappeared into the passageway. Seconds later, the preamble music started playing over the speakers. Ben called out, "Places, everyone."

Within minutes, he found his mark on stage and nodded to the crew member in charge of opening the curtain. Even with the spotlights, he saw the gazes of everyone in the audience land on him from the other side of the window where he'd enter the set. Butterflies fluttered wildly in his stomach, and he looked in the direction of the sound booth. Daisy believed in him.

Most of all, he believed in himself.

After a deep breath, he crept through the window and launched into his first line. "Ho-ho-ho! Nicky and Noelle have been very good this year."

Before he knew it, the play was over, and the cast were taking their bows. Ben held Aspen's hand in his left and Rosie's in his right as they bent in a crisp bow. Returning to an upright position, he connected with his family in the audience. His smile widened as he spotted his father and stepmother in the row behind his siblings and stepsister and their spouses.

Constance came onstage holding a microphone. "Another round of applause for the cast." She waited while the audience showed their appreciation, then continued. "And a round for the crew, including our directors, Ben Irwin and Daisy Stanley."

Daisy materialized from backstage. Constance pulled her aside, whispering something into her ear. The audience applauded the cast and crew until the curtain finally closed.

Daisy's head neared his ear. "Gregson Hill in thirty minutes?" she asked.

Ben nodded and watched her as she opened her arms for the triplets, giving them hugs and praise for their performances.

WITH CHRISTMAS EVE afternoon about to give way to evening, Daisy hurried to Gregson Hill without her three shadows in her wake. Constance promised she'd watch over them, and Daisy passed Crosby and Seth on their way backstage with bouquets of roses for Rosie and Lily and a book for Aspen. The triplets were in good hands.

Speaking of hands, she donned her insulated gloves and wound her scarf around her neck while watching kids on sleds zooming down the hill. Their shouts of laughter and joy filled the crisp mountain air.

Then she caught sight of Ben coming her way, an envelope in his hands. He closed the distance, his dark eyes shining bright, his cheeks rosy even though his Santa makeup had been removed. He kept the envelope close to his heart. "Merry Christmas, Daisy."

The past, the present and the future came into perspective. Life was precious, and she wanted time with him.

She started fast. "I was impetuous yesterday, leaving with the triplets before I gave you a chance to defend yourself."

He neared her, the smell of the spirit gum mixing with his usual scent of pine and lime. "I stayed silent, but I found my voice on the stage today. When I came back to Violet Ridge, I had certain expectations, but doors kept closing. Everywhere I looked things had changed."

She rubbed his arm, the coat unable to hide his strong muscles, strength she knew he'd use to provide a better tomorrow for Violet Ridge. "It's the hope of positive change that keeps us going."

He smiled at her, three fine lines at the crinkles of his eyes deepening. "I love that you be-lieve that. I love that I believe that now."

Passersby greeted them by name. One shouted out, "Hey, Ben! Great job saving the theater. You have my vote for mayor."

Others echoed the same sentiments. Pride in Ben intensified along with her love for him. They found an isolated spot and he tucked the envelope he'd been holding in his jacket pocket. When they were alone once more, she joined her hands in his. "I didn't say it yesterday, but I know you'll do what's best for Violet Ridge. I hope I can be part of that."

He gave a huge sigh of relief, his face light-ening, making him look years younger. "Daisy, will you go out on a date with me?"

"I thought Harvest Thyme and our Smokehouse dinner were our first and second dates, but let's not quibble over that. I'd love to go out with you."

He pulled the envelope out of his pocket and held it out to her.

"What's this?" she asked.

"Your Christmas present. Tickets to a ski lift." He shook his head. "Only when you're ready."

"I'd say tomorrow, but Rosie, Aspen and Lily would have serious issues as it'll be Christmas." Speaking of them, she had to clear the air. "The four of us are a package deal, but I want you to love me for me. After all, I can only be me."

Without another word, he fell backward in the snow and formed an angel. Grinning, she did the same and brushed his hands with hers. They rose and found a pair of connected shapes on the ground.

He removed the glove from his right hand and traced her cheek with his warm fingers. "I fall more in love with you every day—your creativity, the love you have for your family, your innate optimism. I'm warning you so you know my intentions now, Daisy Virtue Stanley. Someday I hope to have many breakfast conversations with you."

Her heart soared. She rose on her toes inside her boots, pressing her lips to his in a kiss that blended his world and hers.

After a minute, they separated, and she pressed her forehead to his. "I'm partial to waffles, so you know. And I'm falling for you, too, Ebenezer Irwin. Who knows? Someday I might act as Mrs. Claus to your Santa."

For the future was in their hands. Love brought about constant change, but together they'd navigate anything life threw at them.

EPILOGUE

BEN'S MAYORAL CAMPAIGN was officially over, and he waited for the results on the stage of the newly renovated Holly Theater. A flurry of activity surrounded him, helping keep his nerves at bay.

Nearby, Rosie and Aspen were playing a card game while Lily was reading a picture book to Ben's stepsister's daughter, an energetic two-year-old who was a delight to everyone she met.

Speaking of his stepsister, Sabrina, she and her husband, Ty, returned to the auditorium, leading the caterers with dinner for the volunteers who helped run his campaign. Sabrina heralded Ben. "Lizzie and Lucky are on their way. Baby Cale just woke up from his nap."

His nephew, Cale William Harper, had made his grand entrance into the world the day after New Year's to everyone's joy and relief.

"Thanks, Sabrina." Ben hugged her and then worked his way around the room.

He started by thanking the co-owner of the Smokehouse, the caterer of tonight's event. He only hoped it would be a celebration rather than a consolation party.

With the polls now closed, more people filed into the auditorium, greeting one another and expressing their support for Ben. He shook a fair number of hands while asking each resident about their family or business. Oren Hoffman showed Ben the latest pictures of his grandchildren while Zelda countered with the notion her granddaughter was the most precocious child in Violet Ridge. While Ben believed his new stepchildren claimed that title, he expressed his admiration to the proud grandparents.

He accepted a cake from Dave Hawk, the man whose battery he jumped last winter. Dave was correct when he said his wife baked the best gingerbread cake Ben had ever tasted. Then Teddy Krengle showed off his dental bridge with the good news it hadn't given him a moment's trouble in the past six months.

Constance entered the theater, and Ben hailed her with the good news about the historical preservation status, which they'd received notice of today. Now the Holly Theater would always be preserved as a Violet Ridge landmark. When Marshall Bayne, Constance's boyfriend, entered the auditorium, Ben excused himself.

From there, he thanked more volunteers, listening as one updated him on their new business opportunity while another showed off the earrings she'd bought from Lavender and Lace last week. Ben never tired of seeing Daisy's beautiful handiwork.

For three months after the play, they'd spent almost every evening together. Some nights, they went out by themselves, while they included the triplets on others. After the triplets were asleep, he'd work on his campaign while Daisy concentrated on her new jewelry line.

One night, three months ago, when the firelight illuminated her face, he knew he was ready for the next change of his life. He sought the triplets' blessing before he asked Daisy to marry him. The following week they had a small ceremony at the Lazy River Dude Ranch and had just celebrated their two-month anniversary.

And there was his wife, entering the auditorium, wearing a light purple T-shirt and a tie-dyed skirt that swirled around her legs. She approached Ben and his gaze went to her earrings, delicate and dainty pastel pieces of glass formed into the shape of a violet.

He kissed her, a sensation he knew would never grow old, just as he'd always anticipate seeing her at the breakfast table, no matter whether there was lively conversation or comfortable silence.

She stepped back with a shrug. "Seth is running late. He's trying to balance the books at Lazy River." She frowned. "We're losing customers to Rocky Valley Guest Ranch. Seth's at his wits' end." The triplets came over and hugged her, a smile replacing her concerned look. "Your uncle Crosby is still in his office. He promised he'll be here in a little bit."

His phone buzzed, the ringtone the one he had set for the elections office. Ben stilled. If he didn't win, what would he do?

The way he figured it, he won the day he found Aspen trying to play hide-and-seek. The election was the icing on top of finding his newfound family where he least expected it. No matter the election results, he'd wake up tomorrow, strong in their support and basking in his wife's love.

Daisy nudged his arm. "It's best to rip off the bandage all at once."

When he reached for his phone, everyone in the auditorium seemed to sense something. Silence descended on the crowd, which had quadrupled in the past fifteen minutes. Daisy squeezed his hand, and he was ready for whatever change awaited.

With a deep breath, he glanced at his phone. The election results were in. Daisy positioned herself so she could see the news, as did the triplets. Together Rosie, Aspen and Lily gave out a loud cheer.

"Congratulations, Mayor Daddy!" Rosie announced with glee.

A cheer came over the crowd. The curtain opened to a big sign: *Congratulations, Mayor Ben!*

From the ceiling, balloons dropped onto the crowd. Aspen and Rosie began throwing them at each other while Lily played peacemaker. His gaze narrowed in on his wife, who kissed him.

"Change is good." She winked at him and brought him close for a longer kiss. "Pearl is exploring her new yard, and Rosie, Lily and Aspen love having their own rooms. Thank you for turning your attic into my personal workshop. That was the best birthday present I could have asked for, just like volunteering for the play ended up being the best part of my Christmas. I love you, Mayor Ebenezer Irwin."

"I love you, Daisy Irwin."

While he still preferred the status quo, he could face change head-on with Daisy in his corner. Daisy's sunshine brought a beam of light, cutting through the darkness, illuminating his world with hope and love. She'd helped him to see that surprises and change were unexpected bursts of goodness to be anticipated rather than dreaded. His house was now a home, and Violet Ridge was bursting with friends and family paving the way to a bright tomorrow.

Daisy changed his life for the better. Happiness with his new family filled him with a lightness that rivaled the balloons surrounding him. Ben had found his peace.

* * * * *

For more great romances from acclaimed author Tanya Agler and Harlequin Heartwarming, visit www.Harlequin.com today!

HARLEQUIN
Reader Service

Enjoyed your book?

Try the perfect subscription for Romance readers and get more great books like this delivered right to your door.

See why over 10+ million readers have tried Harlequin Reader Service.

Start with a Free Welcome Collection with free books and a gift—valued over $20.

Choose any series in print or ebook. See website for details and order today:

TryReaderService.com/subscriptions

RSBPA24R